Target Man

ANNIE DYER

TARGET
Man

Copyright © 2022 by Annie Dyer

writeranniedyer.com

All rights reserved. Apart from any permitted use under UK copyright law, no part of this publication may be reproduced or transmitted in any form or by any means, electronic or mechanical, including photocopying, recording or any information storage or retrieval system, without permission in writing from the author.

Target Man is a work of fiction. Names, places, characters and incidents are a product of the author's imagination and are fictitious. Any resemblance to actual persons, living or dead, events or establishments is solely coincidental.

Please note this book contains material aimed at an adult audience.

Editing by Eliza Ames

Cover design by Qamber Designs

Photographer: Wander Aguilar

Cover image copyright © 2022

❦ Created with Vellum

Also by Annie Dyer

The Callaghan Green Series

In Suggested Reading order (can be read as stand-alones)

Engagement Rate

What happens when a hook up leaves you hooked? Jackson Callaghan is the broody workaholic who isn't looking for love until he meets his new marketing executive? Meet the Callaghans in this first-in-series, steamy office romance.

White Knight

If you're in the mood for a second chance romance with an older brother's best friend twist, then look no further. Claire Callaghan guards her heart as well as her secrets, but Killian O'Hara may just be the man to take her heart for himself.

Compromising Agreements

Grumpy, bossy Maxwell Callaghan meets his match in this steamy enemies-lovers story. Mistaking Victoria Davies as being a quiet secretary is only Max's first mistake, but can she be the one to make this brooding Callaghan brother smile?

Between Cases

Could there be anything better than a book boyfriend who owns a bookstore? Payton Callaghan isn't sure; although giving up relationships when she might've just met The One is a dilemma she's facing in BETWEEN CASES, a meet-cute that'll have you swooning over Owen Anders.

Changing Spaces

Love a best friend's younger sister romance? Meet Eli, partner in the Callaghan Green law firm and Ava's Callaghan's steamy one-night stand that she just can't seem to keep as just one night. Independent, strong-willed and intelligent, can Eli be the man Ava wants?

Heat

Feeling hungry? Get a taste of this single dad, hot chef romance in HEAT. Simone Wood is a restaurant owner who loves to dance, she's just never found the right partner until her head chef Jack starts to teach her his rhythm. Problem is, someone's not happy with Simone, and their dance could be over before they've learned the steps.

Mythical Creatures

The enigmatic Callum Callaghan heads to Africa with the only woman who came close to taming his heart, in this steamy second-chance romance. Contains a beautifully broken alpha and some divinely gorgeous scenery in this tale that will make you both cry and laugh. HEA guaranteed.

Melted Hearts

Hot rock star? Enemies to lovers? Fake engagement? All of these ingredients are in this Callaghan Green novel. Sophie Slater is a businesswoman through and through but makes a pact with the devil – also known as Liam Rossi, newly retired Rockstar – to get the property she wants - one that just happens to be in Iceland. Northern lights, a Callaghan bachelor party, and a quickly picked engagement ring are key notes in this hot springs heated romance.

Evergreen

Christmas wouldn't be Christmas without any presents, and that's what's going to happen if Seph Callaghan doesn't get his act together. The Callaghan clan are together for Christmas, along with a positive pregnancy test from someone and several more surprises!

The Partnership

Seph Callaghan finally gets his HEA in this office romance. Babies, exes and a whole lot of smoulder!

The Green Family Series

The Wedding Agreement

Imogen Green doesn't do anything without thinking it through, and that includes offering to marry her old - very attractive - school friend, Noah Soames, who needs a wedding. The only problem is, their fauxmance might not be so fake, after all…

The Atelier Assignment

Dealing with musty paintings is Catrin Green's job. Dealing with a hot Lord who happens to be grumpy AF isn't. But that's what she's stuck with for three months. Zeke's daughter is the only light in her days, until she finds a way to make Zeke smile. Only this wasn't part of the assignment.

The Romance Rehearsal

Maven Green has managed to avoid her childhood sweetheart for more than a decade, but now he's cast as her leading man in the play she's directing. Anthony was the boy who had all her firsts; will he be her last as well?

The Imperfect Proposal

Shay Green doesn't expect his new colleague to walk in on him when he's mid-kiss in a stockroom. He also doesn't expect his new colleague to be his wife. The wife he married over a decade ago in Vegas and hasn't seen since

Puffin Bay

Puffin Bay

Amelie started a new life on a small Welsh island, finding peace and new beginnings. What wasn't in the plan was the man buying the building over the road. She was used to dealing with arrogant tourists, but this city boy was enough to have her want to put her hands around his neck, on his chest, and maybe somewhere else too...

Manchester Athletic FC

Penalty Kiss

Manchester Athletic's bad boy needs taming, else his football career could be on the line. Pitched with women's football's role model pin up, he has pre-season to sort out his game - on and off the field.

Hollywood Ball

One night. It didn't matter who she was, or who he was, because tomorrow they'd both go back to their lives. Only hers wasn't that ordinary.

What she didn't know, was neither was his.

Heart Keeper

Single dad. Recent widow. Star goal keeper.

Manchester Athletic's physio should keep her hands to herself outside of her treatment room, but that's proving tough. What else is tough is finding two lines on that pregnancy test…

Target Man

Jesse Sullivan is Manchester Athletic's Captain Marvel. He keeps his private life handcuffed to his bed, locked behind a non-disclosure agreement. Jesse doesn't do relationships – not until he meets his teammate's – and best friend's – sister.

Red Heart Card

It's tough being talented and from a footballing legacy, every move you make is under scrutiny. Jude has always been the spoilt baby of the team, which is why he needs to keep what he's up to in private, under wraps.

Severton Search and Rescue

Sleighed

Have a change of scenery and take a trip to a small town. Visit Severton, in Sleighed; this friends-to-lovers romantic suspense will capture your heart as much as Sorrell Slater steals Zack Maynard's.

Stirred

If enemies-to-lovers is your manna, then you'll want to stay in Severton for Stirred. Keren Leigh and Scott Maynard have been at daggers drawn for years, until their one-night ceasefire changes the course of their lives forever.

Smoldered

Want to be saved by a hot firefighter? Rayah Maynard's lusted over Jonny Graham ever since she came back to town. Jonny's prioritised his three children over his own love life since his wife died, but now Rayah's teaching more than just his daughter – she's teaching him just how hot their flames can burn.

Shaken

Abby Walker doesn't exist. Hiding from a gang she suspects is involved in the disappearance of her sister, Severton is where she's taken refuge. Along with her secrets, she's hiding her huge crush on local cop, Alex Maynard. But she isn't the only one with secrets. Alex can keep her safe, but can he also take care of her heart?

Sweetened

Enemies? Friends? Could be lovers? All Jake Maynard knows is that Lainey Green is driving him mad, and he really doesn't like that she managed to buy the farm he coveted from under his nose. All's fair in love and war, until events in Severton take a sinister turn.

Standalone Romance

Love Rises

Two broken souls, one hot summer. Anya returns to her childhood island home after experiencing a painful loss. Gabe escapes to the same place, needing to leave his life behind, drowning in guilt. Neither are planning on meeting the other, but when they do, from their grief, love rises. Only can it be more than a summer long?

Bartender

The White Island, home of hedonism, heat and holidays. Jameson returns to her family's holiday home on Ibiza, but doesn't expect to charmed by a a bartender, a man with an agenda other than just seduction.

Tarnished Crowns Trilogy

Lovers. Liars. Traitors. Thieves. We were all of these. Political intrigue, suspense and seduction mingle together in this intricate and steamy royal romance trilogy.

Chandelier

Grenade

Emeralds

Crime Fiction

We Were Never Alone

How Far Away the Stars (Novella)

To all my readers who have supported me from the beginning, and continue to do so now. Your reviews, recommendations and the time you spend reading my books is so appreciated.

Note to readers:
DO NOT START CHAPTER 11 AS 'JUST ONE MORE CHAPTER'.
YOU HAVE BEEN WARNED!

Trigger warnings - this book contains references to childhood trauma and the death of a parent. There are no graphic detail, and the book charts the character's resilience and growth with the support of therapy.
There is very much a happily ever after.

This is an unproofed ARC edition and should not be redistributed or resold.

CHAPTER 1
Jesse

"CAN I APPEAL?" I was trying to keep my cool. Desperately trying to keep my cool, because I was *this* close to losing the minuscule amount of patience I had left.

My solicitor, Peter Walton, also known as Payoff Pete, shook his head. "I can't get you off again, Jesse. This is as good as it's going to get."

"What the fuck have I been paying you for then?" I slammed my fist down on the table, then lobbed the ashtray against the wall. I didn't know why the fuck there was an ashtray on the table in the first place; no one could smoke inside anymore anyway.

A firm hand pressed down on my shoulder. I shrugged it off, not needing Rhys' attempt to be calming. Rhys was my agent and a damned good one.

"If you got off completely, we'd lose the deal with Shuu. That more than pays for you to have a driver for six months." Rhys sat down, looking way too relaxed for an agent with a player that had just fucked up. "They don't want a face that looks like he buys his way out of shit."

Or rather, fucked up two months ago and couldn't unfuck it.

"You have a six-month ban, a twenty grand fine and a hundred hours of community service. You had a lenient judge. If he'd supported United or City, you could've been looking at a suspended sentence or worse." Payoff Pete stood up, collecting his leather cased tablet. "There's no way you could've walked away with your licence. Not after last time."

I wanted to head butt the table, but all that would achieve would be a headache.

I was captain of my football team. I'd captained the England side for the last two internationals. I never got involved in brawls; I didn't fuck about, keeping company with a couple of businesswomen who had no intentions for relationships or WAG status, they just liked a night full of orgasms every couple of weeks; I stayed away from controversy.

My one vice was that I was a petrol head. A speed freak. I liked super cars and they were my one stupid splurge. I also really liked driving them, almost as much as playing football and having sex.

Speeding on a country road where the Cheshire police didn't have too much else to worry about twice in a three-month period wasn't a vice I could hide very well. The second of those times I'd been clocked going just over a hundred. That made me a bad boy.

Thankfully, the media were too caught up in another football scandal, involving a couple of high-profile players' wives who were trying to sue each other or something. Another good reason to stay unmarried and single.

My speeding had managed a couple of paragraphs so

far and would get a short write up in the press later, which meant I'd been lucky. Really, really fucking lucky.

Only for the next six months, I couldn't drive any of my cars. Anywhere I needed to go, someone would have to take me. Someone would always know where I'd been.

I didn't have the two women I hooked up with come to mine. I usually went to their apartments or houses, occasionally hotel rooms. My house was out of bounds. Getting to see them without anyone other than the two of us involved would now be out of the question.

I swallowed. "Thanks, Pete."

He nodded. "You're welcome. If I'd tried to get you off, Jesse, it would've hit the press. This was the best I could do. My advice – when you get your licence back, don't fucking speed. Go hire a racetrack for a day and blow off that way."

I wasn't going to thank him for that advice.

Pete left, leaving me with Rhys, who tapped at the table with his pen. I'd never seen him with anything to write on. But he always carried a pen.

"The judge has left it up to you to submit how you're going to carry out the community service. He's provided suggestions, but we can put forward our own because obviously litter picking in a public park is going to leave you open to being mobbed." Rhys put his pen back in his pocket. "You have twelve months to complete, but given the season has ended, my suggestion is that you get as much done now as possible. How about the club's summer soccer school?"

I nodded. "I can do that." I had been looking forward to a summer of holidays: a tour round the Greek Islands, ten days in Florida and a quick trip to the vineyard I was considering buying shares in, which was in the South of

France. The last had involved me driving there, the first I'd already missed, because I needed to attend this hearing, and the Florida jaunt was right in the middle of the summer soccer school.

Costa del Manchester it was.

Rhys nodded. That's six hours a day for fifteen days. Ninety hours done. Ten hours at the soup kitchen and you're done. I'll let Pete know and he can get it passed by the judge."

"This isn't your first rodeo, is it?"

He laughed. "I grew up with Rowan Reeves. You have no idea how many bad outcomes I've negotiated him out of."

Rowan was my teammate. This time last year he'd been in hot water after photos had been published of him getting his freak on with a random woman on a sun lounger. It was the last in a long line of incidents that almost had him transferred out of Manchester Athletic.

Rhys and Rowan were friends from school, Rowan getting a professional contract and Rhys turning one down, or so the legend had it. He'd done a degree in sports management and business and had become an agent. I'd gone on his books when my agent had retired.

"Yeah, well, he's got Dee now." Rowan was finally engaged to the sweetheart of Manchester Athletic's women's team. He'd only had to ask her three times.

Rhys gave a short nod. "She makes my job easier. They've picked up a couple of nice endorsements as a couple. Maybe you should get yourself a girlfriend." His eyes narrowed. "Maybe that might cure some of your need for speed. Get some on the regular and you might not need to lose your licence again."

I made a noise that sounded not unlike a hybrid of a

cow and a monkey that had inhaled helium. "Not going to happen."

"Ever?" Rhys looked curious. "You'll never do a Rowan?"

My laugh this time sounded more human. "No. Don't need the hassle."

Rhys shrugged. "Fair enough. Want me to drop you off somewhere?"

I nodded, wishing I could throw that ash tray again. This would be my life for the next six months. Reliant on lifts, taxis and a professional driver, if I gave in and got one. "Nate's, if that's okay?"

"I'm on my way to Rowan and Dee's so it's on the way." He stood up. "It could've been worse, Jesse. You did the right thing, keeping it together."

I nodded, hearing the truth in his words. There had been a good chance that the system might've decided to make an example of me and I'd have gotten a harsher punishment. There had been criticism when a footballer got off with a fine and ten hours of community service a couple of months back; he'd ended up having his character assassinated in the media, which had thrown up a couple of previously well-hidden skeletons, and he'd lost at least two sponsorship deals, and taken a wage cut when he'd renegotiated his contract. Pete had warned me that we had to keep our heads down and not try to justify my speed or throw my bank balance at it.

I'd had the sense to take his advice, fully aware that I wasn't God, even if I could eat for free in pretty much any restaurant in Manchester and find a woman to take home any night of the week. I was more cross at myself than the reality I'd ended up with, because I shouldn't have put my foot down when I was driving the Aston Martin like I did.

But fucking hell, it had felt good.

What didn't feel good was being a passenger. I hated being a passenger. An ex-girlfriend had told me I was a control freak – not with her, I couldn't have given a crap about what she wore or where she went – but I apparently had to have control in every aspect of my life, including in the bedroom, which she didn't complain about.

Rhys' driving was similar to that of a seventy-five-year-old who was about to be reassessed to see if they could keep their licence. He dawdled at lights, wouldn't overtake, and slowed down even when lights were on green.

He also crawled up people's asses while fiddling with the aircon, meaning I almost got a stress fracture from trying to press down on an imaginary brake pedal.

"Will you hire a driver?" He pulled up on Nate's driveway.

"As long as they come with a sedative. Thanks for the lift." I opened the door, knowing that my blood pressure was now high enough to scare our medical team. "I'll sort out the times for the soccer school. Thanks for managing everything, too." Because while he was a shit driver – albeit he still had his licence – he'd looked out well for me.

"Not a problem. Let me know if you get stuck for a ride anywhere. I'm about for the next week or so." He gave me a salute. "And for fuck's sake, don't drive anywhere."

I shook my head. "Unlike some of my esteemed colleagues, I'm not that fucking stupid."

He laughed and tootled off, out of Nate's electric gates and back onto the country roads that were so different than the ones where I grew up.

Nate's front door was open, the man himself leaning

against the door frame with his arms folded, watching me as if studying an animal in captivity.

"How does it feel? No wheels?" His grin was not pretty.

He jumped, his arms moving with no co-ordination whatsoever, which was a bit concerning given he was our first-choice goalkeeper.

Nate Morris was one of the best people I knew. Steady, hardworking, loyal – I'd tell him all of this but I wasn't much of one to talk about such things.

I figured he knew I had respect for him because of the amount of time I spent at his house.

"Amber!" He looked behind him and ended up with a very pregnant physiotherapist in his arms. "You could've made me pull something."

She laughed, her gaze up at him making me feel like an intruder. Which I was, not that I was ashamed of it.

"Hey, Jesse."

Her smile for me was wide too. I'd checked with her a few weeks ago about whether she was cool with me hanging out, and she told me direct that if she wasn't, I'd know about it by now.

Amber and Nate had recently gotten together, the baby they were expecting at the start of October a very big surprise. Nate had two girls from his previous relationship, a marriage which left him a widower and a single dad. Chan had been a good lady, and she'd adored Nate. When she'd died, it had affected all of us, and until Nate had found light again with Amber, he'd struggled.

Amber had him smiling again, and the baby they were expecting in three months couldn't have been more of a blessing, however much of a surprise he was.

"How's my God son?" It was a standing joke from a lot

of my teammates that we all expected to be the baby's Godfather.

She rubbed her belly, Nate's hands covering hers. "Big. He's been really active today. I think it's the heat."

It had been warmer than normal. "Still not going on holiday?" I watched Amber's expression change to a glare, aimed at Nate.

"Staying within half an hour of the hospital at all times." Nate's smile was far more pleasant. "Holiday at home."

I followed them into the house where Nate had moved at the start of the year. He'd wanted somewhere with more grounds, so his eldest daughter, Libbie, could have a horse and there was more security. He'd also needed to start in a place that didn't carry the memory of Chan's passing.

It was a huge home but it didn't feel cold or empty, or full of the usual footballer style décor with tons of silver and glass. They did have a games room with a full-size snooker table and a gym with an indoor swimming pool, hence I found myself here an awful lot, even if it was to babysit.

"We could've gone to Wales or Scotland or the Lake District." Amber prodded him again. "They have hospitals in places other than Manchester, you know."

We went into the kitchen, Amber still giving Nate grief about refusing to go away anywhere.

"We can go to Florida next year. And I'll take you to New York as soon as you're ready to leave the baby for a few days." Nate was unmoved by Amber's protests.

I sat down on a stool at the breakfast bar and listened with amusement, Nate putting a pre-made smoothie from Kitty's Café on the table in front of me. Nate was probably the most stubborn person I'd ever met – quietly stubborn, picking his battles with care, and when he did, he didn't lose.

There had been a couple of scares early on in Amber's pregnancy – I didn't quite understand what – and Nate had since needed to always have her near to her consultant. Hence, no holiday for them either.

Amber shook her head and glared at him but said nothing.

"We heard through the grapevine that you aren't driving for six months." She just about managed to get herself onto a stool. "What are you going to do about getting around?"

I shrugged. I was kind of hoping this was going to be a bad dream. "I can grab lifts to training. Jude and Danny both pass me pretty much. I'm not sure I can sit in a car with Jude driving though." I couldn't help the shudder.

"It took him seven times to pass." Amber accepted the yoghurt Nate passed her, one he'd just garnished with fruit and chocolate sauce.

I tried not to fall off my stool. "Seven times to pass his driving test? What about the theory?"

"He passed that first time. He kept picking up too many minors on the practical though." She inhaled a spoonful of the yoghurt, her eyes closing.

"How did you find out?"

"Neva told me. No idea how she knows though." Amber took another spoonful. "This is bliss."

Nate grinned, his eyes fixed on Amber in such a way I wondered if I needed to make myself scarce.

"Where are Libbie and Zara?" I looked as if expecting them to materialise at the sound of their names.

Nate reached out and wiped a drop of chocolate sauce

from the side of Amber's mouth. I was pretty sure if I wasn't there, he would've licked it off.

"They're with the horse. Jerrica's looking after them today." He licked the sauce off his finger.

I put my smoothie down and frowned. "Jerrica's here?"

Nate nodded. "Yeah, she got back at the weekend."

"I thought she was moving back to your parents?"

He looked at me and frowned, shaking his head. "She was staying at their house to look after the puppies while they went on that cruise, but she's not moving back in with them."

"So she's back living here?" This wasn't what I was expecting to hear. This was almost on the same level as losing my license for six months.

"She was always going to be. The plan's for her to stay until at least after Christmas, then Amber's got some support with the baby while I'm at the World Cup." Nate chugged his smoothie in pretty much one go. "By then she might've decided what she's going to do."

I looked anywhere but at Nate and Amber.

Footsteps that sounded heavier than I knew they actually were padded into the kitchen through the open bi-fold doors.

"Daddy! Daddy! Auntie Jez fell in the pond!" The footsteps stopped. "Uncle Jesse!"

I got off my stool before I was knocked off it and bent down to catch a flying Libbie, even though I now knew a flying Libbie meant that Jerrica was somewhere nearby.

"What do you mean, Jez fell in the pond? There's a fence round it." Nate stood up, heading towards the patio doors.

"Zara's hat blew off and she was trying to get it out of the water." Libbie patted at the short beard I'd worn since the season ended. The plan was to shave it off before I flew on holiday. That wasn't happening, so I'd kept the beard.

A beard I knew Jerrica liked.

My back was to the doors, my muscles braced for seeing Nate's little sister again. I knew I'd see her again; she would always be around because she and Nate were close and she was an amazing aunt, but I hadn't expected her to be back. She'd told me she was going back to her parents while she worked out what she was going to do going forward with her career.

I heard Zara, Nate's youngest daughter, giggling and talking ten to the dozen before I heard Jerrica.

"Fu – flipping heck, Jez! Did you dive in?"

I saw Nate pick up Zara from the corner of my eye.

I inhaled, knowing I was going to turn round and see her, else I'd appear rude and Amber would work out something wasn't right.

"I over-reached." Her voice was just the same, tuneful, with that hint of happiness. "And then I lost my balance. I think I swallowed a fish."

Three. Two. One.

I turned round.

She was drenched, something that looked slimy hanging off her head, mouth curved in a smile.

Her tank top, which had been white, was now sheer and she hadn't been wearing a bra.

She folded her arms, which didn't help.

Then she looked at me, which didn't help either, because instead of scowling at me, like she should, she smiled.

She was still beautiful, even with slime dripping off her head.

CHAPTER 2
Jerrica

THERE WAS something to be said for a good comedic moment. Me standing there in my brother's pristinely designed kitchen, with pond water dripping over every inch on my slightly sunburned skin, and some horrible, yucky, green stuff hanging from my hair in front of Jesse Sullivan would probably make comedy gold in anyone's world but mine.

My two nieces were giggling for all they were worth, Libbie was perched in Jesse's arms, Zara now on her dad's shoulders. My brother was shaking his head but smiling, and my soon to be sister-in-law was doing her best to be supportive and not find me the source of today's amusement.

I was creating a pool on the white tiled floor. I glanced down, noticing that my vest was now pretty much transparent, and I wasn't wearing a bra. Automatically, my eyes went to Jesse and found him looking at me, those dark, dark brown eyes swirling with undecipherable things, as they always were.

I cringed.

This would only reinforce all the more that I was just his teammate's younger sister, and my crush was something to amuse him.

Could I be any more lame? Probably. I probably could do it without even trying.

"I think I need a shower." I looked down at the pool of water that was still growing. "Nate, can you get me a towel so I don't drench everywhere?"

My brother was convulsed with laughter. Amber shot him a look that would maim and probably kill.

"I'll get you one. Nate, grow up." She swatted his shoulder, which was probably just an excuse to touch him.

"Is that green stuff slime?" Libbie pointed to my hair. "Is it like the slime we make?"

I smiled at my niece, not really liking her at the moment because talking to her meant I was looking in the same direction as Jesse. "No, it's real slime and it's gross. Want to touch?"

Libbie clung to Jesse's shoulders, flinching back with fake terror. "No! No! It's a swamp monster!"

I watched Jesse's face battle with not laughing at me and failing miserably.

"Hey, Jez." His grin was wide enough to swallow a ship. "Looking good today."

I shook my head, so glad that Amber was back with a Manchester Athletic towel that had seen better days. I pulled it round my body, too scared to actually touch my hair where that slime and probably a few living things were hanging around.

I was my very own eco-system.

"Thanks, Jesse." I looked at my brother, manifesting the idea of him falling in that pond. "Nate, I forgot to mention."

He did his best to look like he wasn't laughing at my expense. "What's that?"

"I went through all our old photos and found some of you when you went through your anti-clothes stage." I'd hidden all the horrendous photos of me, particularly when our mother thought she could do a better haircut than a professional.

Nate glared. "You got rid of those, though, didn't you?"

I shook my head, giving Jesse a little conspiratorial smile. "Nope. Brought every single one with me."

Amber sat back down, rubbing her growing belly. "How old was he when he went through this stage, Jez?"

"Nine." I shook my head. "Not really any excuse, is there?"

I dripped off to the ground floor bathroom, totally ignoring my brother's protests.

Being under clean water was a relief. I wasn't one of those girls who had to look immaculate at all times; I wore no makeup more often than I did, and I was used to being on the move, therefore sweaty, most of the time. I was only twenty-eight, but I'd already had three different careers and currently would consider most forms of work to ensure I didn't touch my savings from selling my party-planning business.

I could hustle, and you didn't always have to look pretty for that.

I'd gotten back to Nate's a few days ago after spending three weeks at our parents, looking after their two poodle-mix puppies while our parents were cruising round the Med. Nate's house had become my temporary home while I figured out what I was doing with my life. He'd needed someone to help with the girls while his new nanny could start, and I needed to avoid the disappointed look on my parents' faces when I told them that I'd changed my mind about what I wanted to do with my life.

Again.

I actually did know what I wanted to do. I'd had the same ambition since I was nine years old and it hadn't changed, but I'd only recently realised that I could do it as a job. Being at Nate's gave me space and time to work on it, without being pressured, because there was one thing my brother was good at and that was guarding things, which included me.

He still saw me as being his little, younger sister, and because he could – financially Nate, his kids and probably their grandkids, would never have money worries – he spoiled me.

Not that I was taking advantage. While I was here, I pulled my weight with the girls and the house, helping Amber as much as she wanted, and doing Nate's social media. Before the season ended, I was their glue, holding the pieces together when Leon, the nanny, had time off, or the girls had different activities, making dinners, playing games, being a taxi service – my priority had been them.

I'd already had a quick rinse to get rid of the horrendous slime, then rinsed out the huge shower. Now I was luxuriating – not hiding at all – in the hot water, Amber's range of body oils had already been tested, and my favourite, a spicy rose scent, had been topped up.

If I was lucky, by the time I'd finished pruning myself, Jesse would've driven off into the sunset.

Driven.

Fuck. That was why he was here. Today was the day of his court hearing.

My heart rate rose to about what Nate's was when he was saving a penalty. Jesse had been in court and I'd turned up in front of him covered in pond slime.

I tipped my head back under the ceiling shower head, rinsing through my hair again. Jesse had picked up points on his licence for speeding already. Then we'd had a conversation that hadn't gone down very well with either of us, and he'd been caught speeding again on his drive home. Part of me felt responsible, even though it hadn't been me behind the wheel.

I finished shampooing my hair, not able to relax now, wanting to know what the outcome was of the hearing. I dried off, towel drying my hair and slapping on body cream so my skin didn't feel like it was about to peel off an hour later, then I threw on a robe and headed off to the small suite of rooms upstairs that had become my domain to find some clean clothes.

I had a bedroom, en-suite bathroom and little sitting room which I'd converted into my writing den. The landing outside and the bedroom had the plushest carpet underfoot which would've been ruined by pond water, hence the need to use the big bathroom on the ground floor.

This space would probably be Libbie's in the future, when she was old enough to want her own space and Nate wasn't for letting her go far. My brother was like a ball pool: fun and playful, but with huge protective boundaries that did. not. move.

I pulled on jean shorts and a baggy black T-shirt, which I tied at the bottom so I didn't look completely like a slob.

With any luck, Jesse would've gone home or to the gym or to anywhere that wasn't here.

Luck wasn't planning to be any part of my day.

He was in the garden with Nate and Amber, my nieces splashing around in the paddling pool. A pitcher of some healthy looking fruit drink sat on a table, and the pond puddle I'd left on the kitchen floor had been wiped up.

As much as I tried, I couldn't not stare at Jesse. He was almost as tall as Nate, and just as broad, with lean, long muscles and a way of moving that reminded me of a big cat, stalking its prey. His skin was swarthy, his hair dark, and his arms, body, and legs were peppered with tattoos in a variety of designs. He was every father's nightmare and every good girl's wet dream, including mine.

He'd changed out of the suit he'd been in, when I'd presented myself drenched in pond-water, and was now shirtless and wearing a pair of football shorts. Short ones. Not the long, baggy ones that had been favoured a couple of seasons ago.

Every single reason why I'd made a fool of myself that night when I'd made a pass at him was on show. I turned around and headed to the fridge for a glass of white wine.

The fruit punch just wasn't going to cut it.

"You smell better." My brother snuck up behind me, a talent he'd been bettering since I was four and he realised I scared easily.

"I will have my revenge." I found the bottle of pinot I was looking for.

Nate laughed. "I didn't actually do anything! You fell in of your own accord."

I mumbled a list of things he'd actually done, some going back two decades.

He laughed again. "Seriously, not my fault. Bring that bottle out and a glass for Jesse. I think he'll need it."

I put it down on the kitchen island and frowned at Nate. "What happened in court?"

"Lost his licence for six months, community service and a fine."

I swallowed. I knew Jesse loved driving. His fleet of cars was his pride and joy and he'd said one night when we'd been babysitting the girls that if he hadn't been a professional footballer, he'd have either been a race car driver or an engineer who worked on race cars.

"Shit."

"I know. But it could've been worse and fortunately, the press has more interesting shit to focus on right now." Nate referred to an ongoing court case where the wife of one footballer was suing another for defamation. "How's the book coming on? How's the other one selling?"

I smiled. "Both doing really well. I have to get this new one to my editor by the end of the week, but I only have one more read through to do so I'll be early with it." Virtually no one knew what I was working on – steamy romance books that I was self-publishing under a pseudonym. I'd published the first a month ago, and it had done better than I'd expected for a first novel with no real followers of my own. My second would be due out in just over a month, it was a second book in the same series, and there was a little bit of buzz about it already.

That was what I wanted to do. Write. I'd told my parents I'd wanted to be an author when I was a kid and my dad had laughed and said it was a hobby and not a career. Making a living from it didn't seem real, until I'd realised that people actually did. That was about halfway through writing my first book.

I hadn't told my parents. I didn't expect them to rejoice in the fact that their well-educated daughter was writing steamy romance novels that would make my mother need smelling salts should she ever read part of one. They wouldn't understand. I just needed a few more months living off very little money while I worked out my flow, whether I could get by on a part time job or whether I needed to find something full-time and write around that. I didn't want to live with Nate forever.

"How gutted is Jesse?" I tried to hide exactly how much I needed details behind a sympathetic smile.

Nate shrugged, pulling out a big bowl of salad and then putting it straight back. "Barbecue tonight, I think." He looked back at me. "He's gutted because of the inconvenience and implications. He's totally reliant on other people for lifts and he's worried he'll have no privacy. If he employs a driver, or uses a club one, someone always knows his business."

I let a breath go and collected two glasses for the wine, then apologised in my head to Amber for drinking when she couldn't.

"Is Jesse staying here tonight?" Nate had plenty of spare rooms. His house was a freaking mansion.

"Yep. Which I'd glad about. He had a load of summer plans made but they've all been scuppered. Don't speed, kids. Spoils your holidays in the South of France." He popped open a beer. "Come sit with us. Promise I won't call you Swamp Monster."

I rolled my eyes. He was going to do exactly that.

Within the first five minutes of sitting down outside, Nate had called me *Swamp Monster, Swampy,* and the *Monster that Lives in the Swamp.* I tried to not laugh, but it was impossible. I was just glad that no one had taken a photo.

"You didn't take a photo did you?" I looked at my brother.

He grinned. "I'll tell you when you give me those photos you found."

"Not worth it." Nate would have a stag do coming up in the next twelve months – my guess was he was going to propose to Amber soon - and I was sure that whoever he chose as his best man would really appreciate them.

My eyes hovered back over to Jesse, who was now on his second glass of wine, his long legs stretched out in front of him.

He was looking at me, his dark eyes an eddy of mysteries.

"I'm sorry about what happened today." I needed to get it out there before we were left on our own. My stomach churned like I was a fifteen-year-old girl speaking to her crush.

Jesse looked away down the garden. "Well, it could've been worse. I could've had a suspended sentence or - " he shrugged. "It's six months. Then I just need to make sure I don't go speeding."

"What made you think it was a good idea to drive that fast down that road?" Amber topped up her glass of fruit punch.

She'd only glared at the bottle of wine twice since I'd brought it out. I was staring at it now because it beat looking at Jesse while he tried to answer this question without lying.

"Sheer stupidity."

It wasn't a lie, only we weren't talking about his

stupidity, not until he got behind the wheel. It had been all mine before that.

Jesse put his glass of wine down on the table. "I'm going to have to deal with it because it ain't going to change in the next six months."

"The club will provide a driver." Nate glanced up at Zara and Libbie who were sitting together on the lawn, making daisy chains now. "That might be your best bet."

Jesse nodded. "Genny sent me a message to say they could sort that."

"You're not thrilled with the idea." Amber stood up, stretching out her back, Nate's attention automatically going to her to check she was okay.

I loved seeing my brother like this. After Chan had died, he'd been a mess, not knowing what to do with himself, or how to look after himself. I hadn't had a great relationship with Chan, although it wasn't that we didn't get along, she just preferred to have more to do with her side of the family than Nate's, so I hadn't spent a ton of time here, not until Chan was sick and I started to stay to help with Zara, who'd only been six months old when Chan died.

Jesse shook his head. "I don't like being treated like a princess."

"So what're you going to do? Get a bike and pedal everywhere?" Nate raised a brow. "Getting to training every day won't be a problem but getting back from training will 'cause everyone's got different things on. Don't make life hard for yourself, Jesse."

Jesse shrugged. "I'll probably end up hiring someone directly." He laughed. "Anyone know anybody's who's looking for a short term job being at a 'baller's beck and call?"

My heart hammered in my chest, and my stomach did that little thing where it flipped into somersault. I was well aware that this could be the glass of wine talking, but I needed some income for the next few months while I saw how things went with my book sales, and I needed flexibility to write and market – which was a job in itself.

"I am."

Three heads turned to me, confusion and surprise on all of them.

"I need some sort of income short term while I work out what I'm going to do longer term." I paused, thinking carefully as I wasn't fully open with everyone yet about what I was writing about. "But I need flexibility. If you don't mind me waiting around with my laptop, I can drive for you."

I wasn't sure how to read Jesse's expression. He was always guarded, unless he was smiling and he wasn't smiling now.

Maybe I should've offered when my brother wasn't there with us, so Jesse could turn me down without looking mean, because there was a flaw in my offer.

The night Jesse had been caught speeding for the second time, he'd been speeding away from me.

That was the effect the kiss I'd given him had.

CHAPTER 3
Jesse

"THAT WORKS."

I looked at Nate and wondered what his reaction would be if he knew the reason why I'd been speeding.

We'd played together on the same team for four seasons, but I'd known him longer than that because of England's international set up. Nate was a couple of years older than me, but we'd been on the under twenty-ones side at the same time, and both around the full squad after that.

He was a good friend.

A good friend who was protective and knew exactly what footballers could be like. He knew what I had been like, or a little of *what* I liked, and we weren't referring to vanilla milkshakes or thread count on sheets.

After what could've been a publicity nightmare, I learned to keep my private life exactly that. The two women I'd been seeing had both signed non-disclosure agreements quite happily, and there was a reason they were seeing me in a way that didn't involve restaurants and bars, or cosy dates for which they got a manicure and dressed up.

Nate had been the person I'd told when my ex threatened to go to the media with a story that would've seriously affected my career and earnings. I wouldn't be the captain of my team, and my endorsement deals would've been with very different sorts of companies. Not family friendly ones. My life would've been over in so many ways.

As it was, he hadn't judged when he heard the voicemail she left and saw the photos she'd sent. He'd kept me calm and stopped me from doing anything stupid. He'd sat with me while my solicitor had worked her magic, getting an injunction so the story couldn't be published and then I'd settled with her, giving her enough money that she could sponsor a small country and making sure she signed an agreement whereby if she ever mentioned to anyone anything about us, she'd lose everything.

Just like I almost had. I'd almost lost everything in front of Nate.

Which was why when Jerrica had tried to kiss me, I'd bolted.

"I think it's a good idea. Jez needs a job, and you need a driver." Nate stood up. "Want a beer, Jesse?"

I nodded. "I'll get them. You stay with Amber." I looked at Jez. "More wine?"

She shook her head. "I think I'll just get a juice."

She followed me into the kitchen, her perfume musky, the same one she'd been wearing that night.

"I'll find a reason so I can't be your driver. Nate won't let it go." She kept her voice low, as well as standing a good four feet away from me. "And I'm so fucking sorry, Jesse."

I opened the fridge, pulling out two bottles of beer. It was off-season, so our diets and drinks weren't monitored. An afternoon of having a few drinks in my friend's private garden wasn't going to raise any red flags.

The only red flag right now was Jerrica standing there in those shorts that showed off legs that were stupidly long and toned.

"It wasn't your fault."

Her blonde curls bounced as she shook her head again. "I made you feel awkward enough to speed so fast away from me that you lost your licence. I read it wrong. I shouldn't have said anything."

Now I felt like an utter shit. The girl was beating herself up, thinking I was grossed out by her.

"You didn't read it wrong. But there's no way your brother would let me live if he thought I'd been anywhere near you." I popped open one of the beers and took a swig. "None of it was your fault."

Green eyes, just like her brother's, looked back at me. "So if he wasn't my brother, you would've - "

I shook my head. "If he wasn't your brother we wouldn't know each other, so let's not play that game." I sounded like a bastard, but I didn't want to encourage her. She was all sunshine and light, and I definitely didn't walk on that light side when it came to what I liked off the pitch and behind very closed doors.

Plus, Nate.

She nodded, just once. "No reason why I can't be your driver then, is there?"

More beer was needed. "None at all." Other than it was a stupid idea. She had better things to do than be my chauffeur.

"Then why don't we discuss rates of pay."

I frowned. "Seriously?"

"Seriously. I don't sponge off my brother, even though he's tried. I'm working on something now, but I won't know for another six months or more whether I can rely on it as an income. I have savings, but I don't want to dip into that too much. I need a job, but I don't want something that distracts me from – you know – my thing."

I leaned back against the kitchen island while she went in the fridge, bending down to get the pitcher of fruit juice that was Amber's life blood. I didn't even try to not stare at her ass.

It would look good with my hand on it.

I cracked my knuckles. Having Nate's little sister driving me round was going to drive me mad. It would be the worst sort of punishment. Part of me, the side of me that always went for the tattoos where they'd hurt the most, relished the thought. A little torture never did anyone any harm.

It wasn't my job to protect her, not really. If this job suited her and she was offering, then why not?

"What's your *thing?*"

She put the jug down next to Nate's beer.

"I'm writing my second book. Just about to finish it." Her eyes dropped to the floor. "It's romance."

I lifted my brows. "Romance?"

She nodded, looking braver. "Romance and yes, it's steamy. It isn't closed door."

I frowned at her use of "closed door". "What does that mean?"

"I have sex scenes in it. There's description and, you know, people getting their freak on."

I could tell she was trying not to be embarrassed.

"Cool. I take it not many people know? You said this is your second?" Little girl had been busy.

"Second. I'm self-publishing so the first has been out a few weeks. It's done okay. And no, I'm not really telling anyone."

"We all have our secrets." Wasn't that the truth. "How about I pay you thirty grand for six months. Lifts to training and from training, match stuff, and anything to do with my job. Other non-work stuff by negotiation." Because there was some stuff I didn't want her driving me to.

I saw her swallow. "Thirty. That's a lot. Yes."

"Good girl."

I saw her shoulders relax and something in her eyes responded to the praise.

My cock twitched.

"I'm a good driver. But do you want to be driven around in my car?"

That would be a no. She had a VW Golf, which was best described as 'cute'. There was no way I wanted anyone driving me around in one of my cars, which meant there was one solution.

"Send me a list of five cars you like that you think I might like. Tomorrow, we'll go car shopping."

Her mouth gaped open. "And just like that you're buying a car?"

"And just like that I'm buying a car. No Fords, Nissans, VW's or anything like that. Think Maserati. Or Porsche. BMW if you must. No Fiat 500's." I frowned at the thought of being in one of those; my knees would end up around my ears.

"Aren't Maseratis really expensive?"

I nodded. "You okay with driving something like

that?" My theory here was that I'd be better being driven in a car that wasn't one I was used to driving. "You can keep it afterwards. Call it a bonus."

Her chin tipped up. "Of course I'll be okay with driving it."

I frowned. "How many points do you have on your licence?"

"None."

"How old were you when you passed your test?"

"Nineteen."

I'd been seventeen and one day. I'd wanted to take my test on my seventeenth birthday, but I couldn't schedule one for that day.

"How come it took so long?"

"I failed three times. But I'm a good driver. No points. No accidents. I can even parallel park."

She said it in the same way I told people I had an FA Cup winner's medal.

"I don't speed. I keep to the speed limit. I'm a considerate driver. Sometimes I have a tiny – as in teensy tiny – bit of road rage. I don't tolerate backseat drivers. Or passenger side drivers, so if that's going to be you, maybe we need a ball gag or duct tape to hand."

If only she knew.

To be fair, neither were my style. I liked to hear the noises women made when I made them come, and duct tape could be painful to get off, especially if there was hair involved.

"I won't backseat drive. Or passenger seat drive." I had a lot of control. It was how I got my kicks. Control of me, control of my abilities, control of making sure I followed through on my promises.

Not, as my ex had alleged, control of a person.

She met my eyes with something flashing in hers that intrigued me. Jerrica Morris was, for most men, a walking wet dream. Tall and limber, she had an athletic grace that made cocks twitch without trying. She also had an air of innocence that was pure catnip. Finding out she wrote steamy books was the cherry on top of a lot of cream.

Every entendre meant.

"Tomorrow at ten. We'll go to the dealerships. Let me have that list. If after we've spent three hours car shopping you think you still want to drive for me, then we have a deal." I picked up Nate's beer. He'd be wondering what the fuck I was doing I'd been that long.

"Deal." She'd poured herself a glass of Amber's fruit punch and added a shot of vodka. "This is my last alcoholic drink. Just in case you're worried about me driving tomorrow."

I shook my head. "I know you're a good girl. Wouldn't be surprised if you breathalysed yourself first."

She gave me the stink eye. "I'm not that much of a good girl."

I raised a brow, a response on the tip of my tongue that would only be classed as flirting. *How bad can you be? How bad can I make you?*

But her brother was almost in earshot and he knew exactly how bad to the bone I had been.

For now, and if I had any sense, for good, I'd keep my dirty words out of his sister's ears.

I crashed in Nate's spare room, our quiet afternoon turning into a busier evening with Rowan and Dee, then Nicky Pryce-Jones turning up. Genny, the club's operational manager, showed up as well, saying remarkably few words about my driving ban.

"It's your one foible," Genny had said when she found out I'd been caught. "But don't make it any worse."

She managed the media about it, giving statements to the press when they did find out, and doing it in such a way that they didn't dig any further, which took a lot of talent and the hugest pair of balls of any one I'd ever known.

Genny was one of my favourite people. She managed a mainly male backroom team, our moody, temperamental manager and a changing room full of arrogant, egotistical footballers without breaking sweat or losing her shit.

I had heard from Amber that Genny did have a dart board with a regularly replaced photo of our manager on it, I'd seen the evidence a couple of times but I didn't dare ask her about it, for fear of becoming a target.

There was a lot that I didn't dare ask Genny. She was one of the most self-controlled people I knew, pristinely put together and rarely known to not see something coming. She knew the very vague outline of what my ex had said, but didn't have the details, although she had once mentioned something that made me believe she had a good idea about my tastes.

Having Rowan and Nicky there meant nothing more was said by Nate about a possible job for his sister. When I headed down to the kitchen that morning, he and Amber had gone for an antenatal appointment and the girls had gone out with their nanny for the day.

I didn't see Jerrica at first, assuming she hadn't gotten up yet, but then a flash of movement in the garden caught my attention.

I went to the bi-folds, taking my coffee that I'd

managed to get from Nate's weirdly complicated coffee machine, and found them unlocked, so I headed out barefoot into the garden, curious about what I'd seen.

It didn't take long to find the colour. Jerrica was out there, an exercise mat on the patio, brightly coloured booty shorts and a multi-coloured sports bra. She was following a routine on her iPad, her body getting sweaty with the workout.

I sat down on one of the seats Nate had dotted about his garden and watched, knowing full well if she saw me she'd think I was perving at her, which I was.

Jerrica was athletic, with a healthy dose of curves. Her stomach was flat and toned, the product of exercise and a careful diet. Her legs were strong, with defined muscles and her arms were just my right sort of crafted. Blonde hair was tied up in a messy knot on top of her head, with loose strands falling down her face. She was makeup free and pretty, the sort of pretty that you took home to your ma before locking it down.

Not the sort of pretty that wrote dirty scenes in books dressed up as sweet romances.

It didn't take me that long to find her published novel. *Jerrika Pepper* was doing pretty well for reviews, the number of them suggesting that she'd sold a decent amount. Her social media followings were growing too, and if she checked later, she'd see she had a new follower, one whose profile pic was just a tattoo and had a strange name.

I downloaded a copy of the book onto my phone, and ordered the paperback too, then I skim read the first few chapters, getting a little bit gripped when certain scenes came up.

Jerrica Morris wasn't a vanilla cupcake. She was definitely something with a sprinkling of spice.

Just how much of her inspiration was real life versus imagination I wasn't sure, but watching her bouncing around to her HIIT workout fuelled my fantasies. I was just glad Nate wasn't there to see me studying his sister.

She didn't notice me until her workout stopped and she turned round to pick up her water bottle.

"Fuck! Jesse! Give a girl warning." She glared at me, but there was no malice to it. "You could've joined me."

I shook my head. "Too energetic for me. I'll stick to weights with Nicky this afternoon." I'd promised him I'd spot him with some heavier lifts, and the kid was bored, hanging around when everyone else had gone off on holiday. He was finishing his degree and hanging round Kitty's Café pretty much all the time, although he denied he had a crush on the owner.

She gave me a sly grin. "So you just thought you'd watch instead?"

"Yeah. Pretty nice view. Nate's got some nice trees growing in this part of the garden, and that hydrangea's just blooming this year." I leaned my elbows on my knees, watching her get just a little flustered.

"You're terrible."

"I've been called worse. You still want to be my driver if I'm *terrible*?" I managed to keep my eyes on her face rather than her tits, tits that were impossible to miss given she was still catching her breath from her workout.

"I quite like the idea of being the boss of how you get somewhere. Something tells me you're going to hate it."

I'd never seen Jerrica with an evil look on her face until now.

"Probably." I folded my arms. "I'm also not sure it's a good idea."

"What? That you buy *another* car? Or that I drive it."

"Definitely not the first." I let my eyes drop to her tits and then her stomach, looking back up slowly and purposefully. "We can't get involved."

She shrugged. "You do know that my brother is not my keeper and has no say on who I might date, sleep with or have any form of relationship with, don't you?"

I nodded. "Got that. But Nate knows me, and I know if anything happened with us, he'd lynch me. Nate knows shit about me, Jerrica, and that shit means I'm definitely not who he wants getting into his baby sister's bed. I'm the team's captain. He's my vice. Athletic is going to push to win the league this season, and we're in the Champions' League too. Nate and I will more than likely be in the team for the World Cup. If he hates me, it fucks up more than our friendship. I'm not willing to do that."

"What shit does he know?" She walked closer to me.

I saw beads of sweat clinging to the skin just above her sports bra, drops slipping down in erotic little rivulets.

This was self-flagellation. Putting Jerrica in close contact with me every fucking day for six months and not being able to touch was akin to a prison sentence. I already knew I wouldn't be asking her to drive me to either of my hook-up's houses. I was half thinking that this would end up being a period of abstinence, or in translation, me punishing myself for making a huge fucking mistake.

Jerrica was not my usual type. She was too young, too soft and too fucking innocent, despite the hot shower scene I'd read last night that she'd written. I doubted she'd experienced what she'd penned either.

I wondered how much to tell her. "I have a kink. An

ex-girlfriend threatened to tell her story to the media and Nate heard those threats."

"Is this why you don't have a revolving door of women?"

"Pretty much."

"What's your kink?" Her eyes widened. "You're not going to tell me, are you?"

"No. You'll use it as research for your books."

Her pretty mouth curled up into a prettier grin and she folded her arms, which only pushed her tits up. "Maybe."

I wanted to ask her about her writing. Did she get herself off when she wrote those steamy scenes? Who did she picture in her head when she was writing them? Was it me? Had it been me? Or were there other members of the team. She'd chosen to write romance books about a football club.

I wasn't going to ask her any of those questions.

"So that's definitely not a conversation we'll be having."

Her hands dropped to her hips, that chin turning stubborn.

"Are you always this bossy?"

I just grinned.

CHAPTER 4
Jerrica

I WAS NERVOUS.

I was also seriously considering my life choices.

Jesse had offered a preposterous amount for six months of driving him around, which would constitute a lot of hanging around places, giving me chances to binge-write, and having to cope with the sex hormones he exuded. Whatever pheromone it was that he had going, all he needed to do was bottle it and sell it, and he'd be able to own his own football team.

I was also not really able to stop thinking about his kink. What did he mean by kink? I'd read a lot of romance and it was a seriously broad genre. We had women finding their fated mates in the form of wolf-shifters, countless billionaires who liked sex on desks and in the backs of chauffeur driven limos, college boys who fucked like they actually knew where a clitoris was and bad boys who played sports, thrown in with the occasional virgin, and the old classic of the arsehole who's her enemy who turns out to be Mr Hung and Knows What To Do With It. Then there were the mafia bosses, the security guards and the why choose one when you can have three. The last sounded a little too tiring for me to ever consider it as a reality.

Romance covered a lot of kink.

It did not tell me what Captain of Manchester Athletic Jesse Sullivan's was.

"So you like the Maserati?"

Those were the first words he'd said to me since I'd started driving, aware that he was watching every move I made in the car. My hands were sitting nicely at the ten and two position, and even though no one but me drove my little Golf, I'd checked my mirrors were all at exactly the right angles.

I felt like I was taking my test again and given those tests had been four of the most unpleasant experiences of my life, I was not enjoying myself.

"The Maserati Levante. That's my first choice." I gave a little nod. It was the car my brother had bought when he found out about Amber's pregnancy, and I'd driven it a few times and liked it.

I saw a smirk start to grow on Jesse's face, one that told me I'd said something he'd found entirely too amusing.

"What?"

"Nothing."

"You're smirking. I want to know what I've done to amuse you."

"I'm not buying a Levante. You're only choosing that because it's in your comfort zone."

"Don't you want me to be in my comfort zone while I'm driving you around?"

"I want us both to be in our comfort zone. You just haven't found out where your zone is."

"My comfort zone is driving a car I feel comfortable in."

"Obviously. But until you've tried it, you won't know what makes you feel comfortable. I don't want the same car as your brother."

"What's wrong with a Levante?"

"Nothing. Let's look at the Quattroporte. We'll take it out."

I frowned. "Don't we need an appointment to do that?"

His grin was wicked, like a pirate who was just about to rob you blind.

"No. My name gets us a free pass."

He must've noticed me shake my head.

"It's well known I like cars, Jerrica. It's the one thing I use my name for, and I'm not a dick when I go into the showrooms."

I focused on the road, trying to think about cars instead of kinks, but the two now seemed intertwined.

"How much will you miss driving?" It was a stupid question, but I needed to fill the weird silence that was hanging in the air.

"A lot. I can drive on private property though. There's a track that I can use to take a car round – I've done it before a few times."

"No speed limit?"

"No speed limit."

"Does the club know?"

"They don't. No. I don't drive fast enough to be dangerous and I don't take risks, but I do blow off steam." He relaxed a little more into the seat. "How long have you had this?"

"Four years. It's a really good car."

The smile on his face that I could see out of the corner of my eye told me he disagreed.

"I'm not a petrol head, Jesse. As long as my car isn't going to break down or cost me a fortune, it just has to get me from A to B." I slid into the car park at the Maserati garage, feeling sorry for my little Golf, having to be parked near what were supermodels compared to its – well – average form.

His eyes flickered with more amusement. "Let's negotiate. I'm not being driven round for six months in this, although there is nothing wrong with it, it's just not for me. I'll show you what I like, and you choose from that."

"As long as you don't taunt me over my choice. If I make that choice. I might decide that after this morning I'd rather move into Nate's shed than drive you round everywhere." We both knew that wasn't going to happen.

Whatever occurred that night when Jesse drove off, we'd always gotten along well before. He'd hung out a ton at Nate's and while he knew how to push my buttons, I knew that he did it on purpose.

"I'm sure it's a very nice shed. Just like you have a very nice car."

We were out of my car now and he was close enough for me to backhand into his stomach, although my hand was worse off after I hit him.

His abs were officially made of steel.

"Ow." I glared at him. "What are those made of? Did you tense them?"

"You were trying to hit me. Course I tensed them." His hand went to my back. "Can we behave like adults now?"

"We can try." There was a handful of cars in the forecourt all of which could've appeared on a high-end car show. None of them had prices in their windows or at the side. "Is this a case if you have to ask how much it is you can't afford it?"

"Pretty much. This is my one indulgence, Jerrica, apart from my house, so I don't tend to look at the cost."

I nodded, not wanting to ask any more. It felt like a different world.

Nate was part of that world. He had a couple of cars that turned heads and his house was amazing, but his lifestyle was pretty much normal. I knew he invested and next year he was planning on a couple of big holidays, but he'd never flashed any cash, even when he was younger and first signed. Chan had been a little flashier. She'd liked her designer clothes and shoes, and Nate had indulged her, but I knew he had drawn some lines.

He struggled to get Amber to let him even pay for all the baby stuff, which I knew irritated him. There had been a couple of times when I'd found him almost upset because she'd argued her case so hard for going half to some of the stuff they'd bought.

In the end, I'd interfered, explaining it to her from Nate's point of view. He just wanted to look after them both, her and the baby. I knew she'd have a dicky fit when she found out that the house was going to be put in her name in another few months.

I planned to be well out of the way that evening.

Jesse's lifestyle wasn't that different. He didn't party like some of his teammates, although he did go out more than Nate. I didn't remember him ever having a girlfriend and I hadn't heard any gossip from Jude about him hooking up with anyone apart from someone that really was just a regular hook up. Jesse had his cars and his tats and his friends who he hung out with. He trained hard – I knew he didn't drink during the season – and he was seriously involved with Manchester Athletic and their work in the community, which was part of the reason he'd been made captain.

He kept his hand on my back all the way from my car into the showroom.

"Are we going to end up in a gossip column if you're touching me like that?"

His response was to shift closer into me, his hand on my hip. "The salespeople here won't gossip. They're too used to dealing with clients with money, and it might be easier if they think we're together. Less explanation."

"I get it."

His hand didn't move.

My skin was on fire.

If his touch dropped any lower, it would be on my ass.

Please drop lower.

"Can I help?" A woman with perfectly styled blonde hair came over, giving Jesse an appraising look and barely glancing at me.

I shifted closer to Jesse, delivering my best smile.

"I'm looking for a car for Jerrica - "

"Jesse, my man! How's it going?" A rather rotund man boomed over, holding out his hand to Jesse. "Good to see you. I wondered when you'd be looking at one of these to add to your collection."

Collection? I had no idea how many cars he had.

"This one's going to be for Jerrica, so we need to find out what she likes. How's it going anyway, Pete?" His hand lowered, his fingers definitely copping a feel.

I looked at him, giving him my best flirtatious smile, one that I also hoped conveyed the sentiment of *'what the fuck are you doing?'*

"It's great," Pete said, completely oblivious to the fact

that his colleague was throwing serious daggers at him now he'd bumbled through and stolen her sale. "Where do you want to start? What do you fancy?"

Jesse's dark eyes danced with amusement. "Can we take a Quattroporte for a test drive? See how Jerrica finds driving it?"

Pete nodded. "Sure. Let me give you a run down of the car."

"It's being delivered tomorrow to my house." Jesse sat in Nate's kitchen, his phone now on the kitchen island. "You're insured as the main driver."

I sipped on Amber's fruit punch. "You're mad. Spending that much on a car you're not going to drive."

Jesse's laugh was like stained silk. Perfectly smooth, but with just a touch of rough in places.

It sliced through to my core like a very, very pleasant vibration, one I would think about later when I was writing a key scene.

"I'll drive it in six months. It was good to sit in as a passenger. Loads of leg room and the seats were decent. You looked like you enjoyed driving it too."

I had. It had felt like butter, smooth and rich and so very easy. "I think it's ruined me for any other car."

His grin this time was smug. "So the deal's on?"

"It's on. Six months. I don't have any commitments, no holidays planned or anything, so I can work around you." I'd let Nate know already I was taking the job. He'd been pleased, telling me that Jesse was a really decent bloke.

"Have you ever driven abroad? As in Europe?" He sat down on a stool at the kitchen island.

I nodded. "I drove round Europe one summer with a

girlfriend. We took a VW Polo and visited loads of the cities and beaches. I was fine driving on the wrong side of the road."

"Have a think about whether you'd be comfortable going to France with me. There's a vineyard there I'm looking to invest in and I'd planned to visit it this summer. It could be a good break for you – we can visit the vineyard and then stay near a beach or somewhere with a pool for a few days." He toyed with a leather band on his wrist. It was worn and a little frayed. "If you feel weird about it just being us then I'll look at alternative ways to scope it out."

France. It made me think of chateaus and wine and lovely, carby French bread, with cheese and tomatoes ripened under the Mediterranean sun. I'd had an idea for another book, this one not part of my football romance series, but something vacation based, maybe set in Monte Carlo.

Jesse had made it clear he wasn't interested in anything in between us. That didn't mean I couldn't pinch glimpses of him, use him for that inspiration for those scenes.

He never had to know.

"I like the idea. Can we visit Monte Carlo?"

"As long as you don't drive that car like you're in the Grand Prix."

Amber was involved in what looked like pregnancy yoga when I got back, her mat spread where mine had been outside when Jesse found me, some soft music playing from her phone.

She paused what she was doing and assessed me with eyes I knew noticed far more than Nate's ever did.

"You're seriously being Jesse's driver?"

There was no point trying to dress it up. "Six months. He's just bought a new car for me to chauffeur him around in."

"Where is he now?" She looked inside as if expecting him to appear.

"At the training ground with Nicky, Rowan and Nate. He's going to get a lift back here with Nate and I'll run him home." I sat down on the bench Jesse had been on before.

Amber stretched her legs out, her bump exposed from under her tight tank top. "Has anything happened between the two of you?"

"No. It won't either." I wasn't so sure about that. There was a lot of flirting going on, and I'd noticed the way he looked at me. He might be bothered that I was Nate's little sister, but he didn't think of me in a sister-sort-of-way. "At least I don't think so."

Amber's eyes narrowed. She untied her hair that flowed around her shoulders in thick, dark waves. I got why my brother was head over heels for her; she was gorgeous. She was also astute and quick, rational where he could be a little too romantic, and she definitely saw things for what they were.

"Jesse's a great guy. He's a proper professional athlete, but I do wonder what else goes on in his life. He's really guarded about his personal life. I've not known him to have a girlfriend, and all I hear from the other players is banter, really."

"What sort of banter?" I wasn't going to pretend that I wasn't interested in knowing more about Jesse. For a start, if someone was paying attention, they were probably going to notice that my eyes kind of hung around him a lot.

Amber rubbed her belly, pressing a hand down and smiling. "He's moving a lot today. Jesse – so some of the players nicknamed him The Monk because they never saw him hooking up or having a girlfriend. A couple of seasons ago, a player from another team made a comment about Jesse having to tie girls down – I don't know the rest of the context. Jesse just laughed it off rather than being provoked by it. A couple of the players, when they were in the treatment rooms, speculated about it. Whatever he's into, he keeps it very close to his chest."

"He's told me he has a kink. He told me that Nate wouldn't like me to be involved with him." I took a deep breath of air. "That if anything happened between us, it would cause issues for him and Nate."

Amber re-tied her hair. "Nate doesn't get a say in who you go out with. He knows that. But he's never said anything to me about Jesse. I know they get on really well and they've been friends for years. He wouldn't have suggested that you drive for Jesse while he's banned if he didn't trust him."

"I get that. I'm just curious."

"Mystery isn't always that exciting when you get to the bottom of it. His kink might be that he likes his back to be scratched while someone sings Christmas carols to him. Who knows, and unless you really want to find out, who cares? Want me to tell you about your brother's kinks?" Her eyes lit up with mirth.

Mirth at my reaction. "No. For the love of all things cheese, no. It was bad enough when I was sixteen and heard him going at it with a girl through my bedroom wall. I swear I vomited."

Amber started to laugh, hard. "I'll have to ask him about that. Any more juicy stories I can torment him with?

"Tons. Ask him about why he ran out of socks when we were on holiday when he was fourteen. That's always a good one." I was now liking this conversation. "And about the crush he had on a girl called Louise Claire. He couldn't even speak to her."

I had a feeling I'd be on my brother's shit list later. "Jesse drove off that night from here – the night when he got pulled over – because I'd told him I was interested in him."

Amber stilled, her expression changing to serious. "What did he do?"

"He said he couldn't, told me he was sorry and left. I didn't just come out with it, Amber, we'd been flirting and I got the feeling I wasn't reading things wrong. Only maybe I was."

"He's been okay with you since – although, you have kind of avoided him." She crossed her legs and looked very zen, in a pregnant way. "I did wonder if something had happened when you were going to come over and changed your mind when I said Jesse was here."

"Yeah, well. I was embarrassed. I'd made a fool of myself. Yet again." I did not have a great track record with boyfriends or dates. I'd had two longish-term relationships, neither of which had been amazing, just, well, nice. I'd been treated nicely, the sex had been nice, they were both nice men. Oz had been an English teacher, quite hip and trendy, very into his music. We'd ended after we realised we'd gone two weeks without seeing each other and had an awkward conversation about things fizzling out and we'd stay friends – note, we didn't. Carl was an accountant who played cricket at our local club. That ended when he suggested I moved in because then we'd save money, so it was logical. I really didn't want to live with him, which made me question why I was with him at all because it wasn't going anywhere. Apart from Oz and Carl, there had been a couple of one night stands and a few flings, none of which were worth keeping a diary about. There had been a guy I'd been crazy over, and, when I'd declared my love, he'd laughed in my face.

I'd been mortified. Especially when he'd told his mates about it, and one of their girlfriends had spread it around.

"How's Jesse been today?"

"Flirty. Friendly. I don't know – I kind of feel he has an agenda with wanting me to be his driver and I can't work it out. But, I could really use the money. I know Nate would lend it me – he's already offered, but at some point our parents would find out and I can't go through another lecture." I got off my seat and sat down on the mat with Amber.

She tipped her head to one side and smiled. "You'll have fun with Jesse."

"He's mentioned us going to France. Driving there."

"Oh, the vineyard? He mentioned that a couple of months ago. Do it. You get a holiday and maybe some inspo for your books. Jesse's hardly hard to look at – unless he's you know, *hard*."

We both started giggling.

"Have you ever seen him? As in, no clothes?" I was well aware I shouldn't be asking those sorts of questions. Amber was a professional and I knew she kept to those boundaries.

With the exception of bumping uglies with my brother - in her treatment room at the club. That nugget of information had slipped out of his mouth, not hers.

"He's covered with tattoos, and he works out. A lot. His body fats are seriously low and he knows how to train so his body is all that, but because he's an older player he's filled out more, like Nate. Jesse doesn't need to be as quick now because he's got Nicky on the wing to do the running, but he's quick at reading the game and knowing where that ball is going to drop, or where the defender's going to go. But you weren't asking about his football skills, were you?" Her giggle made her sound young.

"Kind of. I know how good he is. He's the team's target man to get the ball to because he'll convert a good assist into a goal, and he's the target man for defenders too." I knew enough about football to write books on it, which I was doing, although the balls I wrote about mainly weren't made of leather. "His body's cut."

"I think he's carrying a decent sized weapon too, because you do see stuff when you're knocking about. You might find out. If you do, you can tell me all about it." Her smile was dirty. 'And I promise I won't return the favour and tell you about Nate's."

"I saw my brother's junk when our parents made us bathe together as kids and I'm scarred from that." I rolled my eyes. I needed no further information. "Does Dee ever share?"

"When she's drunk. Then she doesn't shut up. We should invite them over – Genny, Neva, and Dee for afternoon tea. A boozy one, for you lot anyway." Amber put both her hands on her stomach. "And when Oliver's made his debut, I'm going to rediscover wine."

"You're sticking with Oliver?"

She nodded. "We are. Oliver Morris. Unless he doesn't look like an Oliver, in which case I have no idea."

"Nate's just over the moon and thrilled. I don't think

I've ever seen him as happy as this. Ever." Even with Chan I hadn't seen my brother so damn content and satisfied. When he looked at Amber, especially when the girls were sat with her, he looked like a cat that had all the cream.

Amber tried to hide her smile, but it bloomed anyway. "I think I know the feeling. I didn't ever expect to be this happy. I just hope we get through the next few months and the birth goes well. Then life will get really wild for a while." She gazed at her bump and then looked back at me. "Are you going to go to France with Jesse?"

I nodded. I'd thought about it some since this morning. "I think so. It's my only chance to have a holiday and I love France, so - "

"You can find out all the secrets about our brooding star striker."

"Arguably, that's Ryan O'Connor. He scored one more goal than Jesse last season and played fewer games." I was a geek. I could list stats about the team off the top of my head.

"Mention that to Jesse. See what he says."

I grinned. I might just do that.

CHAPTER 5
Jesse

I WASN'T sure that I was going to enjoy having a driver who liked pointing out to me that my goals per game average was less than my partner's. When pressed, she suggested that I'd missed five opportunities to score goals with my head. When I pressed back, she told me which matches these were and whether it was the first or second half.

I didn't ask my driver, also known as Jerrica the Football Analyst, in for a coffee when she dropped me off, but I did enjoy telling her that I needed picking up for a training session at seven-thirty the next day.

I lay in my bed, staring up at my ceiling, trying not to think about Jerrica in her booty shorts exercising this morning.

Was it only this morning? It felt like three weeks ago. I was a hundred grand lighter after buying a car I couldn't drive, and I had a boner for a woman I couldn't touch. My training session with her brother had reinforced exactly why I couldn't touch as well.

Jerrica's been messed about by men.

Jerrica's finding her feet with what she wants to do. I really hope she can stay focused on this.

Jerrica's really talented at writing; this is what she wants to do. I just hope it works out for her.

Thanks for this, Jesse, I know you'll look after her. I can see you being really good friends.

Friends didn't stare at each other the way I'd eaten up Jerrica with my eyes this morning. They didn't wonder about how soft their skin would feel under calloused fingers, or how their hair would look spread over a pillow.

Those were the tame thoughts. I didn't need any of my edgier thoughts to get as hard as I was now.

I didn't need a psychologist to tell me why I enjoyed the things I did, such as punishing myself through needing to maintain control over almost every aspect of my life. As a kid, I lived all over. My grandma's house in Hackney, my cousin's house in Knowsley, the uncle of my mum's new 'friend' in Cardiff – and there was a reason he agreed I could stay for a summer. When I worked out what that reason was, I stole his wallet and left, managing to get to my aunt in Coventry without being stopped. I'd been eleven.

At fifteen I was sofa surfing on friend's couches, working all sorts of jobs to pay for football boots and kit, and to stay out of the care system, because that experience hadn't been good either.

My mum died when I was sixteen and she was thirty-one. Drug overdose, accidental, or that was how it was reported on her death certificate. I was back living with her at that point in a tiny one-bedroomed flat back in Knowsley, and that night I was late returning home because the chance of a second shift at the takeaway where I was working came up.

If I'd have been home on time, I'd have been there earlier to save her.

When you grow up in chaos, you crave control. When you carry guilt on your shoulders like it weighs the same as your mother's coffin, you learn how to punish yourself.

That didn't mean I didn't enjoy it. There was a perverse pleasure in withholding what I craved, controlling my own enjoyment to a point where I thought I deserved it. Everything was rationalised. Everything was chosen. Even my penance.

Which was why my dick was hard enough to be used as a hammer in some pornographic house reno show.

I would not jerk off to thoughts of Nate's sister.

'Nate's sister' was exactly how I needed to think of her. There was no way I would, one, corrupt her into any of my slightly more wicked than normal ways – not that there was much that could be called normal. Two, she was just too much of a good person for me. Too pretty, too happy, too kind and nice and wholesome. I didn't do wholesome. Three, Nate. Probably the best friend I'd ever had, the only person who knew about my shitty childhood, because no one needed to lavish me with pity and I really didn't need the questioning eyes about how shit things had actually been.

I'd had therapy. I still had therapy. When I'd signed as a kid for Liverpool, the safeguarding lead, Mel, had been passed the details by the social worker who was doing her best to look out for me. She'd interfered in the best possible way, telling me what I was entitled to and why the club wanted to help – because it was in their best interests. There were no favours that would need returning. No pitiful glances. No questions. She'd shown me what to do to live in the accommodation for the trainees, told me to do A-Levels because somehow I'd ended up with a decent set of qualifications after I'd left school, and then she'd in no uncertain terms told me to talk to a professional because if I couldn't unscrew my head, I'd fuck my career up before I'd even tied my laces.

So I'd gone to a therapist she found for me. The same therapist I still saw now.

The same therapist who'd helped me to accept who I was and why I chose to act in the ways I did. I liked me. I had no issue with who I was anymore, and I'd accepted that too.

But that didn't mean sweet women like Jerrica Morris could become a notch on my bedpost.

My cock throbbed. Usually, I'd arrange to meet with Nicola or Polly, very occasionally both of them together. I knew them from a dating service that was very expensive and very discreet. Nicola was married, and the CEO of a huge company dealing with tech. Polly worked in stocks and was married to her job. Both made enough decisions during the course of the day to want to give someone else the job of making decisions in the bedroom. We'd had our arrangement for three years, seeing each other every two or three weeks, whenever it fitted in with the rest of our lives. They'd both signed non-disclosure agreements. I'd signed theirs too. Then we'd had thorough discussions about boundaries and safe words, what they liked, what they didn't. How far we went.

It worked. Only now, I was hamstrung with not being able to get to them without asking for a damn lift, and neither of them ever came to me.

Jerrica had been in my house countless times. I'd had the team over, some of the backroom staff, their families and partners, for parties and barbecues. Nate's daughters had stayed here overnight a few times, especially when their old house was packed up in boxes and they'd started to get a bit angsty.

Jerrica had stayed with them.

In the room next to mine, and I still hadn't changed those sheets.

I groaned. I wasn't going to be able to get to sleep with what I had going on between my legs and as much as I could get off on depriving myself of what I wanted, I'd also learned when it was best to let myself have it.

My en-suite was black marble with gold fixings and my favourite room in the house. The shower was a big, tiled walk in with a built-in seat and handles that looked like they could be used to hold towels.

They weren't for that purpose. They hadn't been used yet either.

I was already naked, clothes in bed seemed pointless, so all I had to do was get under the jets and pretend I was somewhere else, with someone else.

I used my shower gel to lather up my hand, the water turning quickly from cool to hot, and started to work my hand slowly up and down my shaft, the water hitting my back hard.

Images of Jerrica's legs played through my head on repeat. Soft perfect skin, those tiny jean shorts and that cropped top, showing off a stomach that I would've liked to have run my fingers over, delving into the secrets of what lay below those shorts.

I wondered what she tasted like. What sounds she made when she came, if she needed soft, tender strokes or she preferred to be taken to the edge and held there, kept from coming.

I imagined the latter. I imagined how she'd be in here

with me now, holding onto to those handles, my fingers fucking her pussy, finding that sweet spot; my other hand busying with her clit, pinching, holding, rubbing, until she got closer and closer to that edge, then bringing her back from it, until finally I let her go.

That release. Always sweeter when it took longer to get there.

I leaned a hand against the shower wall, keeping my strokes firm and the tempo slow. I was not going to edge myself, not tonight, because that would be a treat, but neither was I rushing to the end.

My imagination was generally limited to plays on the field and plays in the bedroom. When I did this, I usually relived something that had happened already, but I had nothing to go off because I'd not even touched Jerrica.

I could only imagine it.

I came almost without warning, coating the shower wall with my release and filling the room with a groan, my eyelids closed and my head full of ideas about what it would be like to be inside her.

For a minute I stood there under the jets, cock still in hand, still hard. My orgasm hadn't satisfied me. I still felt as if I needed to run a few miles or lift something too heavy. Some way to burn off this energy even if I couldn't do it the way I wanted.

None of those were a possibility. It was late, and in a few hours Jerrica would be here picking me up. That blonde hair and those long legs would be in my house, because while I could make her wait in her car, I wasn't that much of a dick.

I would make coffee, offer her breakfast that wasn't on Neva the nutritionist's approved list, and manage some small talk.

Thinking of small talk managed to send me to sleep.

Jerrica was early. Not only was she early, she was bright and breezy and had a smile on her face that had me smiling straight back.

If I truly was an arsehole, I would have put her down for being so sunshiny at this time of day and made her feel small, but that was the stuff of men who were the same sorts of dickheads as the men my mother had latched onto. I'd told Jerrica we couldn't happen. We both knew where the line was.

"Are you always early?" I let her into my house, noticing how she appraised the entrance hall which had changed since she'd last been here. "Not that I'm complaining."

Her smile was bright, her blonde curls bouncing as she shook her head. "I'm usually on time. Zara was up early and woke me instead of Amber and Nate."

"Another bad dream?" I knew the current youngest Morris was having a series of nightmares.

"About the pond and swamp monsters. I think Nate's going to be spending the afternoon taking her pond dipping there. Can I smell coffee?"

"You can. And there's croissants. Is it too early for you to eat?"

By the look on her face, it definitely wasn't.

"Do you have butter and jam?"

I wondered if her expression was the same when she was close to orgasm.

"I do, but don't tell Neva."

Jerrica laughed. "Neva scares me."

"Neva scares most sane people. She's actually okay." I

led her through to the kitchen. "Her and Amber are good friends, I think." Some of the squad thought they were as scary as each other. Amber was known to be harsh with her treatments and had never been shy of administering a bollocking when someone wasn't following her advice. Rowan had suggested she might mellow with being pregnant, but that hadn't happened; she was even more brutal, although she'd now started her maternity leave.

"I needed to mention something to do with her – and Dee and Genny too. Amber wants to have an afternoon tea, which will involve fizz for everyone bar her. Is there an afternoon and evening where you're not going to need me to drive?" She looked almost hesitant to ask. "I don't have much of a social life, Jesse, so I'm not going to be asking this often."

"Look, just let me know when it is and if I need to get somewhere I'll sort something out. But if you're doing that at Nate's, I'll do a barbecue here for the lads." I poured her a coffee, remembering that she took milk but no sugar. "I don't expect you at my beck and call." There was only one room where I liked my woman to follow what I said, and even then, with one word they could pull all the control back. "If you have something to do, just let me know you're not available."

"Thank you, I will. And thanks for the coffee." She sipped at the drink even though it was piping hot. "Are those the croissants?"

Her eyes lit up again. I checked myself at the jolt of pleasure I got from just doing something nice for her.

"They need about five minutes in the oven. I'll put it on."

"Are you having one?"

I shook my head. "Not today. I'm getting breakfast at

Kitty's after we've finished training." Kitty ran a café across the way from the training complex that specialised in protein rich, healthy foods. Kitty's degree had been in food and nutrition, so she'd clicked with Neva, and we'd ended up with the benefit of a café nearby that stuck to our diet plans. Our winger, Nicky, hung around there all the goddamn time, sometimes helping serve if Kitty was short staffed, so it had ended up becoming a bit of a haunt. We enjoyed taking the piss out of Nicky when he pulled on a Kitty's Café shirt, making sure our orders were hugely complicated and knowing full well he'd come back with what we usually had.

Nicky had less of a social life than me. I'd never known him have a girlfriend or to hook up, which didn't mean he didn't – because most of the team would think the same about me. But what I was absolutely sure of was that Nicky and Kitty definitely had a thing for each other; they'd just not worked it out yet.

"I'll see you in there. I'll get some writing done while you train." She walked over to my fridge. "Is it okay to get the butter out?"

My back tensed to the point where I thought it might snap. I forced myself to blink.

Jerrica would've been in my fridge when people had been hanging out here, but not like this. Not when it was just me and a woman in my house.

"Sure." I busied myself, sticking the croissants in the oven, finding the pre-workout supplements I added to my shakes before training and checking my phone, even though the only notification was that someone had liked a social media post that the company I paid to sort stuff like that out had posted a few minutes ago.

"What is it that you're writing at the moment?"

She blushed, finding oven gloves I'd left on the side and taking the croissants out. "Second in my football series. It should be finished today."

"What's it about? I know it's romance, but every story's got to be different, hasn't it?" I didn't want to give too much away that I'd read some of her first book – now in more detail than just skimming. It was interesting, seeing what could be construed as a healthy romantic relationship. The sex scenes were hot; I just didn't let myself think how they were also insight into what Jerrica might like.

She smiled, that smile that made her face light up. "This one's enemies-to-lovers, you know, they start off hating each other and then they can't keep their hands off each other. A bit like Rowan and Dee."

I frowned. "Rowan isn't like, inspiration for this, is he? Because, just no." I shook my head, taking out the premade smoothie from the fridge Kitty's team had delivered the day before. She had the right idea: we gave her our menus and she – or her team – put together the shakes and juices for three days at a time.

I added the pre-workout supplement and gave it a shake, bracing myself for the taste of grass. This was one drink that even Kitty couldn't make taste decent.

"I don't base any of my characters on a real person. That would just be weird." She laughed. "Although I don't need to imagine how my characters might look. I just need to watch a training session."

I pulled my vest up, exposing my abs, watching Jerrica's face.

She burst out laughing.

"Subtle, Jesse, subtle."

"I'm trying to help. You know, provide some of that inspo."

"Yeah, thanks, but you're just going to make me avoid looking at you completely. How long will you be at the training complex?"

I took a gulp of the drink and winced. It was as bad as I thought it would be. "We're doing drills then hitting the weights for leg day. Probably about three hours. Can you manage three hours at Kitty's?"

I didn't feel guilty. She knew there would be some waiting around and it wasn't that far from the complex that she couldn't come back to Nate's. I also knew she would be able to use one of the rooms in the complex to write if she didn't want to be in Kitty's for that long. I was also paying her a huge amount for this.

"I can manage a full day at Kitty's." She rolled her eyes. "It just means I'll need to go for a run later because I can't resist her cakes." She slapped her thigh.

It didn't wobble.

"I'll run with you later."

She raised her brows. "I'm not sure that's a good idea."

"Why?"

"I'll be too slow for you."

"You won't. I'm not looking to go fast after what I'll be doing this morning. Just build up stamina."

She lifted the croissant up to her lips, still looking at me as if she was appraising me. "Is your stamina not good enough already? Have you had complaints?"

The air in the room became charged.

A lungful of oxygen got stuck in my throat. It wasn't an innocent comment from Jerrica. It was meant the way it sounded.

I should play it down. Mention something about my coaches, pretend to take it innocently.

Even I had my limits.

"Trust me, when I say my *stamina* has never been an issue."

Those gorgeously plump lips curved into a tease of a smile. "I'll have to take your word for it."

My jaw clenched. My eyes dropped to the short skirt she was wearing that exposed those long legs far more than was good for my health. "My word's pretty good." It was a promise.

"Hmmm." Her eyes danced, her mouth full of buttery croissant.

I looked away, fully aware that I was being tortured on purpose.

So this was how the next six months were going to go.

Blaine Richards, one of our strength and conditioning coaches, had gotten wind of the extra training we were doing and turned up as we were getting started. Nate and I had picked up enough over the years to be able to set up some decent training but Blaine had clearly decided we needed some extra evil added, plus some good old competition.

"Charts, lads," he said, pulling in a white board on wheels into the training room we were using which was big enough to do some of the fitness tests. "And a league table. Sprints, sit ups, press-ups, burpees, plank. Plus bench press, squat, deadlift, clean and jerk for those inclined – we'll do that based on your body weight."

He grinned evilly. This was Blaine's idea of absolute heaven.

"What about the rest of the team?" Nicky looked at the board.

I knew the kid would be itching to get to the top somewhere there. He was at that age when he was starting to fill out properly, and he was putting on muscle easier now than a couple of years ago when he'd not been able to eat enough and keep weight on.

"They start when their lazy arses show up here. So if Hollywood Ball's going to spend most of his time cavorting with *ac*-tors this summer, he's going to end up at the bottom of the table." Blaine's eyes drifted over to Ryan, who was already stretching out.

Ryan just shook his head. He was one of the best trainers at the club as he'd shown last season, quietly just getting on with it and treating it as a science.

Like Nate and I, he was on track for an England call up for the World Cup. Nicky and Jude were on the periphery of the squad, which was another reason Nicky was going to be sweating his balls off over the summer break, making sure he was fit enough to start the season not needing match fitness, which meant drills like these. In another couple of weeks, we'd start long runs, ten miles at a minimum, adding in fartleks where we played around with speed, sprints intermingled with slower jogs over a series of miles which better matched the changes of pace in a football match. Nicky had been here before any of us this morning, already starting on speed work. As a schoolboy, he'd been a really decent sprinter over two hundred metres, and he could've taken that higher, but I knew he loved football.

I'd be thrilled for him if he could pick up a few caps for England at the World Cup this winter.

Ryan had beaten me to be the club's top scorer last season, which should've stung more than it had. He was a poacher, the sort of player that could pick up the ball at the half way line, take one glance at the goal and chip the keeper.

He'd had three goals up for the goal of the season award, whereas most of mine were opportune. Headers – although Jerrica was right; I'd missed a few sitters – and powerful first touches that blasted the back of the net. I had fewer classy touches than Ryan, but I'd win the ball in the penalty area, my size and strength keeping some defenders clear.

We started with a good old fashioned bleep test, one with an extension that we'd needed because of Ryan O'Connell, although I was expecting him to not quite be as fresh now he had a high-tariff girlfriend.

Two hours later and I was flat on my back, pouring a bottle of water over my head and wondering if my heart was still inside my body or whether it had managed to burst through my rib cage.

"That was fucking brutal." Rowan Reeves sat down next to me, close enough that I could smell a combination of sweat, aftershave and possibly Dee Jones' perfume. "Someone tell Dee I love her and she's named on my life insurance policy."

Ryan laughed, still managing to look annoyingly fresh. He'd managed to score himself Otter Penhaligon, who he hadn't recognised – he must've been the only person in the modern world not to know that she was an award laden actress – and somehow she'd fallen for him, even though he was the biggest geek ever.

"Dee was outside actually. She was looking for you." Ryan gestured to the door. "Do us all a favour and shower first. You stink." He frowned. "Why do you kind of smell of Dee under the sweat?"

I knew it wasn't just me.

"Er, that would be transference." Rowan could wipe the shit eating grin off his face.

"Were you expending energy before our training session?" I manage to sit myself up.

"I've been expending energy since the end of the season." Rowan squinted at the door. "Is Dee still there?"

"She said she'd see you at Kitty's." Ryan looked incredibly amused, his arms folded and eyes fixed on Rowan. "Are you struggling to keep up with her?"

"No." Rowan was the world's worst liar.

We were all grinning now. This was gold.

"Do you need some little blue pills?" Nate waggled his little finger. "We can always ask coach over there to sort some out."

Blaine spat out his coffee. "Keep me out of this."

Rowan shook his head. "Seriously, I think she's taking something. It's like all the fucking time. As soon as Toby's asleep, or he's at school, we're on our own anywhere – and I mean anywhere – she's on me."

"You're seriously complaining, bro?" Nate frowned at him. "It's the off-season. It's not like you have to conserve your energy. It's good cardio."

Rowan was quiet for a second. "If I didn't know better, I'd think she was trying to get us pregnant."

I glanced at Nate. He was probably the best qualified to respond to that sort of statement.

"Have you talked to her?"

Rowan shook his head. "I don't think she's actually trying, although I'm up for it. We've talked about waiting for another few years until she's ready to stop playing. But I can't exactly say to her 'I think we're having too much sex', can I? What if this is how it's been with her other boyfriends and it's me? I mean, would you guys complain?" His Geordie accent thickened.

"How often are you talking?" Ryan took a bottle of water from the fridge. "Per day."

"Three or four times. She woke me up this morning getting on my dick, then in the changing rooms here – close your ears, Coach. That's twice before seven-thirty. Yesterday there was before we picked Toby up from school and before we went to sleep, so that's four times in twenty-four hours. I think my balls are going to run dry."

He actually looked pained.

Ryan laughed. "I never thought I'd be listening to you moaning about having to put out."

Rowan shook his head. "I need to speak to her, don't I?"

"Take her out for a meal. Drop Toby off at ours tomorrow night and book somewhere she really likes. Get dressed up and have flowers ready for her before you go out. Then seduce her." Ryan put his hands behind his head and tilted back on the chair.

Anyone else would fall over backwards now, but not Ryan. It was like the sun shone on him constantly.

It was a good thing he was a really great bloke, because otherwise we'd all hate him.

"Doesn't that defeat the object of trying to give my dick a break?" Rowan frowned.

Ryan shook his head. "When's the last time you instigated sex?"

"I don't get a chance because Dee practically lives on my dick." Rowan groaned. "I really shouldn't be fucking complaining."

"Before you bring it up, you need to make the first move. Make sure she knows you're still really interested." Ryan finished the water. "Otter was phoning me loads last week, just for stupid things and I worked out it was because I hadn't been texting her what I had for breakfast."

Otter was currently filming something somewhere that wasn't in Manchester. Next week the two of them were off on holiday. A pinch of me was jealous of Ryan and Rowan and Nate because they had these relationships that seemed to ground them, give them a sense of being more than simply a footballer. Maybe I was at the age where I needed to think about what it would mean to have a relationship.

I automatically thought of Jerrica.

Then I shut that door in my head because it couldn't go anywhere. Those thoughts were only going to end up being as frustrating as fuck.

"So she could be this *horny* - " Rowan cringed at the word, "because I've not been making it clear I want her?"

"Have you been making it clear?" Ryan stretched his legs out and crossed them at the ankles. "I might start charging for this advice."

Rowan looked like he was going to choke. "I wouldn't change careers yet, ROC. I think I have but maybe not as much as she's used to. Okay. Meal. Flowers. Hotel room?"

Ryan nodded. "If you can. Then at some point just find out why she's so in the mood all the time. But make sure she doesn't think it's a problem. You could say that you're worried you're not man enough for her."

"I'm not saying that." Rowan folded his arms. "No, man. I'm plenty man enough for her. I just need a day off, or even half a day off, so parts of my dick can grow the skin back."

"Lube." Nate patted his shoulder. "Highly recommend it." He looked at me. "Especially if it's your hand you're seducing."

I shook my head, saying nothing. The fact that last

night I'd jerked off while thinking about Nate's sister was enough to seal my lips shut completely on the topic.

"Are we all off to Kitty's then?"

There was a collective yes and we all managed to scrape ourselves off the floor or various chairs and to the showers.

CHAPTER 6
Jerrica

WE SETTLED on Saturday for an afternoon tea, inviting Genny, Neva and Dee, along with Ryan's girlfriend, Otter, which was a bit unnerving given she was a really well-known actress. A few of the other players from the women's team came too, as well as Leila Downey, whose day job was as a sports journalist, but knew how to leave that at the door so she did hang out with Amber and Genny sometimes. I kind of felt that Leila was lonely. She was in a male dominated environment, and the amount of focus on her looks and how she dressed compared to her talent was ridiculous. She'd told me once that it was cutthroat, and she couldn't really trust many people. She also spent a hell of a lot of time on the road, so her friends from school and college had grown up and they didn't have much in common.

I was glad Amber had thought to invite her, especially when she turned up with a mountain of macaroons and a bottle of Aperol.

Neva fussed around Amber, who didn't usually like being fussed over. I watched from the kitchen, through the open bi-fold doors as Neva insisted that Amber didn't lift a finger.

"She's still trying to make up for how she was when she found out that Amber was pregnant." Genny sat at the kitchen island with a glass of champagne, looking outside as well. "And telling your brother."

I sat down next to her. Everything was ready. Sandwiches were made, cakes were set, the teapots were set out and the kettle had already boiled. Neva had gone to town on the cute napkins and a tea service that she'd hired for the occasion.

"I don't think either of them were ever bothered about Neva telling Nate. It helped, I think." Amber had found out she was pregnant and not told Nate for a few weeks while she got her head round it, as she'd never planned to have children. Nate, being him, had seen the bigger picture, which was kind of what he always did.

"Yeah, well, Neva was a cow." Genny shook her head. "I love her to death but she really can be hard work."

I laughed. "She's one of your best friends."

"Which is why I can say it. But you know what's really bothering me?" She put her champagne glass down, so I knew she was serious. "She's shagging someone and not saying anything."

"Neva?"

Genny nodded. "Neva. Straight-laced, never breaks the rules Neva is definitely knocking boots with someone and my guess is it's someone on the team." Her eyes gleamed.

Genny, full name Genevieve, was the team's glue. She ran the club, apart from the actual stuff on the field. She was the ultimate professional, at least when she was at work. My only tie to the club was Nate and being friends with Amber through Nate, so recently, when we'd grabbed a coffee or managed to sneak a late lunch, she'd started to open up.

"You think Neva's seeing one of the players? Which one?"

Genny shook her head. "I'm not sure. I don't think she thinks it's serious, which tells me it's one of the younger players. Not Nicky. He's in denial about Kitty."

Something we all knew. "Jude?"

"I'm not sure. I can't see her with Jude. He's so much of a baby."

"Is he? Everyone thinks that because he's been in the spotlight since he was a kid, but he's twenty-three. That isn't a kid anymore." He'd been playing out of his skin and had stayed out of the gossip columns for the last few months, which could be a clue that he was seeing someone. I also knew that Jude couldn't hold water. He was one of the biggest gossips I'd ever met.

"I'll do some digging. I've asked Neva if she's seeing anyone and she's outright lied to me and said no." Genny peered outside. "She needs to stop making amends. Amber will flip if she fusses anymore."

That was a possibility. I'd heard Amber snap at Nate twice today, reminding him that she was pregnant and not injured. He'd sensibly made himself scarce for a couple of hours over dinner time.

"I heard you're officially Jesse's designated driver. How's that working?" Genny's eyes danced with the possibility of more gossip.

"He goes to training. He comes here. Next week he starts at the summer soccer school. I get to drive a really expensive car around. There have been no bars or drops offs at women's houses or anything scandalous." I'd say he had a boring life, but I didn't find Jesse boring at all. Anything but.

"He asked you to keep any paddles or handcuffs in the boot?"

"Come again?" I raised my brows at Genny.

She smiled and shook her head. "Rumour has it, and it's a really quiet rumour because Jesse's a good guy who's come through a very, very shitty childhood, that he's a bit of a dom."

"Oh. Ohhhh." A shiver went straight down my spine and lit something in my core on fire. I swallowed, then reached for the bottle of champagne for a top up. "That kind of fits."

Genny looked at me curiously. "Fits what? Your fantasies? Your expectations?"

"He said he had a kink." That was all I was going to say on the matter of the short conversation Jesse and I had. "But I see it now. He's very – dominant, but in a really quiet way."

"I know. He oozes it. He has a smoulder. And he's intense. If I was going to do a player, he would be my choice."

"You like a pair of handcuffs?"

Genny laughed. "I prefer using them on someone."

'Someone in particular?" I suspected who she'd used them on; strongly suspected.

"Twice. I repaid the favour. It was a time when we got on very well. Let's go back to Jesse." Her intense gaze that usually got millionaire footballers to confess every single one of their fuck ups was turned on me. "Would you go there?"

I was a glass and a half of champagne in. That was all. And we were already having this conversation. I'd forgotten what warm afternoons with alcohol were like with girlfriends – it had been that long.

Delicate footsteps sounded against the marble tiles. "Get your backsides out here." Neva's petite frame walked in. "What are you talking about? It looks serious."

Genny didn't pause. "Whether Jez would let Jesse handcuff her to a bed."

"Oh. I'd have to include that in his diet plan." Neva's expression stayed serious. "Outside. Now."

Genny rolled her eyes, because there was no way she was going to do what Neva said without some form of battle.

Amber looked at me through dark lashes as I sat down. "Remember, I'm sober. I will remember everything." She tapped her glass, full of a different fruit punch that Neva had made.

"But will you tell Nate?" I loved my relationship with Amber. We lived together, albeit in a really big house. She was now the mother figure to my nieces and the centre of my brother's world. We'd become friends and I liked everything about her, including how she took exactly no shit from anyone, but I was mindful because her loyalty would always be to my brother, as it should.

She shook her head. "Not unless I think you're in danger of being hurt. But if you want to discuss Jesse's tattoos, cock size or something to do with handcuffs, I'm here."

"Please tell me you and Nate have never done anything with handcuffs?" I felt my heart rate rise as my anxiety levels grew.

Amber laughed. "I think we'd slept together on four or five occasions before I found out he'd knocked me up, so it's safe to say we haven't explored it yet. We'll make time for that later, I'm sure."

"I'm going to vomit."

Everyone else laughed, including Leila, who was now with us, and Dee, along with a couple of Dee's teammates.

"What were you and Genny talking about so intently?" Neva sat back in her chair, her dark hair draping down behind her. "I heard the word handcuffs, so I assume it's something to do with Jesse."

Amber caught my eye and raised her brows. I shrugged.

"I really don't know anything. He's a really nice guy. He's funny, considerate and easy on the eye." It was all true. All I knew was what I'd heard on the grapevine.

"He has a woman he hooks up with. I don't know who she is, but I think she's some high-powered businesswoman. I don't think it's a date type thing. I think it's just sex," Neva said, swirling her drink in her glass. "I know he had a girlfriend a few years ago, and I think she was a wannabe WAG. Since then, he's been so secretive about what he gets up to."

"I can see Jesse having complete control in the bedroom." Amber was smiling at me now. "The question is, would you want your man to be like that all the time?"

"He might not be like that all the time," I said, my imagination starting to go into overdrive. If nothing else, I could get a character out of this, or the basis for one. "It might be like a steak; you don't eat one every night, but when you do, it hits the spot."

"Or anal." Dee reached over the table for the jug of what was definitely not alcoholic. "Although don't tell Rowan it hits the spot."

"What was going on with the two of you last week? He whisked you away somewhere for the night, didn't he?"

The conversation deviated away from Jesse, as it was always going to. I listened in to Dee's tale of tiring Rowan out as a point of revenge because he'd done the same to her a few weeks beforehand, which was both kind of cute and envy-inducing.

I hadn't had sex for nine months. Probably more, because it had been a bit before I'd moved up north to stay with Nate. In two weeks, I was heading off to France with Jesse, driving him to a vineyard in the middle of the French countryside. I needed to get laid before then, else my road rage was going to be off the Richter Scale.

It was close to seven in the evening, our afternoon tea disintegrating into evening cocktails and a debate about whether we would manage to barbecue decently given that only Amber was sober, when Nate turned up with Libbie and Zara, plus the rest of the men who'd been hanging around Jesse's for the day.

I didn't need to look up to know that Jesse was with them, my body already knew. I'd developed a sixth sense where Jesse Sullivan was concerned somewhere around Christmas when I'd watched him score a hat-trick against Arsenal before running up to where I was sitting and sliding down on his knees, our eyes meeting. My little romantic heart had decided he'd scored that goal for me, even though I knew he'd had no clue about who was actually in the stands in front of him. He was high on the euphoria of scoring a hat-trick. Santa Claus could've been sat where I was.

Amber got up to take over from Nate with the girls.

While they had a nanny, he wasn't their parent. Things like bath time and bedtime were done by Nate, and now Amber; even school runs were done by Nate unless he couldn't because of training. I knew he'd been reluctant to have a nanny, wanting his kids to grow up like we had with parents who were there pretty much all the time, but as a single dad, that hadn't been doable with his career. Chan's mum had stepped in, but her illness shortly after Chan's death had forced Nate's hand.

Today, Leon had the day off. He had most weekends off unless there was a match. The girls had been at Jesse's, probably terrorising whatever nature lived in his garden. They were loving the warm days and being outside, which I was glad to see. A few months ago, Libbie was becoming too quiet and shy. That had now reversed.

I tried to focus on their chatter rather than Jesse being nearby, moving to another part of the garden to stay away from his periphery. Neva was talking to Kitty about food and restaurants; involving myself in that seemed like a good way to find a distraction, only every time I looked up, I noticed Jesse.

He was wearing weathered denim shorts, his legs displaying both muscles and tattoos. My eyes crawled up his torso, a muscle top hid some of his skin, tattoos crawling out from beneath the material.

My heart beat out a rhythm that was too fast. My mouth felt dry.

When my gaze found his eyes they were looking straight at me. I expected him to be smirking at the fact he'd caught me drinking him in, but he wasn't. His expression was serious, his eyes dark.

I looked away first. I couldn't hold his gaze any longer, my skin on fire, my chest about to explode.

"You okay?" Kitty nudged me with her elbow. "You've gone all flushed."

"Just the heat." It was a hot day. "And the alcohol."

I noticed Neva had moved over to talk to Genny.

Kitty smiled, but it contained more than just empathy for the heat. "You know what I think it is about Jesse?" Kitty said. "He's got this dangerous vibe going on, but you also know he'd never, ever let anything hurt you. All the thrills and none of the pain."

"Was I that obvious?" I pressed my lips together.

She nodded. "Pretty much. You both were, if it's any consolation."

I shook my head. "It's not going to happen though."

"You tell yourself that and you might just start to believe it." Her smile was sweet.

I watched her as her eyes fell on Nicky. "Does it work?"

"What's that?"

"Telling yourself you're not interested? That you're just friends?" I sipped the Pimms that we'd started to drink. I was pretty sure someone had spiked it with vodka too, as it was feeling like rocket fuel going down.

Probably Genny.

Kitty shook her head. "No. He really is just a friend."

"Okay." I believed her as much as I believed myself when I said I didn't want anything to happen with me and Jesse.

I looked over at him again. He was talking to my brother, who had a beer in his hand which meant Leon was back from his time away and had agreed to stay sober in case anyone needed a trip to the hospital. I allowed myself a minute to just watch him, his slightly too long jet-black hair curling at the ends, still neatly styled; his ridiculously muscled arms covered with tats and I knew each one told a story, I just didn't know the story.

No man had ever had this effect on me. He hadn't kissed me or touched me deliberately in any way that was intimate, yet he was making me feel that I was already on my back underneath him without him even glancing my way.

I was just a girl with a crush on a man that so many women wanted.

Join the queue, Jerrica.

My brother wandered over to Amber, who was carrying Zara, a Zara who, by all accounts, didn't want to miss the rest of the party by going to bed.

Jesse turned away from Nate and looked straight at me, catching me staring at him again. He gave me a look that told me he'd caught me, then a smile that told me he knew why I'd been staring.

I felt the blush cover my face, taking a long pull of my drink to hide my embarrassment, but refusing to look away. I hadn't seen him since yesterday evening, when I'd dropped him off at home after training and then a meeting he had with his agent at a hotel in Prestbury.

I felt like it had been a week since I'd laid eyes on him.

He started to walk over to me, eyes fixed on mine, his smile now teasing, taunting.

"I'm going to leave you to explain why you were perving on him in private," Kitty whispered into my ear. "Just ask him why he was looking at you too."

I shook my head, keeping my chin up and my honesty levels high.

Jesse already knew I was attracted to him. I'd propositioned him already.

When he reached me he didn't say anything, just put

his hand on my arm and moved me away from the crowds in the garden to where it was quieter near the area that had been recently cleared to build a treehouse for the girls. Various trees gave privacy, creating an area that my brother was having cameras put in when the treehouse was done so he could keep an eye on the girls – and one day his son – playing, but for now it was secluded.

"You can't look at me like that and not expect me to respond in some way, Jerrica."

I loved the way he used my full name, never shortening it like everyone else did.

I shrugged, tried to look away from him but couldn't. My eyes were drawn back almost immediately. "I can't help it." I sounded like a six-year-old caught with her hand in the sweetie jar.

He shook his head. "Do you want me to look back?"

"I think I'd prefer it if you said you can't help it either." Clearly alcohol was doing the talking for me at this point, or at least I wanted to blame the alcohol.

Jesse shook his head. "We can both help everything. There's always a choice. I want to look back, but if you don't want me to, I won't."

"Are you always this controlled?"

"Yes."

His eyes were blazing.

"It isn't a magic trick, Jerrica. You can't choose how you feel about someone, whether you're attracted to them, but you can choose if you do something about it. It's just sometimes it's difficult to make the right decision or know what the right decision is." He shrugged. "I've made a fuck ton of wrong decisions. Bad ones."

It was the first time I'd ever seen any vulnerability on Jesse's face. His eyes softened in their intensity, and it felt as if he was trying to read my thoughts. I wasn't a difficult person to read. There were no difficulties at beating me at poker, and I was the worst person to hide the fact I was keeping a secret, not that I let secrets go easily.

"Would kissing me that night have been a bad decision?" Thank you champagne and spiked Pimms for sponsoring those words.

Jesse didn't say anything; he just smiled and looked away, staring at the ground as if it held all the answers.

"Tell me."

He looked back up, slowly, his eyes straight to mine. "Yes."

"What about kissing me now? No strings, just one kiss." I just needed to know how it felt. Would it be as good as it was when I imagined it, would every nerve and fibre in me be electrified? Or would this have been fuelled by my imagination and a seriously long drought of orgasms other than self-induced ones?

"Just one kiss?" He now looked tortured.

I nodded. "One kiss. That's it. No more."

I closed the few steps between us, stealing the space. Jesse didn't retreat or move away. I didn't expect him to, but he didn't move towards me either.

Stepping up on tiptoes, I put my hands on his shoulders and brought my lips to his. His hands finally caught me, holding my waist, his head dropping so the distance between us wasn't as great.

He had also made a choice.

The press of our lips against each other was slight at first, a feather of a kiss. I pulled away, my heart thundering in my chest, every pulse banging out a beat that was almost unbearable.

I made the mistake of opening my eyes and looking at his.

Heat.

Want.

Lust.

Oxygen left my lungs, then my mouth was back on his and this kiss wasn't slight or soft. It was hard and potent and rich.

My fingers dug into his shoulders; my breasts pressed against his chest. He tasted of beer and something sweet, his mouth fighting with mine for dominance, although I knew he was going to win. His hands had dropped to my ass, cupping me closer to him. His teeth nipped at my bottom lip, capturing it and then sucking briefly, the sensation causing need to pool between my legs, sweet heat that I knew wouldn't be cooled down with anything I could do.

How could this be just one kiss?

It was Jesse who ended it. His hands running up my sides and over my breasts, eliciting a whimper from me, while his eyes – those dark, simmering pools of unknown thoughts – drank me in.

One kiss was never going to be enough. I would spend the next five and a half months like a schoolgirl with a crush on her older brother's best friend, knowing he was too far out of my range, having just dreams of him, remembering this moment when I was alone in bed or in the shower.

But at least I knew he wasn't unaffected. The rock hard length pressed against my stomach that I felt grow during the kiss had told me that.

Jesse licked his lips, eyes flashing. "Was that a bad choice?"

I laughed, shaking my head. "No. Because now I know it wasn't just my imagination."

"It was never your imagination. But the rest of it might have to be."

I caught a butterfly in my throat, escaping from my stomach. "What if I want more?"

He shook his head slowly. "It would be a lot more. And it could ruin us both. Probably me more than you."

Jesse bent his head, pressing a kiss to my cheek.

"Some things are better imagined. Use that kiss for your books." He stepped back. "We should get back before your brother realises we're both missing."

"Sure."

Only I wasn't sure at all.

CHAPTER 7
Jesse

I WASN'T the sort of guy who partied in clubs and bars. I went to bars occasionally, usually to keep an eye on the younger players who were likely to do something dickish, or to watch out for a more senior player who was going through a rough patch and might end up doing something he'd regret later. Not that I was a buzzkill. I liked to socialise and I generally liked being with my teammates, but clubs were something I tended to avoid, unless they were exclusive and underground, with NDAs signed at the door and phones handed in.

Tonight I wasn't in a nightclub because I was babysitting baby footballers. Tonight I was doing something I forced myself into doing at least once a year; seeing my cousin.

As a kid, I'd ended up living with him and his mum for a few months here and there. We'd briefly played on the same football team together, me doing odd jobs for elderly neighbours to earn enough to the pay the subscriptions; Lyle nicking the money out of his mum's latest boyfriend's wallet. He knew what my childhood had been like, but unfortunately, when he saw me, he wanted to talk about it. He wanted to compare how it had been shit for both of us and I'd "got lucky" getting a football contract, while he'd ended up as a labourer or doing odd jobs. Lyle had never been in the care system, although his mum hadn't been too different from mine, and he'd never had a lot of looking after. But he had lived in the same house while he grew up and stayed in the same two schools. He'd been fed at least once a day, and I knew he'd had big Christmas presents every year, although my aunt had been shit at remembering his birthday.

I arranged to meet with Lyle when he started getting frequent with his text messages, usually building up to accusing me of being too up my own arse to bother, or too rich to remember him. It also usually coincided with him having had a 'business deal' gone wrong, which basically meant he owed money to a loan shark.

It wasn't that I hadn't helped Lyle out. I'd given him grants – as we'd called them – in my early professional days, when he'd had ideas for the next big thing, fancying himself as an entrepreneur. I knew that once he had the money, he'd pissed it away on booze, drugs, gambling and women, then panicked and borrowed when I'd asked where my investment was up to.

Now, to ease any guilt I had that I was living the dream and he was still living in the same house where he'd grown up, I'd drop him a birthday gift in the form of a few grand and check up on him. Lyle trod a fine line between keeping clean and dipping his toes in a bit of illegal shit, so me keeping my distance was in my best interest, which I'd explained to him once.

It had gone down exactly as you'd have expected it to.

We were meeting at a club on the outskirts of Manchester, not a dive because that would've been an outright no, but a new venue that was aiming itself at trendy clientele. Lyle said he knew the owners and they'd asked him to invest, something I was finding hard to believe, but I went along with it, asking Jerrica to drive us out there, parking in a secure spot and taking a cab the short journey to the club.

It was exactly a week since I'd kissed her, or she'd kissed me. I'd filed the moment in a box labelled with a warning sign and let myself open it twice a day; when I was in the shower first thing in the morning before I saw her, and just before I went to sleep at night.

Jerrica was all the things I couldn't have and everything I shouldn't want. She was curious and had an innocent air that a life like mine would only taint. I knew her childhood had been good overall. Nate had told me on an away game, when we were back in our hotel, that his growing up had been nothing like mine, with both his parents being as fully present as they were able to with him and his sister. They'd moved house three times as children, each time to a bigger property with more land, his father and his mother both climbing in their careers. Birthdays were celebrated; Christmas was a big family event.

I didn't scorn Nate's childhood, or the difficulties he'd gone through that were his and his alone, but I knew that I carried scars that sometimes became inflamed and someone like Jerrica didn't need to be the person who had to put balm on them.

My therapist had asked why I didn't think I deserved a woman who I thought was perfect and I hadn't been able to answer her, which was why I was taking Jerrica with me tonight.

She'd meet my cousin. She'd see a less charmed life. She'd learn a little bit more about why she needed to make a better choice about kissing me in future.

"We'll get a taxi back." I put my hand on her back as we walked toward the club doors. "Have a few drinks if you want."

"What about the car in the morning?"

"Nicky said he'd give us a lift in. He's coming into town tomorrow to pick up the books on his reading list for uni." The bouncer looked at me and nodded.

Lyle had used my name to get him, whoever he was with, and us on the guest list. My suspicions were that he'd bragged about me being his cousin and that if I came here, so would my teammates, which would bring in punters who'd spend.

The club was standard plush. A VIP area with table service, a couple of dance floors, booths and an area that was separated off with privacy glass. I'd been in worse places and I could see how this would attract a certain crowd, probably some of the younger players whose egos still enjoyed being stroked.

"Any time you want to leave, just say," I whispered into Jerrica's ear. "My cousin will be okay – he'll be trying to show off."

"Why are you meeting him here?" She leaned into me, her perfume making my temperature rise.

She was dressed in tight fitting black trousers that had a sheen to them, and a strappy top that showed off her stomach. She'd changed into heels when we'd parked up, and her make-up was heavier than normal, not that she wore much. If I was round Nate's during the daytime, she was always bare faced.

Tonight she looked fucking gorgeous. It was a side to her I hadn't seen before, and I'd already clocked at least four other guys eyeing her up.

Not that they'd approach. There wasn't much chance that they wouldn't recognise me, and it definitely looked like she was with me, and not in just a friendly way. My arm was around her waist, keeping her close as we headed into the VIP area where Lyle was.

"Jesse!" He saw me before I saw him. "You're fucking here! Nice one!"

I let go of Jerrica to be enveloped in a huge embrace. He smelled of expensive cologne, but too much of it.

My chest hurt for him. Lyle had tried so hard to be someone. To have something. He just always went that one step too far to try and get it.

"Good to see you, Cuz." I slapped his back and pulled away carefully. "This is Jerrica.

Lyle smiled, leaning in to give her a peck on the cheek. "Really good to meet you. Jesse is one of the best people I know."

Jerrica smiled, glancing at me with a slightly querying look. "He's a good guy."

Lyle nodded. "I'm so glad you came, man! I really want to see what you think of this place. I'm seriously thinking of investing. You might want to join me on that."

"It's cool so far." It was. Nowhere near the dive I'd been worried about. "But my agent wouldn't advise it. Clubs and shit like that won't work with the endorsements I've got." Which was the absolute truth. I also didn't want to invest in a nightclub, most of which had short lifespans, and the drug association would not work for any part of my image or the club's.

"Shit! Really?" Lyle looked put out. "Fuck. I was really hoping this was something we could do together."

I put my hand on his back again. "Look, it seems class so far, but the club would be down on anything like this. Most clubs would be. They don't want us associated with alcohol and shit like that. All about the clean-living lifestyle, man."

He looked crestfallen. "Shit, man. I didn't think. Let's have a good night anyway. We've got champagne coming over." He looked over at where a bartender was, ice bucket in hand, followed by another woman who was carrying glasses.

It was popped and poured. I accepted a glass, making sure Jerrica had one, and ordered a water, sharing a moan with Lyle about how strict it was even off-season. It wasn't, not at this point, but he didn't need to know that, and I didn't want much to drink.

Something was making me feel on edge, although so far the atmosphere in the club was good, lively. Lyle was chatting to Jerrica, telling her about our shared childhoods and shit about how close we'd been, trying to win her over.

His current set of friends were around us, all dressed in designer gear, their girlfriends made-up so they only needed a filter and they'd be Instagram ready. They seemed like an okay crew, although at least two of them were being too open about the blow they were heading to the toilets to take.

This wasn't my scene.

"You okay?" I pressed my mouth close to Jerrica's ear,

my arm back round her waist. She'd been talking to a couple of the girls, her genuine friendliness sparkling.

She nodded, leaning a little more into me. "I'm getting the feeling this isn't your scene?"

I nodded. "I'm here just to see Lyle. He wanted to show it off."

"And get you to invest."

"That was always going to be the case. If I shot him down straightaway, he'd end up blowing my phone up with how I'm not giving him a chance."

She was moving with the music, which was pretty decent.

"He's very different from you."

"Maybe. Maybe not. Do you want to dance?" I knew if she said yes, I'd be torturing myself.

"I was hoping you'd ask."

"A couple of tracks and then we'll head to a bar that's a bit more chilled." This week she'd driven me around a lot, with a couple of late nights because of dinners with my sponsors and a club thing that Genny managed to rope me into.

I took her hand as I led her through the crowd to the dance floor, which was packed with people already.

I wasn't a bad dancer, unlike Jude who was terrible. I also liked dancing occasionally, and I had a feeling I was going to like dancing with Jerrica, although this was probably going to be one of those bad decisions; something else to box anyway with a warning on the lid.

She didn't even try and keep space between us, her arms going around my neck, her body pressing up against mine, and she started to move to a beat that was fast enough to make sure we didn't spend too many seconds too close to each other, because there was no way in hell I was going to be able to hide my body's response to her.

I turned her round, my arms crossing over her stomach, keeping her moving, feeling her shimmy up and down, her ass pushing into my body a little too much, so I placed my hands on her hips, my fingers grazing against the soft, smooth skin of her exposed stomach.

I was engrossed in the feel of her, the sense of being so intimate even though we were surrounded by people. But right now, there were just the two of us, and for now I was going to enjoy the moment.

I was, until the atmosphere changed.

People on the dance floor parted like they were the Red Sea, a woman I all too easily recognised tearing through them, whatever she was shouting drowned out by the music until she was closer, her hands reaching for Jerrica, and she wasn't about to hug her.

"Fucking bitch! Stealing him off me - "

Gayle-Ann Robinson was someone I'd hoped I wouldn't have to deal with again. If I never saw her again it would be far too soon, or however the adage went. I had no idea why she was here, unless it was because she was still keeping an eye on people who I was connected to, and she knew about my cousin. Right now, seeing her lunging towards Jerrica, hatred oozing from her and a madness I hadn't seen when we dated, my blood turned cold.

I didn't ever lift a hand to a woman unless she was lying across my knee with her ass bared and pussy wet and asking me to do it, but I wasn't going to let Gayle-Ann lay a finger on Nate's little sister.

I pulled Jerrica behind me, Gayle's hands smacking straight into my chest. Phone camera's flashed, people were filming, the music continued, and security were there quicker than Jude-the-media-whore to the start of a press conference after he'd scored.

Knowing that this would be all over social media and probably hitting gossip websites before I even left the building, I stretched out my arms, palms outwards and stopped her from getting any closer.

That was all I needed to do. Security bundled her away. Someone shielded Jerrica and I as we left the dance floor, the music now just an annoying drill.

"We're so sorry about that Mr Sullivan. Is there anything we can do?"

I figured it was the club manager offering his favours, probably worried about publicity or what I'd pass on through word of mouth.

"Not your fault," I said, because it wasn't. "I'd appreciate you making sure none of your employees embellish what happened."

He nodded. "We'll prepare a statement for the press. What else can we do?"

I looked at Jerrica, my arm still around her, although she didn't seem anxious or fazed by what had just happened. She had been uncharacteristically quiet though.

"Can you arrange a lift? I think we'll head somewhere closer to home. Great club though." It wasn't a bad place, just not somewhere I'd be returning.

The door to the room opened and Lyle breeze in, words spouting from his mouth at a million miles per hour.

I waited for him to finish, a combination of apologies and excuses, with requests for damage limitation all mixed together in a panicked verbal vomit.

"Lyle, it's cool, man. Just chill." I lifted my palm – a stop sign – and eventually he did. "She's an ex-girlfriend from years ago and doesn't seem to be in the best frame of mind. Maybe you need to get a bit heavy on your drug policies." Gayle had definitely been on something, which didn't surprise me. She'd dabble some when we'd been together, and had asked me at one point to make good with her dealer as she owed him money.

That had been one of the reasons why I'd ended it; that and my innocent ass finally worked out that she wasn't that into what we did in the bedroom, it was a ruse to try and reel me in.

The manager's face paled.

I knew the score. They were using their own dealers, but somewhere there would be someone who started their own side line. At fifteen, sixteen, Lyle and I had seen how it worked on our own streets, with my mother. Using kids as runners, targeting those who couldn't stick up for themselves, fear – then there was the other side, that pretty rainbow where chemicals and powder could take you.

I'd stayed clear. There were other highs I was starting to discover by then. Sex. Orgasms. Women.

Lyle didn't have the same motivation to stay clean. He dabbled. Still did.

"I'll make sure my staff know what to say if they're questioned by the media," the manager reiterated.

I nodded. "There'll be enough of an explanation on social media by now. But I'd really appreciate a lift. Good tunes, by the way. Your DJ is mint."

That made the manager smile. Lyle started to speak again. I let him finish but didn't respond.

"Call you in a few days, Cuz. We'll meet for lunch or something."

He nodded at me, his smile wide.

I wouldn't call him for a couple of weeks. He'd want to avoid me after this. Lie low. That suited me.

. . .

A black cab picked us up, the driver informing us that the fare would be paid by the club, which was a nice but unnecessary gesture. I phoned Genevieve, who answered after two rings, and gave her the lowdown as to what had happened. She searched the internet while I was on the phone, finding a video of it already.

"This is the ex with the NDA, right?" She always sounded far too alert at any time of day or night.

"Yep." Genny knew the finer details but not to the extent of Nate.

"Leave it with me. I'll call Rhys and your solicitor. We'll get a polite reminder sent as to the terms and conditions she had." Genny had seen the deal that had been made. It was her job to bullet proof or deploy the troops if something looked like it could be breached. "Go calm the fuck down somewhere – are you still with Jerrica?"

"Yeah, we're on our way to Casa Negro." It was a quiet bar in Alderley that required a membership. Their wine list was just what I needed right now, because I had the sneaking suspicion that Jerrica was about to throw a dozen questions at me.

"I'll call you if I need to, but get down to the club for lunch tomorrow and we can make sure we've covered everything. Look after Jez."

She hung up without me confirming the time because she knew I'd be there anyway.

The bar was quiet, not because it wasn't busy – it was – but because it was designed to feel discreet. There was space between the tables and partitions between the booths, the lighting was low and intimate, and the wait staff knew when was not a good time to come to the table.

The membership fee was high, the privacy priceless. We were met at the door with a slight smile and a discreet nod, before being led to a table where even if anyone did overhear us, no one would repeat anything.

As a teenager, I never knew places like this existed. The cost of a single light fitting probably would've fed me for six months; the price of a drink would've paid for my football subs for a month or longer. When the teammate who brought me here sat me down in one of these seats, I thought I'd been transposed to an alternate dimension where the other version of me was living a life that was someone's fantasy.

My teammate had been called Andy; he was thirty-five to my twenty-two, and he'd figured out a lot about my background.

"Take a look around you, kid. This is your life now because you've made good choices and you've got talent. Accept your talent – nowt you can do about that - and reward yourself for those good choices. This is one of those places where you can reward yourself. It's safe here." He'd also been the person who took me to another exclusive club, the first place I saw people having sex in front of me, and the first time I understood what it meant to own control.

Andy lived in the States now, coaching for a college soccer team. Occasionally I got an email from him, telling me I was doing okay and to keep it up. Whether he meant at football, my standards, or my cock, I wasn't exactly sure.

"A large St Emillion," I told the waiter what I wanted. Red wines were my favourite, as long as they were good. "Jerrica?"

"The same, please."

"Make it a bottle then." I gave the waiter a nod and he disappeared, leaving me with Nate's sister.

"This place is amazing. Nate brought me here last year and it was the highlight of my month." She gave me a smile that suggested she hadn't just been on the receiving end of my clearly unhinged ex-girlfriend in the middle of a very public nightclub.

"Whatever you want tonight is granted."

Her brows raised. "Whatever I want?"

"Here. From the menu." I couldn't stop the smile.

Jerrica laughed softly. "Damn. I was about to call it in. Who was she, Jesse?"

I owed her an explanation and maybe a little more. "She was the ex-girlfriend who tried to blackmail me. We were seeing each other about four years ago. It wasn't serious, and I called it off because I'd started to get the feeling that she was playing a part, that she wasn't into what we were doing."

"Which was?"

I shrugged. "Edging – orgasm deprivation. Light bondage. Toys. I like to be in control." I listed it as someone might list sandwiches on a menu.

"More than what people experiment with?"

"Very much so. She was a one-night stand who became more of a five-night stand and she worked out what I was into. She played along." I shrugged. "I figured she was faking it and then I overheard her on the phone to a friend – or she said he was just a friend. After I ended it, she threatened to go to the press and do a tell all of what I'd 'made her do' unless I paid her seventy-five grand. It was just as I was about to play in two international games for England and it would've jeopardised my international career. I passed it to my solicitors and they managed to get an injunction and we settled a payment with her."

"Why not go to the police? It was blackmail."

"Because then it would become public. She was making noises about how I'd forced her to be tied up – the way I tie, you can get out if you want – and if any of it had slipped into the media I'd have been fucked and not in a good way. So we settled and she signed various bits of legal paperwork." I saw Jerrica's eyes darken when I mentioned ties.

She was curious, if she hadn't tried anything like that already. Something not to talk about when we drove round the south of France.

"Have you heard from her since?"

He nodded. "If I've made headlines. She follows my career. I'll get a text that's obviously from her, but not her old number – that was blocked. That's the first time I've seen her since it got shitty."

"What will happen now? Will your solicitors get involved?"

"We can look at pressing charges. I imagine we'll be in touch with the police and then her solicitors will agree that she doesn't contact me or come within whatever distance. I've seen that happen before with a couple of older teammates. But are you okay? You weren't out for that to happen, Jerrica."

"Nate had girls hanging round from him being eighteen. Some of them, if I was with him, would think I was his girlfriend – which was icky on so many levels. It isn't the first time that's happened. You remember his stalker?"

I laughed, even though I shouldn't. We'd given Nate a ton of shit about it in the dressing room, but it was more serious than something to mock. It had ended up being serious, with this woman hanging around Nate everywhere he went and sending messages, saying that she was married to him. It had ended when she'd started to make threats to hurt Chan. "I do. That was ages ago."

"Four years. Hence his house is like Fort Knox."

"Your brother was the only person who knew the details of what was happening with Gayle. He was just there and solid." Which was why I knew I shouldn't have brought his sister out tonight. I shouldn't have put her in this position.

I shouldn't be thinking about her how I was.

"That's Nate. He's a good man. But so are you." The tips of her fingers brushed the top of my hand.

Our waiter came over with the wine, pouring a drop into each glass first so we could taste it. I'd done wine tasting events and had private tours of vineyards, the whole history and process of making wine fascinated me, but this in a restaurant always made me want to make some embarrassing comment because it all felt too posh and a little pompous to be real.

Jerrica clearly felt the same, smiling at me while she rolled the wine to the edges.

I nodded to the waiter, telling him that the wine was good, and watched as he topped up our glasses. It was a wine I'd had several times here before, and the waiter wasn't unfamiliar. He wasn't going to cork a bottle.

"I feel so awkward when they do that. I haven't met a wine I didn't like – well, not until the next day." Jerrica rolled her eyes.

"France means wine tasting. You'll have to practice your skills."

Her smile was full of sunshine. "I think I can manage

that." She took a good sip of her wine. "I meant what I said, Jesse. You're a good man, too."

I'd tried to pretend she hadn't said the words. I didn't think I was a bad person. I tried to make amends for not being there to stop my mother from dying; I made good choices, measured ones, about how I lived. But I didn't perceive myself as *good*.

"Am I?"

"You've read some of my book, I guess?"

I nodded. "Some. Not all of it, but the key parts." I couldn't stop the grin then.

She shook her head and looked away, a hint of embarrassment on her cheeks.

"You're a good writer. I have lots of things I want to ask, but I'll save them until you've had more wine."

Jerrica shook her head, laughing. "Just because you get your rocks off a certain way doesn't mean you're a weird reprobate, Jesse. If you read other romance books you'll find that most sex scenes have a little spice in there."

I stretched, needing to move and do something with my arms. "Like what?"

"Monsters are a bit of a thing at the moment. Retellings of fairy tales like *Beauty and the Beast* – so imagine what happens there. Shifter romance, where the woman falls for a man who's also a werewolf or some other creature - "

"This is sounding a little like bestiality."

"Hmmm, not quite." She tipped her head, studying me. "We then have praise kink - "

"So that's like 'come for me like a good girl' sort of thing?"

There was a nod. "Yes. There's falling in love with your captor or kidnapper, spanking happens *a lot*. Whatever bad sex you see online, there's the good version with characterisation and usually positive, healthy relationships in romance books. And really, really good sex. Sometimes the sort of sex women fantasise about but isn't likely to happen for them other than on the page."

I sat back with my glass of wine. "Sex clubs?"

"Whole series set in them. But the authors put believable storylines in and characters who can be seen as real, so it isn't just turning and watching two people get it on. And there has to be a happily ever after, or a happy for now – a happy ending and not just the one in the bedroom, or on the kitchen counter."

"Kitchen counter sex is overrated."

She smiled again, her eyes dancing. "Good to know. But don't think you're not a good person because you like to be the boss in the bedroom, Jesse."

I wanted to ask her what she liked. What was it that got her hot, where did she get her ideas for her scenes – was it from experience or imagination? I knew she hadn't had a boyfriend since she'd moved up to Manchester.

I drank more wine instead.

Then I told her something that Nate didn't know.

"Most people have their thing, their kink, but they vary it. I don't. I have to have control, I can't give it over to the woman I'm with. My – girlfriends is the wrong word – lovers give me the power over their bodies so I can give them pleasure, but I can never be that caring partner, the one they cuddle up with afterwards, or lets them take the lead. That balance isn't part of it."

She didn't say anything for a moment, circling her wine around her glass and I wondered if I'd just given her the most massive overshare of my life.

"I'm sorry, I shouldn't have said that."

"Why? Why can't you let go and go with the flow of

sex? I'm guessing – I'm only going off what I've read or watched – that you have scenes you create so everything is planned, maybe you can switch scenes or change different elements on the spur of the moment, but have you ever just had cosy sex on the sofa when Netflix is really boring? Or a quickie squashed into one of your cars? No planning, just lust? Quick decisions, that you don't really need to think through?"

Her fingers rested on my hand that was now back on the table. Her touch feather light.

"That sounds very normal."

"Have you though?"

"Before. Before I found what I really liked."

She nodded, her touch feather soft. "Have you ever had a relationship? A proper one, that wasn't just about sex."

I hated thinking about what her opinion of me would be after I answered.

"No."

"Have you been on a date?"

"Gayle was the last woman I kind of saw regularly." It was a dodge of answer.

"What about recently? I know you have a couple of hook-ups."

I didn't want to know how she'd found that out. "I do – did. Neither of them wants a relationship and we just see each other for sex."

"Booty calls?"

"Pretty much. It works."

"Then why haven't I been dropping you off at wherever you see them?" She drained the rest of her glass, the waiter there almost immediately, topping up both our glasses.

"Because it was private. And I couldn't ask you to do that. Not after you told me you were interested."

She smiled, a soft, knowing smile that made her look like an ethereal woman in a Renaissance painting. "So when's the last time you had sex?"

Fuck. Or not. There hadn't been much fucking at all. "Two months ago. What about you?"

"Ten months. I'm jealous."

I was hard. This conversation, probably the most open and honest one I'd had with anyone apart from my therapist – which was obviously a one-sided conversation - was not easy on my control.

I wanted to do exactly what I said I didn't do and drag her into a bathroom and fuck her against the wall, or have her sit on the side of the sink while my mouth devoured her, finding out exactly how she tasted and what it took to make her pull my hair with her hand.

I swallowed. Drank more wine. I was at my limit now for what I would have in one night. It was late. We'd had a night that was going to take some explaining tomorrow.

And my cock felt like it was going to explode.

"Maybe we could further our arrangement to take care of other matters." Jerrica's hand left mine, her fingers pushing her hair away from her face.

"No." I shook my head. "Nothing good would come of it in the end."

She smiled then shook her head. "It's a cliché, but it's the journey and not the destination. Every relationship that someone starts leaves them at risk of heartbreak and rejection, but you find your self-worth in there and rebuild stronger, if it ends badly, and not all relationships do. What do we have to lose?"

I searched for my words, feeling the seriousness of this.

We spent a lot of time together. I valued her as a friend and as someone who was really helping me out. So I took the coward's way out.

"Are you trying to use me for your research?"

We slipped into Nate's house, the taxi dropping us both off there. I could've stayed in it and gone back home, but I didn't feel like it right now. After Jerrica had laughed at my answer and joked back, we'd talked more about what had happened, Gayle storming towards her on the dance floor, the vibe in the club, my cousin, more about my childhood and his – no detail. I'd overshared enough for one evening.

She poured herself another glass of wine, and gave me a beer, bringing it over to the sofa where I sat, feeling slightly guilty for being here with Jerrica in Nate's house.

We didn't carry on talking about the night, or her books, or those scenes. Instead we talked about wine and France, the car I'd hired that we picked up at the airport, because that was a more sensible way of getting there rather than Jerrica having to drive all the way.

"Hang on here a second, Zara." Nate's voice quietened us both.

"Are you checking for monsters, Daddy?" Zara sounded excited rather than scared. I wondered why she was up at this time, the very early hours of the morning.

"No, just your aunt, which is kind of similar." Nate peered around the door, his eyebrows raising when he saw me.

"I heard that!" Jerrica laughed, her tone bubbly.

Nate beckoned Zara in. "I thought you were on chauffeur duty for Jesse?"

"She was," I said, figuring he hadn't really noticed me yet.

I was standing near the fridge, still holding my beer. Jerrica had moved to the kitchen island, her glass of wine almost full still.

"I had a drink so we left the car. We grabbed a taxi back here." Jerrica said, not quite explaining it as it happened.

"Decent night out?" He looked from me to Jerrica.

We glanced at each other and shrugged. This could be a long answer.

"A little bit of drama," Jerrica said. "I said Jesse could use the spare bedroom. Is that okay?"

Nate shrugged. "Sure. What was the drama?"

I shook my head and looked at Zara, who was hovering next to Nate and listening to everything. "Tell you tomorrow. Let me guess, this one's after milk?"

Zara nodded, beaming. "Strawberry."

I grinned and glanced at Nate. "Did you know that if you drink strawberry milk at midnight, you wake up in the morning with your face looking like a strawberry?"

Zara looked horrified. "What if it's chocolate milk?"

"Same thing. Your face will look like chocolate."

"What about banana?"

"You'll look like a banana, which would be really funny – for us." I opened the fridge and pulled out the cow's milk, plain and simple, passing it to Nate when he walked over.

Jerrica followed Nate back upstairs, carrying the milk and water for Zara, Zara happily following her.

Five minutes later she came back downstairs, heading straight to the stool where I'd sat, checking my phone for any updates, although everyone seemed to have gone quiet.

Jerrica didn't say anything, putting her hands on my shoulders, waiting for me to look up, and then catching my lips with hers in a kiss that was brief and anything but sweet.

"Goodnight, Jesse." She stepped away. "I'll see you in the morning."

I didn't respond, just watching her ass as she walked away from me and fought the urge to follow.

CHAPTER 8
Jerrica

AT MONTPELLIER AIRPORT there was a Porsche Boxster waiting for us, a very keen and enthusiastic person waiting to hand it over to us, despite it being after midnight because the flight from Charles De Gaulle airport had been delayed.

I hadn't driven on the wrong side of the road for a few years, and I hadn't been expecting to drive at night. I could feel Jesse's eyes on me as our rather starstruck new friend talked me through where things were on the car, making it almost sound like the car could drive itself.

Since I'd kissed him in Nate's kitchen, we hadn't spent as much time together. He'd got Nicky to pick him up most days, as Nicky was hanging round at Kitty's Café, trying to get his uni work done, and Jesse was at the summer soccer school, just across from the Café. After the soccer school finished for the day, he, Nicky and Rowan would train, then Nicky would drop Jesse back off.

I didn't know if he'd been taking a taxi to see either of the women he had his relationship with, or whether my kiss had scared him off, but he'd only asked me three times over the last two weeks to chauffeur him around.

I'd missed him. I'd become addicted to his company, the sharp banter we had, the conversations. I missed the scent of his cologne, the curl of his smile, the way he watched people through interested eyes.

Spending just over a week together in the south of France, touring vineyards, was either going to be immensely painful or I was going to embarrass myself further, and then it'd be even more painful.

"It's thirty-five minutes to the chateau where we're staying." Jesse put his hand on my shoulder as he spoke, the lad who had delivered the car to us heading over to the small little Fiat that was waiting for him. "Think you'll be okay driving there?"

I nodded. The roads would be quiet given the time and that their destination was based in the countryside, and the airport was on the outskirts of the city. "I'll be fine. It's what you've brought me here for."

He didn't respond, just loaded the luggage into the small boot, somehow managing to fit it in. I climbed into the driver's side and started up the engine, feeling the car's low purr.

Jesse absolutely loved cars. In the last few weeks, I'd learned more about them than I'd known altogether. As well as the Maserati Jesse had bought, I'd driven two of his other cars, taking them out just for fun along the Cheshire lanes. He'd talked about the cars, explaining in easy terms how they held the roads so well, how they were designed and how to get the best out of them by driving in a certain way. I wasn't a car lover; as long as it got me where I needed to be without breaking down, I was happy with whatever I was driving, but Jesse's passion was absorbable.

I felt more confident than I would've if I hadn't had those experiences, so although I set off tentatively, having to keep telling myself that driving on the right was correct, by the time I was at the second junction, I felt okay.

The sat nav was easy to follow, and the roads were almost empty. Jesse started to check the map on his phone when we knew we were getting closer, the dark lanes meaning it was difficult to judge when turnings were coming up. I slowed the car, using my full beam to spot the turning, catching a wooden sign with Chateau de la Lumière written on it.

"We're there." I felt that tinge of excitement mixed with tiredness from travelling for most of the day. "I can't wait to see this in the daytime."

"It might not be as spectacular as you're thinking. Remember it's still being renovated."

"I know. But even from the photos when they first bought it, it's still like something from a fairy tale."

Jesse laughed. "Does your imagination ever stop?"

"No. And you really don't want to know *all* the things I imagine." I said it on purpose, because I hadn't forgotten either of those two kisses, or even come anywhere close to forgetting.

Jesse didn't reply, something that made me feel uneasy and question whether I'd gone too far, but then I hadn't exactly hidden that I was interested in more than being friends, even if he said it couldn't happen, it didn't change how I felt.

"Look ahead. You can see it."

He was right, the outline of the chateau appeared, a couple of lights making it easier to spot now. We were driving along a tree-lined single-track road, the trees clearly the tall cypress trees that were common throughout the area.

For a week, we'd be based here at the chateau, or rather, the building that had been a chateau and was being painstakingly restored by a family who'd moved out here for a new life. They'd had a vineyard in southern England, which they'd sold, wanting to swap English greenery for French skies, so they'd bought an old chateau with several acreage of vineyards as their next project.

The chateau would be an intimate luxury venue, for weddings or cookery escapes, or bespoke breaks. The vineyards had been kept running as a business, making wine that was local to the area, and according to Jesse, fucking gorgeous.

This was an investment that didn't need Jesse's face marketing it. The owner was the cousin of Manchester Athletic's manager, and it had been Guy himself who'd suggested to Jesse that he might want to be a silent partner. Jesse was here to decide for himself whether he wanted to, as well as to tour some of the other vineyards in the area just for the hell of it.

I pulled up after cruising onto a long drive that felt smooth, tall old-fashioned street lamps now illuminating the way. The chateau doors were open, a light on in the hallway. Jesse had phoned ahead to let them know of our delay and give an approximate time; Carina, the owner, hadn't been fazed at all, her response was 'we'll still be drinking wine then! It's been a long week.'

She did indeed meet us at the door with her wife, Suzette, and her son, Gideon, who, after gawping at the car, grabbed our suitcases.

"Bonjour!" Her accent was definitely not French. "Welcome to Chateau de la Lumière! I'm so sorry you were delayed in Paris."

Jesse smiled and shook his head. "That is not your fault. I'm sorry you've been kept up waiting. This place looks spectacular."

"It will be once it's finished. We had the spiral staircase installed last week – it runs up four floors and, honestly, I could've bought four kidneys for less money. Most of the rest of the house is still a work-in-progress slash disaster, but we are on schedule with the restorations, which is a miracle." She inhaled, walking up into the hall, which was where the staircase was, a combination of dark wood and metal, contrasting against white walls and a tiled patterned floor. "Shall I take you up to your bedroom and you can freshen up? Suze has got a light supper ready for you and we have wine, of course."

"That would be great, thank you." Jesse either hadn't picked up on the mention of the single bedroom or had chosen not to mention it. "Supper would be good too."

We hadn't eaten since we'd grabbed a snack at Charles De Gaulle airport, and by snack, it hadn't exactly been the finest French cuisine.

"Follow me."

The chateau was half a modern architectural masterpiece and half construction site, although it seemed like most of the heavy building work had been completed and they were now onto the end pieces, the part where it would all really come together. The stairs we went up I knew had been lifted into the building, with part of the roof removed, the story of which had been documented on their social media.

"This must be an incredible project to be part of," I said to Carina as she led us away from the stairs and along a corridor with rooms leading off both sides.

"It is. We've basically lived in a building site for three years, so in another twelve months, we're hoping to be finished. While you're here, you'll be able to use the pool that was signed off just yesterday, and tomorrow night we have a friend of ours who's going to cook. She's a chef, and we're looking at her coming out here to offer cookery school holidays." Neva had moved over to talk to Genny. She was that combination of tired and excited, and I had a feeling she'd been in that state since she'd moved over here. "Here's your room. I'll let you find your own way down when you're ready – we'll be in the dining room with the doors that lead out into the garden."

I glanced up at Jesse.

"Is it just the one room?" he said, flicking a gaze at me. "We're not a couple – just friends."

"Oh." Carina looked mortified. "Fuck. I'm so sorry. I just assumed - " She put a hand to her forehead. "I'll sort out another room. My son's here at the moment, as are his two friends – we've got them labouring as a summer job, and I have a room set for Simone and her husband Jack for when they get here tomorrow. Let me see if - "

I stopped her. "We can share. Is there a sofa in there?"

She nodded. "There is, but - "

"I can sleep on that for at least a night. Don't worry." I looked at Jesse, worried at his reaction because there was every reason for him to really not want us to stay in the same room.

"Jerrica's right, we can manage." He put his hand on the door handle. "Honestly, Carina, don't worry. We're both tired from travelling."

She smiled. "Lots of wine and you won't care who's in bed with you when you sleep!"

. . .

The room was gorgeously luxurious. A huge carved fourposter bed was in the centre of the room on a massive plush grey rug, wooden flooring underneath. Two large windows looked out over the gardens from what I could make out in the night, a decent sized sofa in the middle of them. Adjoining was a bathroom with a brass-coloured bath in front of another large window, planned so you could look out, but no one could see you. A walk-in shower dominated the back wall, and there were two sinks, along with the toilet.

I looked around there first, working out what to say to Jesse.

Humour. Always humour.

"This is a romance trope, you know."

He had been looking out of the window. "What's a romance trope?"

"Like single dad, or enemies-to-lovers. This is the one-bed trope."

His lips curved into that beautiful smile. "Does this mean you're going to jump my bones in that bed?"

I tipped my head to one side. "Do you want me to?"

He looked away. "Of course I want you to, Jerrica. I just don't think we should."

"Oh."

He looked back. This time his eyes had darkened and there was an expression on his face that made me feel like I was prey for a hunting tiger.

"What are the chances of us sleeping in the same bed and nothing happening?"

I shook my head. "You're Mr Self-Control, so you tell me."

"I'll sleep on the sofa."

He was one of Manchester Athletic's and England's best players. There was no way he was sleeping on the sofa.

"I'll take the sofa. I'll fit better."

"Let's argue about it after we've eaten."

"And had wine."

He smiled and nodded, pushing his hand through his hair, which was less styled than I'd ever seen it before.

I wondered what he looked like first thing in the morning and realised I was probably going to find out.

We freshened up, taking turns in the bathroom to change out of the clothes we'd travelled in, Jesse grabbing a quick shower, me grabbing a slightly longer one.

It felt blissful to be in clean things, the grottiness of airplanes and airports washed away. We left everything else still packed, the words around who was sleeping where unsaid, and headed out into the corridor, tracking back our steps to the staircase and then down into the hall, finding a door that led us through to another wide corridor, this one with stone floors that were smooth and felt cool under my bare feet.

The kitchen, when we found it, had Carina and Suzette in there, a bottle of red wine open, and plates of sliced meats, breads, cheeses and olive oil laid out on a table that could've been used for banquets in the time of the crusades. The kitchen was a blend of modern convenience and traditional French; I was just too tired and a little overwhelmed to really take it in.

"Will you be okay in that room for tonight?" Carina looked concerned, her glass of wine full enough to suggest she hadn't had any of it yet.

Jesse nodded. "We'll be fine. It's an amazing room."

"The bathroom's incredible." I picked up one of the empty plates on the table. "Is it okay if I help myself?"

"Please." Carina stood up, coming over to me. "These meats have all been cured locally. The cheese has been made at the vineyard too, so all local products for you to try. We're trying to source everything within the region. Even the toiletries are from a woman in the village who has her own cottage industry going on."

I had used the shower gel and body moisturiser already. "They're fab. We both managed a quick shower and I used what was in there." I waxed lyrical a little about them, sensing that Carina was really embarrassed about the mix up with the rooms.

She relaxed some, watching Jesse fill his plate with meats and cheeses. "Have you tried the wine from here? I sent Jesse twelve bottles a couple of weeks ago, but he hasn't given me a review yet."

Jesse chuckled, sitting down with his feast. "Not yet. I wanted to try it here first. Don't worry about the bedroom thing, Carina; Jerrica and I will be just fine."

We were fine until we got back to the room. I switched the lamps on, working out that there was one switch near the bed that pretty much controlled everything that was switched on, which saved that trip out of bed to sort everything out.

It also made the room sultry and intimate. Which might've been Carina and Suzette's intention, but probably not what Jesse and I had in mind.

Awkward was an understatement.

"Do you think we can share the bed?" Jesse looked from the sofa to me. "It's a huge bed."

"We can share the bed. Do you snore?"

He shrugged. "I have no idea. I haven't slept in the same room as anyone apart from Nicky for two years, and he sleeps like the dead, so he's never given feedback. Do you?"

"No one's ever told me." My head was caught up on *two years*. "Do you want to do that thing where we put a line of pillows in the middle?"

Jesse laughed. "Not really. I could sleep on the sofa, Jerrica."

"But you don't want to choose that."

He shook his head. "No. I don't."

"Good. We're adults. We can do this. We might be doing it all week." Which really did sound like torture. I'd spent too long on the plane with his leg pressing against mine, that one touch heating my whole body, especially that spot between my legs.

It was warm there now.

"Do you want to get ready first? Bathroom?"

Was I imagining it or were Jesse's eyes heated. His gaze flicked down to my chest, my thin T-shirt probably not doing much to disguise what was underneath. The plan tomorrow was to explore the chateau, the grounds and I had every intention of spending some time in my bikini by the pool with a book. I'd finished writing my second romance and it was now with my editor, so I'd given myself this break to relax, read and decide what the next in the series would focus on. When I had that bikini on, he'd be seeing a lot more.

"If that's okay?" I'd already found my toiletries bag. "While you're in there after me, I'll get changed."

"Sure."

I brushed my teeth and used the toilet, giving my face a quick wash and putting on moisturiser.

Jesse was lying on his back on the bed when I came out. "What do you think your brother would say about us sharing a room like this?" He stared at the ceiling.

An owl hooted somewhere nearby.

"I don't think he'd say anything. I can text him and tell him, or tell Amber?"

Jesse sat up. "He wouldn't charter a plane out here and rip my balls off?"

"Only if you did something really horrible to me would he do that. Bathroom's yours. I'll get changed." I'd found the vest top I brought to sleep in. It was a tight fitted, cropped top, which was soft and old and comfortable. It revealed a lot of skin, and I knew Jesse would be able to see the outline of my nipples through it, but it was dark enough in the room to not look too indecent.

I wore that and my underwear, smothering a grin at the idea of him sleeping in his jeans or something.

That grin was wiped straight off when he came out of the bathroom in just a pair of shorts.

Smooth skin over cut muscles was only highlighted by the glow of the lights. A saga of tattoos was patterned over his body, each an unknown chapter that had been read only by him.

I sat up, letting the sheets drop to my waist. His eyes left mine, dropping to my breasts and lingering there for a moment.

We'd opened the windows because the night was warm, and the air con hadn't yet been fitted in this room. A cool breeze ruffled the drapes at the window and chilled my nipples.

I didn't hide how they'd hardened.

Jesse didn't try to hide how he was looking at them.

He climbed in bed next to me, his weight only slightly moving the mattress, and he lay down on his back.

"I can sleep on the sofa if you want."

I lay back down and faced him, keeping to my own side. "I'm fine with you there. Let's make an agreement though."

"What's that?" His voice was raspy, maybe with tiredness.

"Whatever happens, neither of us are embarrassed about it." Because the chances were I'd wake wrapped around him or he'd have morning wood.

"Fine. I promise not to tease you about your snoring." His eyes closed.

"I don't snore."

"I'll let you know in the morning."

I stretched a leg out to kick him under the cover, but instead stilled it as soon as it touched his skin.

Maybe we should've made a wall of pillows after all.

CHAPTER 9
Jesse

SHE DIDN'T SNORE. While there could've been times during the night when she did because I was asleep, they were few and far between. Every muscle was tight, my cock was hard. At one point, I risked it and got out of bed and jacked off in the bathroom like a fifteen-year-old with no chill, because I was hitting the point where I needed *some* satisfaction. That bought me an hour and half's sleep. Jerrica's hands woke me up, like some tortuous dream just as sunlight started to peek through the windows.

She moved a lot in her sleep. Starfish was too minimal a word for how she spread out. Her legs entwined with mine, her arm ended up over my stomach, which made my cock think all its fantasies were about to come true, and her ass grinded against it at one point.

And I knew that if I woke her with a kiss, either to her mouth or her tits or between her legs, she wouldn't stop it. She'd made a decision that we wouldn't be a bad idea.

I still wasn't sure that we would end without someone getting hurt, including me from her brother's fist.

The sound of voices outside told me it was an acceptable time to get up. I moved out of the bed slowly, not wanting to disturb Jerrica as I was sure it wasn't yet seven, and there was no reason why she couldn't sleep later.

I pulled on thin sweats and a T-shirt, slipping on slides and headed downstairs. The next few days were off plan completely; rest, good food, more alcohol than usual if I wanted it, and no restrictions. I'd done enough over the summer so far to keep me in the same shape I was during the season, so a week and half now wasn't going to set me back for pre-season.

Suzette was in the kitchen pouring a mug of coffee when I got down there, her hair damp from either a swim or a shower. I had only spoken to her a couple of times when I was discussing the possibility of investing, as most of my conversations had been with Carina. From what I'd learned, Carina was the figurehead of the business, while Suzette worked behind the scenes, co-ordinating the work that needed doing. I gathered she was the organised one, while Carina was creative and had the vision.

"Coffee?"

I nodded. "Thank you. Is anyone else up yet?"

She shook her head. "No. It was a late night, but we had an early delivery scheduled with furniture, so someone needed to be up to sort that. How did you sleep?"

I accepted the mug of coffee, adding a splash of milk. "Not well, but that's not because of the room. Just not used to sharing."

She shrugged and offered a half-sympathetic smile. "Carina is mortified – she thought you were coming here with your girlfriend, or rather she assumed, and we all know what that does. I don't think we're going to be able to sort a second bedroom for you until just before you're due to leave. The decorator is finishing off in three of the rooms and the electrician has final fixes to do in the others. I'm so sorry – I don't know what to suggest."

"We'll manage." Part of me was glad; part of me wanted to adapt the bath into a bed.

All of me knew that this wasn't going to end on platonic terms.

"Are you sure? You seem like more than just friends. I mean, bringing her to France to see the place you're looking at investing in is hardly what you do with a girl who's just a friend, is it?" Suzette's eyes narrowed. "And I am totally being nosy."

I smiled, sipping my coffee and avoiding her eyes so she couldn't read anything that was there. "Jerrica's my teammate's sister. She's working as my driver as I managed to get myself banned for six months."

"Ah. So the UST I felt was your frustration at not being behind the wheel?"

"UST?"

Suzette laughed. "Unresolved sexual tension. I take it you're frustrated at not being able to drive in more than one sense of the word."

Was there any point in denying it? "That's one way to put it." I sat down at the table. "How long have you and Carina been together?"

Suzette opened a cupboard and got out a milk jug. "Fifteen years. We've known each other nineteen."

"How did you get together?"

Suzette smiled at me and raised her brows. "Really? You want to go there?"

I nodded.

"Okay. Carina was married, two children. I was in a relationship with my then girlfriend and I started working for her at the restaurant she managed – I was the sommelier. We were friends for a couple of years. Her marriage wasn't good – it wasn't bad either, but to all intents and purposes, they were friends who lived together. They split; we carried on as friends. Me and my girlfriend also ended things – it was amicable but we weren't going anywhere, so one of those.

"One night, Carina and I had a few drinks after the restaurant closed and we ended up kissing. She was curious, so was I. It kind of developed from there. It hasn't been easy, especially for Carina, not fifteen years ago when the world was a different place. But here we are. We want this place to be a wedding venue for everyone. It feels so free here and open. The place where you can be yourself."

She studied me for a moment, her eyes not moving from my face. "What's the story with you and Jerrica then?"

"No story. I'm not who her brother would want her to be with."

"And who says that? You or him? Does he know you're interested and is he her keeper?" She spoke to me while fishing out coffee beans and a grinder.

"No to both."

"So who made you god?"

I laughed. Her directness was gold. "No one."

Suzette shook her head, tipping beans into the grinder. "You know, the only person you can ever have any say over is you. That includes kids. I've been blessed with being a stepmother to Carina's two, and it's been one of the best things I've ever done, or still do. I've seen them grow their wings and flutter round, back to the nest and away from it again, worried about branches in the breeze, but knowing we're still here to be that stability. Carina tried to be a helicopter parent at one point – that lasted two minutes. People are made to walk their own roads, Jesse. That includes you and Jerrica. Don't try and clip anyone's wings but your own, and before you do that, ask yourself why."

"It's too fucking early for this conversation." It was a weak response.

"So have it with me over wine and cognac tonight."

"I might just do that."

Footsteps halted our conversation, blonde hair and green eyes made my focus be solely on her. Jerrica looked awake and bright, her smile beautiful when she saw me.

"Is that coffee? I usually drink tea, but the smell of coffee woke me up." She looked hungrily at the cafetiere.

Suzette smiled warmly and glanced at me. "Why don't you two sit outside and I'll bring you a pot and milk. Half an hour and we'll have fresh pastries delivered for you to try, too."

"Sounds divine." Jerrica looked at me. "You're up early."

"I wanted to make the most of the day." Which wasn't a lie. I did. But if I'd stayed in that bed any longer, I would've made a choice I wasn't sure I was ready for.

We ate breakfast, made by Suzette, and sat outside on the terrace, an area set in the newly established garden, the nearby pool rippled by the soft morning breeze.

Carina joined us, apologising once again about the rooms. I was relieved when Jerrica reiterated that it had been fine and we could make do, adding in something about sleeping better when she wasn't on her own anyway. How true that was, I didn't know, she'd never mentioned anything about it before, but Carina started to smile again.

"Shall I still tour you round this morning? I can show you the chateau and the grounds and explain the next phase with the outbuildings." She topped up my coffee. I'd drank more of it this morning than I'd done in the last three months.

"I'm looking forward to seeing it," Jerrica leaned forward, taking another slice of watermelon. "Are we touring the vineyards too today?"

Carina gave a firm nod. "Late this afternoon. There's wine tasting and we'll serve you dinner in the building we've refurbed down there. It'll be a twelve-course tasting menu – we're letting the chef we've appointed have a practice. It should be good."

"Are we okay to use the pool this afternoon?" Jerrica glanced at me. "I know we're exploring, but I really fancy a lazy day."

I couldn't help but smile. She'd mentioned a few times on the way here that she was looking forward to lounging in the sun, and to be honest, I was looking forward to seeing her lounging in the sun.

Maybe I was going to hell, but at least I'd have some good memories to think about when I got there.

"The pool's all yours. The work being done at the moment is focusing on getting the rest of the rooms ready inside the chateau and the carriage house at the back. The barn we can use as a wedding venue amongst other events, and that's almost finished, so any work that's happening today won't be around the pool area. You should have peace." Carina's smile was content and bright now. "Just tell me what time you want your first Aperol Spritz."

Jerrica laughed. "I'm so looking forward to today. Just being here is lovely. The décor in the chateau is amazing – I didn't get to notice much last night."

I didn't follow much of the conversation that followed. I was too busy noticing Jerrica. Her shorts were cotton, exposing almost all of her thigh. The top she was wearing was strappy, showing more skin, skin that was tanned and smooth.

I pictured her lying naked on the big bed, her blonde hair fanned out across the pillows, tanned skin contrasting with the white of the sheets.

I wondered what it would be like to run my mouth over her curves, to taste and tease, find those sensitive spots and see how I could make her whimper in the best possible way.

Determination and self-control made me pull my attention to the pool, trying to take in the construction, the design around it, which had been really well done. Carina and Suzette were after investors to help finish some of the third phase of the work, and get the staffing off the ground, as well as expanding the distribution of the wine. The offer was promising, a ten percent stake for what wasn't a huge chunk of change, and it included a stay here each year too. They only wanted three investors, my manager Guy already one of them. Nate had said that if I was in, he'd join in too. He'd seen plans for one of the outbuildings that would have its own pool, and he'd been all over that as somewhere to stay with the kids and Amber.

That was what I was here for. Not to perv at his sister and imagine what it would be like to feel her tighten around my cock.

I was starting to consider exactly what decisions I wanted to make.

The tour of the chateau and the grounds took a couple of hours, the setting idyllic and lush, despite the gradual rise in heat. Carina showed us photos of the works as they'd progressed, the two staircases that were statuesque in their design, the inspiration behind the themes for the different suites and the curated pieces of art that fitted the air they were going for.

It was impressive.

What was also impressive was how Jerrica asked about different aspects, not just the choices behind the décor, but also their business model and marketing plan. I shouldn't have been impressed; I knew she was a lot more than most people already, but in all the conversations we'd had, we'd never talked about anything serious business-wise. I knew about her writing, or the little she'd told me. Jerrica didn't want to talk too much about what she was writing; when I'd asked her about it, she'd said the bare minimum while being polite and I hadn't pushed for any more.

We lay by the pool just after midday, a light breeze taking the edge off the Mediterranean heat. Jerrica had been reading her kindle, her bikini the stuff of my teenage fantasies, and most of my adult ones too, the ones that were tame, anyhow.

"You know more than me about marketing." I sat up, reaching for the sunscreen I had the sense to apply. "Where did you learn all that?"

She put her kindle down and looked over at me. I'd caught her eyeing up my abs and chest a couple of times already and I'd be lying if I said I hadn't preened. It was harder, being far away from home and her brother, to remember the reasons why I shouldn't be wanting her.

"It isn't just about writing all the words. I have my own website, newsletter; I run ads – and I have to manage them myself. I've created a brand, which involves knowing how to post on social media – or trying to know. It's not an easy industry. And I ran my own business before too – so I learned a lot from that."

I studied her, trying not to let my eyes wander down to her bikini top that wasn't going to make sleeping next to her tonight any easier. "Still waters run deep."

She laughed. "You should know. Man of mystery."

I lay back down, hands behind my head, the sun blaring down on us. "Really isn't much to be mysterious about."

Jerrica shifted so she was on her side, watching me. "Your cousin. I guess you didn't have my leafy-green childhood."

"Concrete grey rather than leafy green." Maybe it was the sun, or the blue sky that was so rare in Manchester, or her bikini, but I told her a little about how I grew up. Just the bare bones, my mother, how we moved, how she'd left. How she'd died.

It didn't feel like I was telling someone else's story now. The first time I'd gone through my childhood with my therapist, she'd made me tell it like it had happened to someone else. She'd told me to tell her about that boy, how he'd felt, as if it hadn't been me, then over the years, I'd begun to own those feelings, to reconcile what had happened to me as a child without blame or guilt. Even regret.

I was almost at peace with how I'd grown up. It had

made me the man I was now, even though he wasn't perfect.

Jerrica didn't say anything while I gave her the bones of my story, her eyes wide pools of something I could drown in. I didn't want her sympathy. Maybe I wanted her understanding. Maybe I just wanted to give her something of mine to take away, something I didn't give freely. Maybe it was the sweet air of the South of France and tang of the grapes and the wine we'd already sipped at.

"The fact I'm here now, thinking about investing in a place like this, makes me feel like a god." It sounded conceited, but I didn't mean it that way. "Or at least some god gave me strength from somewhere."

Jerrica sat up, the movement drawing my eyes to her tits again. I'd given up trying to not look anymore.

"The media has never worked out where you came from?"

"No." I shook my head. "It's part of the reason why I try to keep a low profile. Being captain helps, because I can have a club profile and that seems to keep them happy. Genevieve has kept them at bay too a few times when they've managed to dig something up."

"Why wouldn't you want them to know?"

"I don't want to relive it in public. It's in my past and I've dealt with it on my terms, which makes me sound like a selfish fucker. You're one of the few people who know." I sat up, hearing footsteps that sounded like Carina's.

"I won't say anything."

"I know you won't." I didn't think for one minute she'd prove me wrong.

. . .

We toured the vineyard, Gérard showing us round with the same amount of pride as Rowan after scoring a hat-trick, his broken English not a barrier in explaining the process of moving the grapes from the vines into wine.

Jerrica wore a yellow sundress over a different bikini that she'd had on while we were sunbathing. Her hair was tied up in a messy bun, her sunglasses overly large, making her look like a movie star. I managed to take in some of what Gérard was saying, but most of my attention was on her, the way she smiled, the way she nodded at what he was saying, how she gestured with her hands when she was enthusiastic.

The winery was a decent size – I'd visited several in the last few years to be able to compare, but it wasn't really kitted out for tours. Carina and Suzette planned to convert one of the nearby outhouses into a visitors' centre, complete with restaurant and shop, where they could sell more of the wine and the cheeses they produced too. The chateau was close enough to the town to make it easy to get to, and part of the plan was to offer a pickup and drop off service from some of the main hotels.

So far, I was liking everything I'd seen.

"So, it is time for your wine tasting. If you come with me, I'll take you to the table we have laid out for you." Gérard's glance at his watch told me his tour had probably ran over.

That didn't matter. We had nowhere else to be today, nothing else to do apart from drink wine and eat food in the late afternoon sunshine. Carina was busy with the deliveries they'd had this morning, styling rooms and getting testy with Suzette who was trying to sort out another team of builders who'd arrived.

Sitting down at the rather rustic table, laid out for two,

underneath a pergola with climbing flowers tangling up it, felt rather like a date. Gérard pulled out our chairs, talking us through the first wine. The dinner was more of food with wine pairings, a menu that Neva would never in a million years approve.

"So what are your thoughts? Are you going to invest?"

Jerrica sipped the white wine, her expression showing that she liked it.

"Probably. It seems like a no brainer." Being by the pool had made my mind up; the place was a little piece of paradise, and I could see how the chateau would look when it was finished. It was exclusive without being pretentious and had a casual vibe that I could see being addictive for those looking for a place to escape where it wasn't about who they'd be seen by.

"Think they want a writer in residence?" She took off her sunglasses, putting them down on the table. "I'd be happy to volunteer."

"Live here from May until October, spending your days writing and evenings holding workshops? That sounds like a plan. Mention it to Carina." The thought of her not being around Manchester didn't sound like a plan to me. I bottled away that realisation to think about later.

"There's a group of writer friends I have who would definitely come out here for a retreat, you know, to get some writing done and sample the wine." She looked around the fields that laced where we were sitting, the early evening sunshine bathing everything in a golden glow.

"Have you met any of them?" Since Jerrica had moved in with Nate, I'd not seen her with any friends who'd visited, although I was aware she'd had a weekend in

London where she'd met up with some people from university once.

She nodded. "Just two. Most of my writer friends are in America. Amy's in Stoke and Elizabeth's in London, and we've met once. The rest are online." Her smile was half sad. "That's been the most difficult thing: my event planning job was facing people every day, sometimes seven days a week. I now spend days just with the people in my head, so there are times when I think I'm going a bit mad."

I smiled with her, because she wasn't mad at all, but I got what she was saying. "Living with Nate suits you then."

"Most of the time, although I feel bad sometimes because I'm pretty sure he'd like some time with just him and Amber and the girls. Not that he's ever said that."

"I think he's glad you're about to help. Especially keeping an eye on Amber in case anything goes wrong."

Nate kept it well hidden how much he worried over Amber's pregnancy, even from her. It wasn't a high-risk pregnancy, but it was bordering on it and they'd had a scare earlier on. He'd mentioned to me before we left for France that he was having nightmares about things going wrong and that Amber's due date couldn't come soon enough. I also knew he hadn't shared this with his sister, and especially not Amber.

Jerrica smiled, sipping at the wine. "But once the baby's a few months old, they'll be ready for more space. I can't stay there indefinitely."

"You can. That house is big enough." I'd managed to polish off a whole bowl of olives without even realising it. Some sort of bird of prey hovered in a nearby field, looking for dinner that definitely wouldn't be olives.

She shrugged. "It is, but that's not the point. I might

look at a shared house in Didsbury or somewhere like that. I don't want to live on my own, because then I'd end up only speaking with the people in my head, and therein lies the madness." She looked completely fucking amused at the idea.

I chuckled, topping up both of our wine glasses.

Gérard popped back up, bringing little plates straight from the kitchen, talking us through what they were and where the ingredients were from. The carafe of wine was replaced too, with fresh glasses.

"I think the writer in residence idea might have legs. I could live like this every night."

Her eyes were bright with enthusiasm and laughter, the light catching her hair and making it appear as if it was threaded with gold. I'd noticed before how pretty she was, even when I'd turned up at Nate's at stupid o'clock in the morning and she'd just gotten out of bed with wild hair and creases on her face from the pillow. Tonight though, she glowed with the sunshine from the day and the warm air, her enthusiasm for being here and talking about her books, lighting her even more.

We carried on talking and eating, sampling the wine that Gérard appeared with every so often. I found out more about her books and what she had planned, listened to her talking about the marketing that went on behind the scenes and how she was figuring out what was working for her at the moment.

The sun dipped down for the night, candles were lit, the night air was filled with the sound of crickets.

It felt like a date.

Or what I imagined a date felt like. I hadn't been on a whole load of dates, especially recently.

I hadn't been with a whole load of women who made

me want to give them a flower just to make them smile, or make sure they were warm enough in the evening air because the idea of them not being comfortable just wasn't okay.

Panic bubbled under the surface of my smooth, the same sort of feeling I had when I fell in the deep end of a swimming pool and I couldn't swim – swimming lessons weren't on my mother's agenda when I was a kid, and when they were taught at school, I was rarely in.

I hadn't been taught how to do this either. Healthy relationships weren't something I'd had much experience of watching, other than the ones my teammates had somehow managed to evolve into.

Even Rowan Reeves seemed to manage it.

As we carried on talking, laughing, eating, I checked myself. This was Nate's sister, and her brother knew too much about my tastes.

Jerrica Morris was too perfect for a boy like I'd been.

CHAPTER 10
Jerrica

I'D REALLY THOUGHT he might've kissed me.

It was one of those nights I would write about in a book some time, one of those moments which was almost too perfect to be true. Jesse was easy to be with, his bad boy exterior melting the more I got to know him, his interest in me felt genuine and his smiles were given freely.

I caught him looking at me when he thought I was distracted by food, little glances from smouldering eyes that made me feel warmer than I had done when I was sunbathing.

When we'd walked back to the chateau along a newly paved path in white stone, lit subtly with spotlights placed next to it, his hand had brushed against the small of my back, light touches that sent shivers over my skin and I longed for the guts to stop in my stride and kiss him like I'd done before.

The chateau had been quiet and still when we got back, the time after midnight. We'd spent longer than anticipated at the barn, sipping wine then coffee, dining on small tapas style plates that were delicious and light, easy to eat, and working with the wines that Gérard talked us through.

We paused at the bottom of the grand staircase, and for a second, I wondered if Jesse was going to pick me up and carry me up to bed. I wondered whether in that slight moment we were on the same paragraph on the same page.

He didn't.

Instead he moved me into an awkward hug and said he was going to make a quick drink before heading to bed.

That quick drink took longer than the hour I was awake for, trying to read my book but spending more time with my head flitting between a scene for the new novel I was starting and wondering about Jesse.

He was avoiding me.

By the time he came to the room, I must've been asleep. When I woke up to the sound of birds singing and the voices of children outside, the bed was empty of him, if he'd even slept there.

What I knew, as I summarised while making myself a breakfast platter from the meats and fruit and cheese that were laid out on the table, was that Jesse was avoiding what we could enjoy.

I knew why. He'd explained as much but it wasn't enough to make me believe it was worth it.

I slipped away from the kitchen with my food and my phone, aware that it was only just after seven back home in Manchester, but that was not a reason to not phone my brother.

Nate picked up on the third ring, sounding pleased to hear from me, rather than annoyed from having been disturbed from sleep or something else.

"You okay, Jez? Everything good?"

"Everything's fine. This place is gorgeous." I spent a few minutes telling him about the chateau and the pool. "We're heading out to see two other vineyards today before Simone Wood and her husband cook for us tonight."

"If you think it's a good investment, see if they'll accept the same as what Jesse's putting in. Is he still planning to invest?"

"Definitely. I think last night made his mind up."

"What was last night?"

I talked him through the food and the wine, leaving out the details that were clearer in my mind than anything to do with the meal or the drink.

"It sounds amazing." He groaned. "I'll see about taking Amber next summer."

"How is she?" I'd only been away a few days but I did miss them, Nate, the kids, and the woman who would probably be my sister-in-law before too long. I'd seen the hearts in her eyes when she looked at my brother. He didn't even try to hide his.

"Doing really well. Actually resting. The girls keep trying to look after her which isn't always ending well. When you're back, would you babysit for a night so I can take her for a spa break?"

"Course." Leon the nanny was around, but Nate was fixed on him only having the girls overnight when he had away games. He preferred my nieces to be looked after by friends or family if he was away playing. "Just get it booked. Nate?" My heart raced a little.

"Jez?"

"I wouldn't usually discuss things like feelings with you - "

He laughed. "Thank god for that."

"But how would you feel if I asked Jesse out? He's your friend and teammate, and I wouldn't want to make things awkward for you."

My brother was quiet, which worried me. Nate was rarely completely quiet; he laughed a lot and while sometimes he didn't say much, what he said was generally filled with a smile.

I broke his quiet. "I know you know about the ex-girlfriend. The one who tried to go to the press."

"Jesse told you?" Nate sounded surprised.

"Yes. I'm not asking your permission, Nate, that would never happen, but I don't want to create an issue between you and your teammate." I truly had too much love for my brother to fuck up the good things he had going on in his life, and his football career and playing for England.

"It's your choice, Jezzy. Jesse's a good bloke, but he doesn't do relationships and I don't want any details if you hook up with him. Ever. So whatever you share with Amber or anyone else, I don't want coming back to me." There was an odd quiet to his words. "Don't take this the wrong way, but is Jesse interested in you like that? I wouldn't have thought you were his type, and I didn't mean that to sound as shitty as it did."

"I don't think I'm his type but I do think he's interested. I think he's bothered about what you'd say."

More silence.

"Nate?"

"Sorry, Jez. Your life, your choice. But unless it gets serious, like ring and wedding bells serious, I don't want to know from either of you."

"Sure. I don't want to sneak around behind your back though."

"It isn't sneaking; it's just not being obvious so I don't need to think about it. Remember I know *a lot* about Jesse."

"I know. How's Amber?" I changed the subject, needing to take my brother's head out of wherever it had gone.

"Good. She's started sleeping well the last couple of nights, which means I'm sleeping well too." He told me more about the girls and very quietly, about the plans for the big tree house in the garden, as well as his latest plans to propose.

By the time we ended the call because Libbie was up and wanting his attention, Nate's voice was back to normal and I half wondered whether he'd forgotten the reason why I'd phoned.

A text message from him half an hour later told me he hadn't.

Your choice always, but if he fucks you about I'll hire a hit man.

Jesse was drinking coffee with Simone Wood and her husband, Jack, two of their children playing in a playpen that had been set up far enough away from the pool that there would be no sudden splashes.

He smiled when he saw me, standing up and making introductions. I kind of knew Simone through Amber's sister-in-law, Ava, as she was a friend of Ava's family, and I'd eaten at her restaurant a few months ago when I'd been in London. Both she and her husband were chefs, owning and running three restaurants in the capital, and holding at least a couple of Michelin stars.

"Ava sends her love." Simone stood up too, pulling me into a quick hug. "She wanted to come with us but things got in the way."

Jack hugged me after, his arms as solid as Jesse's. "And Simone's not allowed to give you any more details, even though she's dying to."

I raised my brows. Ava was one of seven siblings and they'd been working hard to make sure there would be another large generation of Callaghans to terrorise the world. 'I won't ask, but I will speak to Amber later."

Jack nodded. "You do that. But you never heard anything from us. How was your meal last night?"

Carina joined us as we talked through the menu. I took a chair next to Jesse, trying to ignore the scent of his cologne that seemed to do things to destroy my brain cells. A discussion started about local produce and what Simone and Jack would need for dinner tonight as they were taking over the kitchen as a trial.

"The debate we've been having - " Simone started.

"Argument, babe. It was an argument." Jack wrapped an arm around her shoulders.

"It was a debate. We were having a professional conversation." She gave him a glare that could've been classed as a weapon of mass destruction.

"Professional conversations don't end with make-up sex." His smile was smug.

Her glare was even more lethal.

My eyes found Jesse's and we exchanged a small smile.

What was also lethal was how he looked this morning. He was wearing a sleeveless T-shirt, his tattooed arms bulging, legs stretched out in front of him. Sitting on a lush lawn in the South of France, surrounded by vineyards, was not a place he should've looked at home. On a motorbike somewhere, kicking up dust, was more in keeping with the darkness he exuded, but the smile he gave me and the light in his eyes told me he was happy being here.

I wanted the right to touch him, to reach out and put my palm over his bicep, to twine my fingers with his.

"Let's park what makes a professional conversation till later and find out whether the people we're feeding want vegetarian or meat." Jack pulled her onto his knee, wrapping his arms around her, both of their attention going to their children as the eldest, a little boy, tried to use his sister as a trampoline. "Leo! Stop it! Now!" The peaceful French countryside was ruptured by Jack's yell, followed by a yell back from his son.

"He so takes after you." Simone glanced up at her husband.

Neither of them had moved, but Leo had stopped what he was doing and was now helping the little girl line up the toys she'd been playing with.

"Well you definitely don't do what I say that quickly, so I'd agree." Jack picked up her long hair in his fist, wrapping it round.

The gesture made me feel as if I was a voyeur, intruding on a private moment, especially as Simone's cheeks pinked.

"No one's vegetarian," Carina said. "So just cook whatever you want with the ingredient. Shall we head into the town for the market?"

There were various comments made about what to buy and a debate between the two of them about which dishes to focus on. The plan was for them to hold two or three culinary breaks here over the course of the year, some being where they would teach, others where they'd just guest chef in the kitchen. I knew from Jesse that they were designing the menu that would be used in the restaurant most of the year too.

"We should head off – we have a vineyard tour at midday." Jesse stood up, stretching, which made him look even more of a mammoth than he had seated.

Carina left her seat too, nodding. "Are you sure you don't want a lift? Suzette said she would."

"It's fine. I'm here as Jesse's chauffeur anyway, and you have enough to do. What time are we eating tonight?" Carina had offered yesterday to ferry us around the two vineyards, feeling like I was missing out if I didn't wine taste. I really wasn't bothered – Jesse had already said he didn't actually drink much of the wine, and wine was something I preferred to have with food or if I'd had a Very Bad Day.

Carina shook her head and gave me a wry smile. "I think you're more than just the chauffeur, but have it your way."

I didn't argue, just carried on listening in to the arrangements for dinner and trying not to stare at Jesse.

"Maybe when I retire from football, I'll move here."

We were outside our second wine yard of the day, the first tour having felt quite commercial and not particularly in depth. The scenery though had made up for it, surrounded by fields and flowers, a pretty river running next to the large barns that were used to make the wine.

"Don't you think you'd be bored?"

He shrugged. "I don't know. I'd have to try it to find out." He'd changed into a white linen short sleeved shirt before we'd headed out, the material and colour making his skin look darker. Jesse caught the sun easily, his skin already darker where the tops he wore for training didn't cover his skin. The summer so far in England had been hot, hotter than normal, and he now looked like a bad boy pirate, something I was coming to realise was my catnip.

"What would you do to occupy yourself?"

"Maybe have my own vineyard. I like the idea of a simple life, one where you don't need to race around town or have meetings or shit like that to do, but not one where I don't have a project. What about you?"

"I think I'd like to write full time if I can make a career from it. I can do that from anywhere."

"Including a house share in Didsbury?" He raised his brows at me. "I just don't see you feeling comfortable doing that, Jerrica. When's the last time you lived with someone other than your brother?"

"When I was at uni." I wasn't sure it was such a great idea either, but it might end up being all I could afford. I couldn't apply for a mortgage until I had three years of accounts to show, and I didn't want to commit myself to paying out a huge amount of rent either.

"What if I bought a house as an investment and you rented it from me?"

Jesse's suggestion almost made my head implode from the shock.

"I'm sorry, you said what?"

"Rent off me. It might be a fixer-upper, but you can have a say in what decorating goes on and things like that, but then you get more space and a rent you can afford." He looked incredibly smug with himself. "Problem solved."

"Why would you do that?" I knew what I wanted his answer to be.

"Why not? Let's look at some houses when we get back

to Manchester." His hand went to the small of my back again, just above my ass, his little finger resting just where the curve began.

My whole body felt as if it was melting from the inside.

"I spoke to Nate this morning."

I heard Jesse swallow.

"What about?"

"You." I watched his expression darken, his hand moving to my waist. "I asked him if it would cause trouble between you if anything happened between us."

"Jerrica - "

"He said it wouldn't because what I chose to do was up to me."

Jesse nodded, looking away from me.

"You can't use my brother as an excuse, Jesse. If you're not interested, that's fine. I won't bring it up again. If you are, then why not have some fun?"

"You deserve better than what I can give you." He spoke quietly, with gravity to his words.

I shook my head. "The only person who gets to decide what I deserve is me. My brother probably thinks I deserve some version of god, but even he has the sense not to tell me that." I took advice but not at the expense of my own decisions.

I also knew that Jesse's reticence to get involved with me on any level apart from this wasn't just down to him worrying about Nate; there was a whole lot more going on in his head.

"Sorry. I didn't mean to do that. I know you're perfectly capable of making your own decisions." His fingers pressed a little harder against my hip. "What would you want from anything that happened between us?"

I laughed, a little surprised that he was asking that. Most men acted first and thought if it ever became necessary, or at least that had been my experience so far. There were exceptions that I'd seen, but none that I'd experienced.

"Good sex. It's been too long since I had an orgasm at the hand of someone other than my self."

Before he answered, a woman walked out of the building to greet us, a badge on her top that was the same as the emblem on the sign.

"Bonjour! You're here for a private tour, I think?" She gave us a wide smile. "I am sure you will enjoy it. Please, follow me."

By the time we returned to our chateau, my knowledge of wine had more than doubled. It had certainly grown enough to have a conversation in the car with Jesse on the way back that turned into something of a debate about types of wine, although I stopped when I realised I was arguing myself into a knot.

We hadn't restarted the conversation from earlier, about what I wanted from anything that might happen between us. I'd caught him looking at me a few times, his eyes stormy, and I wondered whether it was some internal turmoil that was causing it or whether he was irritated that the way in which he was trying to keep me at arm's length wasn't working.

As much as he'd told me about how he liked to be in control in the bedroom, he wasn't a controlling person outside of it, or that was what had come across. I'd expected him to be something of a backseat driver, given his love for driving and frustrations that he couldn't be behind the wheel, but he hadn't once told me how to drive or been anything other than a relaxed passenger, which was handy, because otherwise, he might've ended up being dumped by the road somewhere.

When we returned, a table outside had been decorated with flowers and greenery, some vice type contraption holding up a bar above the table from which a flower had been hung. It was Insta-worthy at its finest and I suspected that it was partly made up for that purpose. The table was set for eight of us, making me wonder who else was joining, along with Jack and Simone, and Carina and Suzette.

"You're back!" Carina materialised from the kitchen into the garden. "How was it?"

I glanced at Jesse, wanting his opinion to be what she heard first. I was here as his chauffeur, friend as well, so it was his thoughts she needed to hear, not mine.

"Interesting. The first tour was very basic. The second probably too much – I think Gérard had it about right with the balance of information and hospitality. Were you thinking of doing tours without food?"

Carina shrugged. "We've talked about both and haven't come to a decision. There's a market for group tours, with a cold buffet at the end, that we could put on once or twice a week. Some of those people might return for a meal or even a stay, but I think we want the bulk of it to be more fine dining around when we don't have events on."

I managed to stay quiet. I hadn't worked in the hotel or restaurant business, but I had organised events from elaborate parties to weddings and christenings, so I did know a little about pitch points.

Jesse turned to look at me. "What do you think?"

"I – I - "

He laughed. "No, Jerrica, you do have an opinion and we'd like to hear it."

The look he gave me contained enough heat to mull all the red wine in Carina's cellar.

"Offer monthly or fortnightly tours that can be booked directly through you, with the buffet that you suggested. Keep it to limited places so it feels exclusive and price it at that, too. Push the dining experience, but maybe think about having it only certain days of the week but available for private parties. Make your guests who are staying the priority. Focus on them first. That's what I would do, but I don't know the area or this particular industry." I gave them both a smile, stepping back a little.

"Tomorrow, can we talk some more?" Carina gestured at me with her finger. "Tonight, we're eating like royalty. Dress for expanding stomachs." Her grin was only slightly dirty as she looked at Jesse. "Although I'm not sure yours expands. Too much muscle in the way."

I laughed, enjoying Jesse's half self-conscious gaze down at his feet.

He followed me up to our room, which surprised me. I'd figured he'd wait for me to have first shower, staying outside with Suzette. His feet behind me on the stairs made my breath catch in my throat, anticipation burying a bomb in my stomach.

"Carina's left something for you in our room." His voice was velvet behind me.

"What is it?"

"A surprise. She said it was a treat for you for being my driver."

I walked a little quicker, hearing him laugh.

The surprise was visible as soon as we entered the room; a bottle of champagne in a cooler and the scent of roses coming from the bathroom.

A bath had been run, filled with rose petals, a note beside it that told me the roses and the oil used in the bath had come from the chateau's gardens.

A tray of macarons had been placed on the bed too, along with a hand-tied bouquet of roses and lavender next to it.

"This is a really sweet touch." I picked up the note left with the flowers.

Check the water isn't too hot x

Good advice. You should always check the temperature before you jump in.

"Carina and Suzette are good people." He wasn't smiling; his expression was almost stern. "You want me to open the champagne for you?"

"There are two glasses. I think we're meant to share." I picked up the champagne myself, twisting the metal and popping it open with no spillage.

Jesse's eyes stayed on me all the time, his smile never breaking through.

"I'd offer to share the bath with you, but I think I know what your answer would be." I poured him the first glass, passing it to him with a smile.

He accepted but didn't take a sip. "I don't do relationships, Jerrica."

"Disagree. We have a relationship already. What you're saying is that you don't do intimate relationships." I poured my own glass, putting the bottle back in the stand. "I'm not suggesting a ring and a church, Jesse, just a night or two, and this is the last I'm saying about it. I can only take so many semi-rejections before I start to consider writing crime fiction and basing a victim on you."

He managed a smile, looking away.

"I'm going to enjoy my bath. I'll leave the door unlocked in case you need to come in."

The door stayed shut, but I hadn't expected anything different.

My ego wasn't bruised. I didn't feel like I'd been rejected, despite the bath – which was big enough for two, even when one of them was the size of Jesse – only containing one of us.

I was different from the women Jesse usually hooked up with. He made them sign non-disclosure agreements and agree where their hard no's were. Everything was about them, only on his terms.

I wasn't someone who agreed to anyone's terms and conditions without negotiating my own.

Even if that someone came in a viciously sexy package with enough of a broken hero complex to fill a trilogy of romances.

I drank champagne in the most glorious bath I'd ever been in and let my mind drift off to the next book I was planning to write, trying not to think about the release day for my second book which was in just a few days. Escaping into a world that I could control without risk to anyone else was blissful, the view from the window next to the bath full of fields and blue skies. A moment of bliss, although another man-induced form of bliss would've been equally welcome.

I wasn't going to hold my breath though.

CHAPTER 11
Jesse

I'D BEEN LESS frustrated watching my team play from the bench than in the bedroom while Jerrica soaked in that bath.

The scent of the water stayed with me long after Simone and Jack served their first course; it overtook the taste of the wine and fucked with every thought that I tried to have that didn't include Jerrica.

I'm not suggesting a ring and a church.

Those words had reverberated through my head on a loop at least every three minutes, the absolute truth to them a banging drum.

Every relationship I'd chosen to walk into had come with a set of rules that I had set. My boundaries dominated the bedroom even if my lover got to choose exactly how she came.

But it was never in my house. It was never she who left. I never stayed overnight, leaving before I could fall asleep, even if waking would mean another round. If they phoned me, I didn't answer, returning their call when it suited me and it had been long enough for them to know I wasn't at anyone's beck and call. We didn't go on dates; I didn't share meals with them. It was an arrangement that suited us both, or us all, and it didn't involve feelings.

I wasn't their ride or die. I wasn't their friend. We fucked and shagged and came and that was the start and the beginning of our relationship.

I already had more than that with Jerrica.

Telling her that Nate would hunt me down and turn me into fertiliser for the pitch if I hurt her wasn't the truth. I wasn't enough of a fool to not realise that her getting hurt wasn't a problem. It was the opposite.

She wanted just a few orgasms to break a drought: I wasn't sure I could walk away after just a few.

"So, Jesse, what are your plans for tomorrow?"

I focused on Suzette, who was looking rather contented, mainly because we'd had probably one of the best meals ever created.

"Not much tomorrow. Maybe hang around here and use the pool." I looked over at Jerrica who'd spent the evening chatting to Carina and Simone. The two chefs hadn't needed to serve the food: Carina had a couple of members of the team she'd employed in to work with them, which was part of the trial to see how it could work in the future. Jack and Simone's two children had gone to bed at their usual time, baby monitors with screens set up so they could be checked on easily. Jack's eldest was still in England, grown up enough now to spend her holidays as she wished. Neither had woken, mainly because Jack said they'd spent most of the afternoon in the pool and had knackered themselves out.

"Those are the best days," Suzette smiled. "Just relaxing with nowhere to go and nothing to do. We're having a late breakfast tomorrow, but if you get hungry early, just help yourselves to croissants and pain au chocolat, or whatever's in the fridge."

"Thank you, but I don't think I'll be eating for at least twelve hours." Jerrica stood up, and I saw her stifle a yawn. "If it's okay, I think I'm going to head to bed."

Carina also stood. "I'll be following you in. Jules and Danny will tidy all the plates away so no one needs to bother."

There were good nights and thank yous, a few hugs and then footsteps tapping over the ever-present sound of crickets.

I followed Jerrica to our room, my eyes fixed on her ass which was fine in a dress that clung to her every curve. When the door closed behind me, I leaned against it, watching Jerrica as she slipped off her shoes, rubbing a hand over the top of her feet.

"You just want to experience an orgasm that isn't from your own hand?"

She froze, her eyes on me.

"I can give you that."

I saw a smile grow, slowly, owned by a woman who had figured out – probably a while ago – that she was the one in control.

"How? Tell me how you'd make me come." She sat up straight, looking like she was ready to listen to a story.

I moved to the chair near the window, the shutter still open. "Come sit here." I gave my knee a single pat.

Jerrica slipped off the bed and walked over to me, sitting straight down on my knee, her back resting against my chest. Her dress was short; when she was standing the hem was just above mid-thigh, when sat down it rose higher. I put a hand on her thigh, knocking down one of the thin straps of her dress with the other.

She wasn't wearing a bra underneath, her nipples pebbling, her tits rising as her breath became deeper.

"I'd make you sit on my knee to tell you a story, but you'd have to be a good girl and not move."

"I can do that, but why not move?"

"Because this is about you coming. Not me." I was as hard as steel which I knew she'd have worked out by now. Her moving would push my control too far.

"I promise not to move. Until I come. Then I won't be able to help moving." She sat up straighter, making her tits more prominent.

I ran a finger down her arm, pulling that strap a little further down, then ran my finger slowly back up and along her collar bone, working my way down to the line where her dress started.

"Spread your legs for me, baby."

She'd held them closed together, a little primly.

Her legs parted, her dress moving higher up her thighs. My other hand ran up and down the inside of her thigh, just to the point where the dress ended.

My hand on the top of her chest feathered its way over the material of her dress, pushing it a millimetre lower.

I felt her exhale. I felt the beat of her heart.

Slowly, I pushed her dress down over her breast, exposing just one of her nipples, hard and deep pink. She squirmed on my lap when I trailed a single finger over the bud, the faintest of pressure such a tease. I followed it with a hard pinch, which pulled a gasp from her lips that sent a jolt to my dick.

He wasn't getting any action tonight unless I found ten minutes in the bathroom afterwards. She'd asked me for an orgasm at a hand that wasn't hers, and I would give her that.

"Do you like that?" I circled her nipple with my finger, my other hand teasing her inner thigh, never moving close to her underwear.

"Yes. I liked it when - "

I gave her nipple another sharp pinch, pulling on it a little more this time.

Jerrica groaned, her hips lifting. Her hands stayed on the arms of the chair.

I waited for her to settle down again on my lap before cupping her breast, feeling the weight of it in my palm. She had bigger tits than she should for her frame, full and pert, ones that I knew would bounce if I fucked her. One last pinch, another gasp from her and I pushed her off my knee.

"Take the fucking dress off, Jerrica. I want to see you." I hadn't planned on being so blunt or demanding, part of me worried that it would have her running from the room. The women I'd been seeing I'd met online, we'd discussed exactly what they – and I – liked before they even knew my name. A non-disclosure agreement had been signed before they saw my face. I knew nothing about what Jerrica liked, apart from what I'd read in her books, which gave me some idea, and the idea of doing something that stopped her from liking me – as a friend or whatever else – was almost enough for me to bolt out of the door myself.

She turned to face me, slowly pushing the strap that was still on her shoulder off it, the material catching round her breast, meaning she had to pull it down further, exposing herself to me, for me.

She bent over, giving me a chance to take in her tits bare at last, my own groan when it came as needy as hers had been.

When she stood back up, wearing just a lacy pair of

panties, her eyes were wild, her hands coming up to pull her hair away, her body on show. There was nothing brazen, just brave exposure.

"You're fucking beautiful, Jerrica. I need you to take your underwear off, so I can finger that pussy."

Her cheeks reddened, either from embarrassment or lust, or maybe a mixture of both.

"Turn around when you take them off and bend over so I can see what I want."

I expected hesitation, but there was none. She moved around slowly, bending over and pulling her underwear down those smooth, long legs, spreading them slightly, which gave me a better view of her ass and a glint of wetness that was smeared down her leg as her panties came down.

"Good girl. Come sit back on my knee. Lean back and spread your legs." I reached forward, taking hold of her hips in my hands and pulled her back to where I wanted her. Her legs parted, her shoulders pressing back partly into me and partly into the side of the chair, giving me full and obvious access to her tits. My arms wrapped around her and I pressed a kiss to the side of her neck, then a little bite, my hands coming up to cup both of her tits, squeezing both nipples at the same time.

My guess was that she was close to orgasm and a few touches would detonate her. That wasn't going to happen.

Her arms spread higher and further back, a hint to do that again, which I would. My guess was that a little light bondage would suit her, that she would happily hand over control to me. I circled her nipples then petted them, seeing arousal glisten between her legs, her clit visible.

"What do you want me to do, Jerrica?"

"I want you to fuck me."

My cock almost exploded.

"I'm not fucking you tonight, but I promise I'll make you come. Do you want me to carry on doing this - " I pinched her nipples again, harder than before, clamping them between my finger and thumb for longer. "Or do you want me to finger your cunt?"

"Both."

"Greedy girl." I slipped a hand down and over her stomach, stopping just on her pubis. She was waxed and smooth, just a scattering of neatly trimmed hair left. I didn't much care how a woman choose to have herself there, it was their choice, whatever made them feel comfortable, but I liked how she was. I would enjoy having my mouth there at some point.

I raised my hands and gave a quick slap between her legs, nothing that would sting, only quickly stimulate. Jerrica's moan and her legs widening told me everything I needed to know about heading in the right direction.

"Did you like that?"

"Yes. Again."

I obliged, doing it twice more before resting my hand over her centre, keeping any pressure off her clit. I pinched her nipple with my other hand and then pushed a finger inside her. She was tight and hot, tensing around my one digit while I slowly plunged it in and then removed it, taking it up to her mouth.

"Suck it. Taste yourself." I pressed it down on her lips.

She opened her mouth obediently, sucking on my finger with desperate enthusiasm. I pulled it out, trailing it back down between her tits, over the slight curve of her stomach and gently over her clit back to her opening.

This time I pushed two fingers inside her, curling them to find where that little raised spot was, applying just enough pressure to have her buck in my arms. I started slowly, gently. She was tight and I knew it had been awhile since she'd been fucked. Her body started to tense. I bit her neck, quickening with my fingers, her juices making them slick, the sound of her arousal only making mine build.

Quicker and quicker, I fucked her with my fingers, speeding up to take her to a point where she was strung tighter than a violin. I shifted my other hand down to her clit, pinching it between my thumb and fingers. Jerrica grasped hold of the chair's arms and she started to come, hard and noisily, my arms keeping her grounded, my hands forcing her to ride out her orgasm, her pussy and thighs slick with her wetness, probably more than she was used to.

My cock had grown harder, furiously needy and jealous of my two fingers buried deep inside Jerrica's pussy. My balls had tightened and before I could even pull together any self-control, my own groan was pulled from me, and I ejaculated into my trousers, my cock pinned between my stomach and Jerrica's back.

"Fuck!"

Her hands went to my knees as her body started to relax, my fingers still in her, my other hand now over her tits, memorising the feel of her skin, the warmth of it. Everything.

"Jesse - "

My name sounded like a prayer.

"You okay?" My orgasm finished. I had no idea if she realised I'd just come, too.

"Yes. No."

I laughed, removing my fingers straight to her clit, ignoring the wetness in my clothes. I circled softly over her clit, the gentle touch in complete contrast to what I'd just done. "Come for me again. Be a good girl. I want another orgasm."

She braced herself, her legs open again, almost as if she had an audience in front of her. If we did this again, I'd have a mirror there so I could watch her show, make her watch it so she could see just how fucking lovely she was.

"Your pussy is so fucking tight. I'd love to have my cock in there. I'd love to find out how it feels when you come on my cock." I strummed a little quicker, a little harder. "Would you let me fuck your pussy?"

"Yes." The word was long, almost a hiss.

"Such a good girl for me."

She came with her hips bucking, her feet looping behind my calves to hold her down, curses on her tongue that another night I'd have told her off for in the best possible way.

Usually, when that had happened with another woman, I'd move them off my knee, clean myself up and leave. That was always the deal.

That wasn't happening tonight.

I pulled her higher onto my lap, one hand on her ass, my little finger playing close to that puckered hole I was curious about – had she been touched there? Did she know how good it could make her feel?

"Are you good?"

Her eyes flickered at me. "I've never felt better. But I want to pay back the favour."

My laughter was wry. "No need. You didn't even need to touch me, but I do need to clean up."

"You came?"

"In my pants like a teenager. How do you want me to play this now?" All the confidence I had with what I'd just done to her was flying out through the window. I had no idea what happened next.

"Clean up and get in bed, but I need you to at least try to hold me for a few minutes. Can you do that?"

I nodded. I didn't actually know if I could, but this – she – was different. I could try. "Spoons?"

"Spoons. You're the big spoon. Tomorrow – we see what happens. Don't worry about it. If this is it, it was good, Jesse."

She was giving me a way out, but I wasn't sure I was going to take it.

I cleaned up, taking a quick shower while she did something in the bedroom, the atmosphere between us unsure and tentative. Jerrica headed into the bathroom after me, sounds of water running and the toilet flushing, the shower on for just a couple of minutes, before she came out, slipping into bed first.

"You didn't kiss me."

It was a statement rather than an accusation.

"I know."

"Will you kiss me now? A goodnight kiss?" She sat up, the tight vest she'd put on clinging to those curves, her nipples still visible through the material.

"I've never given someone a goodnight kiss." I wasn't ashamed of the words. My therapist would tell me to be proud of saying them.

Jerrica nodded. "Then let me show you something. I've never done anything like what we did on that chair before."

"How do you feel about it?" Because I didn't want her to feel ashamed or embarrassed.

"Like I bossed my body. Or rather you did."

"But you let me. The moment you say stop, I do."

She nodded, moving down the bed towards me on her knees. "I know. And the moment you say stop, I will."

I'd never felt lightness from my shoulders, but I did then.

She raised high onto her knees, her hands grasping hold of my shoulders, her mouth slowly finding mine.

It wasn't a kiss that was a prelude to sex. It was a kiss that promised everything and demanded nothing.

Rarely had I been able to trust someone. As a kid, I had me, and that was it. I'd spent a few nights when I was thirteen, fourteen sleeping rough. I'd sofa surfed as a sixteen-year-old, found a hot meal where I could. Promises were made by family members, my mother, social workers, friends and they were broken with more ease than it took to tear an ageing love letter.

When my hands found Jerrica's waist, her thin knickers doing nothing to hide the warmth from her skin, I didn't have the urge to let go any time soon.

Her kiss was chaste, soft, not that of a woman who wanted more right now.

"Get in bed with me." She moved away, making me follow, getting under the sheets with her, her hand stretching out to turn off the final light. "I promise I won't make any move on you."

She turned on her side and curled into me, pulling one of my hands onto her and down to the soft sheets under us.

"Isn't that a weird promise to make to a man?" My teammates would laugh if they ever heard those words.

"I don't think anything is weird, Jesse. I just accept it."

Her hair smelled of honeysuckle and summer. My eyes closed as I sank into the pillow, my body relaxing, her warmth enveloping me.

I decided not to overthink this. In the morning I'd know what to do.

I woke to the scent of woman and fresh air, my brain taking a few minutes to become cognisant of where I was and who I was with.

It had been years since I'd woken up in the same room as someone else until this week, let alone the same bed. And definitely not with my arms wrapped round someone, my hand somehow under Jerrica's top, my palm cupping her tit, my other hand under her body and then on her ass, over her knickers. Her head was lying on the top my chest, one of her hands on my hip.

My dick was hard.

It had now been months since I'd had sex, or an orgasm at anyone's hand but my own. I knew the same was true for her until last night. In fact, she'd used those words.

If I slipped my hand lower on her ass, my fingers would be between her legs.

Was she wet?

Was she still asleep?

Her nipple was hard under my palm. I ran my finger over it, feeling it tighten. Her legs scooted higher up over my hip, nudging against my cock.

Did I try to gently move her off me and head straight to the bathroom? Did I freeze? Move my hands off her?

I didn't want to do that.

I wanted to fuck her.

I wanted to feel my cock deep inside her heat, feel her pulse around me as I made her come just like she had around my fingers. I wanted to tell her when she could come, when she could touch me. I wanted to step out of my controlled, boundaried expectations about what I could deserve and venture further into the unknown. With her.

All with her.

I needed some control here if I didn't stop what was possibly about to happen.

Swallowing any indecision, I started to toy with her nipple, gently pinching it between two fingers, running my finger around it, stretching her top with the movement of my hand.

I hadn't fixed on what she was wearing for bed when she kissed me last night because I knew that wouldn't end well. Her tits were just a bit more than a handful, plumper at the bottom, which meant her nipples sat high. The top she wore was white and fairly see-thru; I figured she'd consciously decided to wear it, knowing what reaction she'd provoke from me, because I knew that Jerrica was just as controlled as me, she just understood better when to hand that control over.

I slipped my hand lower on her ass, just enough movement available as she was lying on my arm. The knee of her top leg moved higher and a slight moan came from her lips. I pinched her nipple again, this time a little harder. The movement of her fingers under the waistband of my shorts told me she was awake.

I pushed my fingers over the material between her legs, finding a wet spot that told me exactly what I needed to know.

I just wasn't sure exactly how she'd expect me to be as a lover.

I carried on stroking her there, teasing that nipple,

applying pressure over her covered entrance, not quite reaching her clit.

She started to move in my arms, just slightly, as if she was pretending she was still asleep for fear that if I knew she was awake, I'd stop.

I slipped my finger under the material of her knickers, the smooth liquid heat of her arousal making it easier to tease. She twitched her ass, just enough so I could possibly think she was still asleep, but enough to give me the go ahead to continue, just a little.

This time I tugged at her nipple, like I had last night, enough so that there was no way she could pretend to still be asleep.

"Don't stop. Whatever you want to do, don't stop." Her words were breathy, still laced with sleep and tinged with need. They were like catnip for my dick, her hand now creeping towards it, shifting her legs so I had better access.

I could finger her easily now, so I slipped a digit into her tight heat, feeling her squeeze around it. Slowly I moved it in and out, my other hand still on her tit.

"How far do you want me to go?" Jerrica's hand was trying to clasp my cock now under my shorts, clever fingers playing with the tip. I needed her boundaries before I snapped.

"I want you to fuck me and make me come. I'm on the Pill and I'm clean." She opened her eyes and tipped her head to look at me. "Are you?"

"I'm not on the Pill but I'm clean. This all stops when we get home. That's my boundary." For now. That was my boundary for now. "It's between us."

Her lips parted as I carried on fingering her, adding

another digit, trying not to think too much about how tight she was going to feel when I got inside her.

"Fine. Take these off." She tugged at my shorts.

"I have to pull my fingers out of you to do that, and I like them there at the moment. Take your hands out of them."

She did as I told straight away. My cock was liking this.

I carried on with shallow thrusts of my fingers, not enough for her to get anywhere near an orgasm. Her breath was becoming harder, her body moving instinctively to try and get to the end.

I wasn't going to go hard core edging with her now, but it wouldn't hurt to play.

I let her have a little more depth, finding that spot inside her core again that would send her over the edge eventually, and giving it a couple of nudges, before I pulled my hand away from her sopping centre.

"Take your clothes off."

She opened her mouth as if she was going to reply, then stopped, sitting up and pulling her vest over her head, leaving her tits exposed for me to look at.

And I looked, holding up one in my hand then the other.

"Good girl. You're perfect."

Her back arched, any embarrassment at me seeing her naked held back once again.

"Take your knickers off and then spread your legs for me." I lay on my side, elbow propping up my head. Noise outside told me it was still early, but late enough for others to be up.

Jerrica's hands went to her underwear, pushing it down and lifting up her ass to slide it off. I watched as she became exposed, creamy skin on her stomach leading to her untanned mound, that slight scattering of hair my new idea of perfection.

She pulled her underwear off and pushed it off her side of the bed, tentatively spreading her legs.

I didn't touch her; I just looked. "Good girl again. You're fucking soaking, aren't you?" I could see her pussy glistening with her juices.

"Yes."

"I like how you answer me. Do you want me to touch you?"

"Yes, I do. Do I need to say please?" Her eyes widened.

I laughed quietly. "No. Only if you want. Where do you want me to touch you?"

"My clit."

"Will you come if I do? Be honest?"

"Probably." She nodded, spreading her legs wider.

I could smell her scent. I wanted to taste her down there, to play with her clit and her slit with my tongue, but I'd save that for later.

"Lie back and put your hands above your head. I want you to try not to come until I'm fucking you."

She lay down, looking at me while she slowly put her hands where I'd asked, taking hold of the pillow.

I stayed away from touching her between her legs, leaning over to take a nipple in my mouth instead, sucking it hard, then running my tongue around her areole. Jerrica whimpered, but her hands stayed fixed.

I moved over to the other nipple, keeping my hands away from her, aware that her legs had pushed together so she could try and create some friction.

"I said to spread your legs." My mouth left her nipple.

She moved them apart. "Sorry."

"This bed is perfect for tying you up. Then you won't

be able to not do as I say." I watched her face as I said it, seeing lust and want, desire. She was into this. Maybe I would find something to tie her up with before we went home.

"Good girl."

She moaned. I licked her nipple, once, twice and then I took it in my mouth, aware that her hips were moving.

I put a hand on them to still her back to the bed, rewarding her with running one finger down over her clit to her opening, feeling her slickness. I wasn't going to push a finger inside her again, but it was too tempting not to.

"Jesse - "

I found her eyes with mine and I stilled the digit inside her. She was so fucking tight.

"You're going to be amazing round my dick."

Her pussy pulsed.

"Such a good girl."

She moaned, pulling at the pillow.

I laughed, loving her frustration. "How much do you want to come?"

"I want you to fuck me more. I want to touch you."

"You can when I say so."

I was going to let her touch me before I finished, something that I didn't usually do. I liked to do the touching, all of it. I couldn't do that with Jerrica; I knew it would be too anonymous for her. I knew I didn't want her to be the same as the other women I'd been with. I knew a lot of things right now, but I didn't understand them.

I moved off the bed, watching her while I took off the shorts I'd slept in. Her eyes drank me in, moving down my body and fixing on my dick.

"Now I understand when heroines in romance novels ask if it'll fit." She didn't move her gaze.

"It'll fit. It might be uncomfortable at first." Because I was big. I'd had one woman change to give me a half-hearted hand job because she'd decided I was too big for her to manage. I'd been nineteen and hadn't known much better. "But then it'll be good. More than good."

She parted her legs more, giving me a better view that made me groan. Her hands stayed fixed on the pillow.

I moved over her, taking my cock in my hand and teasing her clit with its tip, watching her mouth open more as she gasped.

She was going to come quickly when I was in her. I probably wasn't going to last much longer than her.

I lined it up at her entrance, sensing her tense a little, which wasn't good. I leaned back down and sucked a nipple hard, lifting a hand to tweak the other and then I slid in, her slickness making it smooth, keeping going until I was seated all the way and then pausing, giving her time to stretch around me, get used to my size.

I limited my kisses, but it was too tempting not to take her mouth in a messy battle while I started to move. I kept it slow for the first couple of thrusts, her hands still above her head, her knees lifting up, giving me more space and letting me go even deeper.

She was vice-like and responsive with the little noises she made, sounds that were going to haunt me every time I grew hard again. I moved high over her, pushing on her leg and started to fuck her faster and harder, knowing she'd be sore after and thinking of me all day. That thought was potent, scary and heady, because I didn't want her to walk away from this room today and for this to be it for her. I wasn't even going to think what it was going to do to me.

Her eyes widened, her tits bouncing with each movement, her chest flushed and mouth parting.

"Need to come!" She spat the words out.

"So come round my cock." I moved harder inside her, feeling her explode, her hips jerking, her pussy getting obscenely wetter. She squeezed my cock tight, over and over again, her whimpers and moans driving me almost to the very edge.

"Good girl. That felt amazing." She was still whimpering as I spoke. I pulled together every last ounce of my control. "You can move your hands now while I come inside you."

Jerrica grasped hold of my shoulders, her nails digging in my back, while I fought not to lose it too soon. I wanted to savour this, to try and be aware of everything that was happening, just in case this never happened again. My balls tightened, that pull that told me my own happy ending was beginning.

I came with a roar, far too soon, my cock deep inside her, her pussy pulsing again. My head dropped to her shoulder, sucking the skin there as I poured into her, the feeling potent and frightening at the same time.

I stayed inside her as my heart rate came down, my mouth finding hers in a series of sweet, hard kisses, realisation dawning along with the growing light that fanned into our room.

I'd fucked Jerrica.

I'm come inside her, a decision I'd made with the right head.

We had another four nights in this room. In this bed.

I pushed myself up and looked at her beautiful face, flushed and sated from her two orgasms.

I had absolutely no regrets.

I shifted to my side of the bed, not wanting to crush her, and needing to lie down after expending some sort of rare energy.

I wasn't a cuddler. As a child, hugs had been infrequent, usually when my mother was sober and not high, and she didn't have a man around to devote her attention to. Those three things were rare by themselves and virtually never happened all at the same time. I'd talked about it with my therapist, why I found physical contact other than sex so hard, the one exception being when one of Nate's girls needed a hug. She'd listened, asking questions, making no suggestions, coming back to it over the course of a few sessions, asking me why I thought I couldn't hug, or cuddle. Was it about me not being able to give physical affection or receiving it.

The answer was simple.

I didn't know how to do it. My brain when I was young hadn't understood that hugging or physical contact was nice and safe, it wasn't used to the chemicals such contact would chuck out, and my fight or flight – in this case flight – reaction kicked in. It was all more complex than that, but in short, little boy Jesse had no idea how to hug.

Rubbing wrists and ankles after you'd loosened the ties was a lot easier to emotionally deal with, because that touch served a purpose, just like giving a woman an orgasm.

Lying next to Jerrica, after fucking her bare, after

saying some very dirty things to her that I had an inkling hadn't been said before, and the fact I wasn't stupid, I knew I needed to either explain or make some contact.

I reached for her hand, intertwining her fingers with mine.

She gripped back.

"I'm not good at hugs or the after bit." I turned my head, my heart racing almost as much as it was when I'd been inside her and about to come. "It's why I'm not good at relationships. Part of the why."

"Sleeping you is good at hugs."

"What do you mean?"

She smiled. "I woke up in the night and you were asleep still spooning me. You were cuddled up right behind me and your arms had me seat belted in."

"What did you do?" I squeezed her hand back.

"Snuggled back in and went back to sleep." She turned over on her side, her hand coming back to mine once she'd moved. "Not going to lie, I kind of need something after that. This is fine; as long as you just don't get off the bed and leave, I'm good."

I was quiet, just looking at her, her blonde hair utterly mussed.

"You usually just go, don't you?"

I didn't deserve her smile.

"Usually, yes." I wasn't going to lie.

"Okay, how about this. I need a shower. That shower's huge - why don't you shower with me? Wash my back."

"Because I'll end up fucking you again."

"That's a bad thing how?" She sat up, her hands not even trying to cover up any of her skin.

I sat up too, something in me wanting to pull her close to me, something else wanting me to hide away.

She got off the bed, our combined wetness glistening between her legs, a shock of pride going through me at how I'd marked her so very intimately.

It had been years since I'd gone without a condom, not since I was young and even more stupid than I was now.

"Come, shower. Wash my back. Rinse my hair." She walked round to me, offering her hand, comfortable with her nakedness, admiring mine. "I'll do the same for you."

It was intimacy with a purpose. Maybe she knew that, offering an in between.

I pretended to grouse as I got up, the sheets a messy white puddle at the bottom of the bed. I took her hand and let her lead me into the bathroom, the daylight now streaming through the window. I didn't notice anything else, except Jerrica's bare ass and her long, now messy, curly blonde hair walking in front of me, leading me into the shower.

She turned it on, spraying us both with cold water at first, our laughter bouncing off the walls. I was starting to get hard again, the sight of her tits and the mark I'd left near her neck making me become focused on one thing.

The water warmed up, Jerrica stood under the spray, droplets running down her hair and over her tits, her nipples hardening again.

For a minute I watched her, not needing to hide my gaze. She started to lather up her hands, then rubbing them over her skin, her arms, her breasts.

I swallowed, a lump hard in my throat. Something else was hard too.

"Let me."

She handed me her soap. My pulse fluttered as I rolled it in my hands, before putting it down, then running my palms over her skin as gently as I could, kneeling to wash her skin on her ass and then her legs, my fingers lingering as I washed the place where I'd just been, her pussy still slick with my cum.

My dick was hard, keen to be back in there, half my instincts wanting to turn her round and press her back against the tiles, picking her up so her legs wrapped around my waist and I could drive into her.

The other half, the side I didn't recognise, wanted to do this slowly.

Differently.

Without my usual dirty words that quickened and slowed desire in exactly the ways I planned. Those words that dominated and dictated.

Fear was a beautiful thing. People talked about fight or flight, but there were more instinctive and basic reactions than that. Freeze, flop and friend were there too, and given that flop wasn't going to happen, and I didn't know how I could freeze, there was one other option.

I was opting for friend. For the first time. The very first time.

Jerrica turned around, her hands on my arms, running over my biceps.

"I can't tell you how much I've wanted to do this." Her smile was shyly victorious.

"Do what?"

"Touch you."

I knew I had frozen, despite not thinking it possible. "How do you want to touch me?"

"Like this." She picked up the soap, lathering up her hands and then starting to cast a spell over me as she moved her hands over my skin, not complaining when I touched her back, needing to find a way to ground myself before I floated off.

Although I did think I could. My feet were rooted, every focus I had was on how my skin was alight against hers. Nerve endings where her hands brushed were on fire, when her breasts brushed against me I was seared. My eyes didn't leave her, watching how she moved, where she was, catching sight of every subtle shift she made.

And there were no words. She told me nothing about what she would do next, leaving it for me to try to predict, which I couldn't. She dropped to her knees to wash my hardened shaft, running her hands up and down it, teasing my balls with her fingertips, brushing her lips over the tip.

My hands stayed on her shoulders, lax and unmoving for the first time ever. I'd received blow jobs, but I'd always taken control I wasn't being afforded now. My hands didn't stray to her hair or the back of her head. I didn't give her instructions or encouragement.

There was no praise.

Jerrica licked her way up my cock to the tip then stood back up. "I think you should sit down."

I looked at her through the spray from the shower. "Sit down?"

"Sit down, Jesse."

There was a padded seat in the shower, probably designed so it was easier for someone to shave their legs or wash if standing wasn't a good idea. I managed to walk backwards to it, my hands on Jerrica's waist.

"What am I going to let you do to me?"

She kissed me as I sat down, bringing a knee onto the seat at the side of me, then to other, straddling me.

"Tell me stop if you need."

My head tipped back as she sunk down on my cock,

slowly, slowly, taking her time to be fully seated on it, her hands on my shoulders.

My fingertips pressed into the flesh of her hips, steadying her, steadying myself.

"Is this okay?" She paused, her pussy gripping me.

I nodded. "Can't promise we'll finish this way."

She started to move, slowly up and down, a tortuous dance that was leaving me desperate and needy, pushing at my limits because not taking control here, allowing her to be the one in the lead felt completely foreign.

"Everything is okay. There are no rules right now, just feel good. Does this feel good?"

"It feels fucking fantastic."

"That's all that matters." Her hips angled so her clit pressed against me, the dig of her hands in my shoulder becoming sharper.

I let go of her hip to dip my hand between us, finding her clit and pressing down on it, wanting to speed her release so I could find mine.

"You feel amazing inside me," she gasped out the words, still bouncing up and down on my cock.

My hips were working in time with hers, somehow finding the same rhythm, neither of us seeming to be completely controlling it now. "It feels amazing inside you too." The words felt completely flat of what I wanted to say.

Her head tipped back and her muscles tensed around me, her breasts flushed, presented there for me to see.

I wanted more time here, more chance to learn all the ways she could break apart and let me piece her back together. I wanted to know every way there was to make her find that high and learn how to ride it out with her, to be that person who could take her to those stars and steal them for her.

When I came, buried deep inside her, I found peace as well as panic, a tightening of my chest that made me want to race from the room and find a ceiling high enough to let me take in enough oxygen to breathe.

I didn't.

Not because I couldn't. Jerrica wouldn't have stopped me. I could've lifted her off me, set her on her feet and walked away, taking space, finding air.

I didn't want to.

I found breath. I found the world in her eyes as she regarded me with a blend of fear and something else, because for all I knew she wanted to run too.

"What do I do now?" My words were husky and overfull.

"We kiss. And then we try not to slip when we stand back up and somehow, we finish showering. I need to wash my hair."

"I'll help you." I didn't intend those words. They just fell out and hung in the damp, warm air around us. "If you want."

"I want."

My heart pounded as if I was about to take the stage for a performance that I'd never rehearsed while I shampooed her hair, trying not to get suds in her eyes.

I didn't want to make her eyes water.

I didn't ever want to make her cry.

CHAPTER 12
Jerrica

SOMETHING CHANGED. Maybe the breeze altered direction. Maybe a sea witch released a spell to calm troubled waters. Maybe my brother finally remembered to squeeze the toothpaste from the bottom.

But something felt different that day after we had shower sex that fragmented my mind and left me not wanting to piece it back together.

"So you finally did the deed?"

My head twisted round fast enough to give me whiplash, Suzette standing in front of the fridge with a knowing smile on her face.

"Sorry?" I had no idea how to reply or how she knew. Had she heard us? We were at a different side of the chateau to everyone else, although there had been open windows and people had been milling about outside. "What do you mean?'

She laughed, smiling in a way that told me she was amused, nothing else. We were in the kitchen where I'd been getting a drink of water for Jesse and myself, trying to slip about the chateau unnoticed in case someone else tried to wait on us.

"You both have that freshly fucked look. He also looks like he's just been bowled over by a hurricane." She pulled out a pitcher of water with fruits drenched in it from the fridge. "Carina and I wondered what was going on with the two of you."

"We're just friends."

She raised her brows.

"Friends who have slept together. It wasn't in the plan." Kind of. I wanted to. I came here with Jesse knowing there would be a lot of time when we were alone and I wanted it to happen, I wanted there to be something more because he fascinated me.

And I liked him. More than a lot. I had done for a while, and I thought I was right to, especially after last night and this morning.

Suzette shrugged. "It usually isn't in the plan. Those are the best things that happen, usually. This French air is good at drawing out the romance in us, too. Everything moves slower here, especially the builders." She gave a look of irritation. "Jesse has offered to invest. He mentioned your brother wished to also."

I nodded. We – myself, Jesse and Nate – had video called this morning. Nate was taken with the idea for many reasons, especially the cottage on site that was on the renovation list for autumn, with a view to being ready in spring. The plans were for it to have its own pool, self-contained enough to maintain privacy, but with the use of the chateau's restaurant too. "They're both set. I think Jesse pretty much was ready to go before we came out here, but seeing it has made his mind up completely."

"It's a good place and it will be a success. I think it will be a big success." She nodded, a flash of determination in her eyes. "Carina dreamed about this from when we first met – a sanctuary where people could relax. Be themselves. Find themselves." Her smile was bigger than I'd ever seen it. "You know, we had an amazing gastro-pub back in England, a small village in Norfolk, too small really for us to be much. But we created this fantastic place where people could escape, and found a chef who had aspirations for a Michelin star. Moving here was a risk. We slept in a caravan for the first nine months, until this became habitable."

"You really followed your dreams."

"Which is how you should spend your life. I know you want to write – Jesse told me. He said you had a successful event planning business."

I nodded, wondering where this was going. I respected what Carina and Suzette were doing here: I could only imagine the life changes they'd made and the finances they'd put on the line, but that didn't mean I needed a lecture.

"He's proud of you. He said your book is really good, too."

I saw her eyes dance.

"He's read it?"

She nodded. "I'm looking forward to seeing how things work out between the two of you, but even if they don't, remember how it felt to be here, when you have that flight of first lust, because nothing's more magical than that, however long it lasts."

"How do you and Carina keep it like that? Magical?" I knew relationships changed. My parents had been married more than thirty years, but I still saw my dad looking at my mother like she'd hung the moon and the stars as well.

I'd seen Nate's marriage to his first wife Chan change, and I had wondered just before she was diagnosed with cancer whether she was content to be Nate's wife, looking after their girls. I'd seen her head turn, not that I'd ever let my brother know that and I never would.

"I don't think a relationship can always be magical. There are times when it is, and times when it's hard work and difficult, like treading through treacle based on sinking sand, but maybe it's those parts that let you know what that person's really like and you know the bones of them. Maybe those are the bits that matter." Suzette shook her head, smiling at me as if I was a butterfly about to flutter for the first time. "But now's not the time for you to think about treacle, unless you're licking it off him."

I smiled, feeling my cheeks grow hot, that blush I'd never been able to master pushing through any tan I'd managed to develop.

"I don't know what's going to happen. I think it might be a holiday romance." Because that was what he'd said. *Just while we were here.*

Suzette shrugged. "In that case, go and enjoy your holiday. I'll bring you some of this that I made." She gestured to the pitcher. "Go sit back with your beau."

I smiled, nodding, hearing the wisdom in her words and letting it stop my mind from galloping after notions of what might happen.

We lazed by the pool, spent an hour with Simone and Jack and their kids talking about food and diets and restaurants in Manchester, and walked around the grounds and the vineyards, the hot Mediterranean sun sultry on our skin.

As we walked, Jesse took my hand. It was tentative,

his gesture, his fingers brushing against mine, the back of our hands meeting briefly, before he caught my hand in his.

I didn't ask, but I didn't think he'd ever held a girl's hand before.

We talked about home, about his schedule when we got home because pre-season was starting, the first game six weeks away. There would be friendlies, fitness training and a whole remit of media for him to attend as club captain. There was also the build-up to the World Cup which was happening through November and December, when I'd definitely be with Amber and the new baby, plus my two naughty nieces, as we wouldn't be travelling to the Middle East. The heat would be too much, and the travelling, plus the amount we'd see of Nate would be minimal. All of his focus – and Jesse's – would be on the games and the competition, as England pushed to be world champions, something they hadn't done for nearly sixty years.

We didn't talk about what was happening when we got home. I didn't ask him if we'd still steal moments together, or whether we would leave last night and this morning here in France.

Or this afternoon, when he kissed me in a vineyard and I felt like I was seventeen again, falling in love for the first time with a boy who held all my happy endings in his hand.

It was a kiss that relegated all of my other kisses to just faint memories of things that barely ever happened. His hands were on my waist, almost chaste in their touch, and his lips met mine tentatively, as if he wasn't quite sure what to do, or how I was going to respond.

A light breeze whispered through the trees shielding

us. No one else was around. The only sound the breeze and the call of birds.

I pulled myself closer to him, my arms around his neck, body pushing against his, letting him control the speed of the kiss, how deep it went, how much it demanded. My body responded too easily, the pulse between my legs growing stronger, heavier, need increasing.

The night before, when he'd told me what to do, had been a new experience. My previous lovers hadn't had that confidence or that craving to take control in that way. Jesse had owned it. In that time, he'd owned my body, or at least I'd loaned it to him.

This morning I'd been surprised. Part of me hadn't expected a repeat of the night before at all, let alone more, with him coming inside me. Jesse sheltered behind a wall he'd carefully constructed, one with a moat and a defensive system designed to repel any attack on his emotions. For some reason, he'd let me breach them without so much as a warning shot.

In the shower, I'd felt that moment when he didn't even try to put those defences back up, when he'd made that careful decision to keep his arms down, letting me step into his territory.

In this field, filled with wildflowers and fruit trees, the chateau rising in the distance like some maternal goddess, I didn't try to analyse and work out his strategy; instead I just was.

Here. His arms encircling me. A kiss that tasted of summer and hope and want. All the sweetness of that brush of what love there could be.

"I don't know how I should be doing this." His words

were the finest of whispers, barely overheard even by the bees hovering nearby.

"It doesn't come with a playbook, Jesse." I pulled his hand down so he sat with me, the ground warm and dry. "It's just meant to feel good."

His eyes darkened, that pirate look that made me want to hear him call me his good girl again and feel his hand sting intoxicatingly between my legs.

"I know lots of ways to make you feel good."

I laughed. "You've only shown me a couple."

"I can show you more. Did you like what we did last night? This morning in bed?" He swallowed, and I saw concern cross his face.

"A lot."

"Did you prefer the shower?"

I shook my head, pressing the palm of my hand against his jaw, feeling the stubble that had grown there. "I liked both. I enjoyed both – I wouldn't prefer one over the other."

He nodded. "Are you saying that because you know what type of sex I've been into?"

"No. If I didn't like how you were on the chair or in bed, I would tell you. I don't believe in telling lies, Jesse."

He didn't answer, his dark eyes studying me like I was some rare creature he'd just encountered for the first time.

"Did you like the shower?"

"Yes. It scared me."

"Why?" Although what he'd said didn't surprise me, I was just surprised he'd said it so bluntly.

"Because I've never had sex – not since pretty much my first time – where it wasn't me in control."

"You were in control in the shower."

He shook his head. "That was all you."

"Disagree. You could've moved me at any time. You could've told me to stop. You could've picked me up and had me against the shower wall – which I know you thought about but you chose not to do it. So you can't say you didn't have control, Jesse. It was just different."

He looked to the ground. "Just like you could've said no on the chair or in bed."

"Or now."

He looked back up at me. "Now? We're outside – "

I laughed. "Have you never had al fresco sex before?"

"Al fresco? How very middle class."

I laughed back, lying now with my head on his lap. The sky was azure blue, cloudless. No thunderstorms or showers lurked right now. "So you've never fucked anyone against a wall outside? Even as a kid?"

"No. Always indoors. Not necessarily in a bed. Often not in a bed."

"You mean you have a dungeon? A sex dungeon? Can I see it? It'd be really good research." I tugged at his T-shirt.

"So that's what this is all about. I'm research?"

There was enough teasing in his tone to know he wasn't serious. "Completely. I have writer's block and I can't possibly finish my next book without seeing your sex dungeon."

"Jerrica, I don't have a sex dungeon – "

"What about one of those sex benches? Or that horse thing? A selection of handcuffs, maybe?"

He was laughing hard now, his body vibrating through to mine.

"Okay, I have handcuffs. I have rope. I don't have a switch or a paddle because I prefer to use my hand to administer a spanking, which I'd be quite happy to do here if you carry on about sex dungeons."

There was a glance of seriousness that was doing all the wonderful things to my girl-parts.

"Would you tell me I was a good girl?" The air froze.

"Only if you were a good girl." His eyes darkened; the lightness that had tinted our conversation became shadowed, hunger starting to be exposed in his look. "Do you want to be a good girl for me now?"

I pushed up my best top over my stomach, exposing skin, trailing my own hand over it. "Yes. I think I do."

"Here?"

"It's a perfectly good field. And no one can see unless they're looking."

He shook his head. "Your argument is lacking, Jerrica. People would look. They'd want to see you."

"But only you are close enough to see everything. We can go back to our room if you want."

He was quiet for a moment. "Take your shorts off. And your underwear."

I lifted my hips without questioning, without letting myself question, sliding both down together, placing them next to me. The sun felt immediately warm on my exposed flesh, adding to the heat that had been building since Jesse had held my hand.

"I want to watch you make yourself come." He stroked my hair as he spoke. "I want to see how you touch your clit or if you finger yourself. Are you wet?"

"Yes."

"What made you wet?"

"You holding my hand. Then the kiss. But I was wet already because you came in me before. Twice."

I moved my hand between my legs, dipping a finger to my entrance and spreading the wetness that was plentiful, smoothing it up to my clit. Jesse's hand moved from my hair to my breast, cupping it through the thin material of my vest. I hadn't bothered with a bra, my bikini top left on the bed when I'd changed, so his touch was potent.

I expected him to get rough with my nipples, like he had this morning and last night, but his hand was more reassuring, a caress, almost a tease. I felt exposed, lying here outdoors, my bottom half exposed even though it was only Jesse who could see.

"Give me your fingers. I want to taste your pussy." His hand moved onto my arm, guiding it so my fingers went to his mouth. He sucked them softly, just enough pressure to make me gasp.

"Sweet. You taste like I thought. Carry on." He dropped my hand, moving his to roughly pull up my vest so my breasts were exposed, my nipples hard.

He didn't touch them, just looked at them. I watched his gaze as he seemed to appraise them, my orgasm creeping even closer.

"Am I allowed to come?"

His eyes went back to mine.

"Good girl for asking. Yes, you can come, but I want you to keep just using your clit. If you do that, you'll get a reward."

My hand was moving quicker now, the heat, the air, his attention on my body, the fact that the only place he was now touching me was my collar bone.

"What's the reward?"

"My cock." He brushed his hand over my breasts, my nipples in almost agony as he grazed them. "Either in your mouth or your pussy. I haven't decided yet."

I came with a moan, my body jerking, my hand struggling to keep the rhythm I needed.

I heard his words, praising me, telling me I was beautiful and for a moment I had a flicker of a vision of other women he'd said the same words to. Pushing them away, I opened my eyes to look at him, sensing movement.

His shorts were undone, his large, thick cock exposed. I turned my head, close enough to not have to move much to take him in my mouth, sucking tentatively, as if someone was going to take my treat away.

Jesse's hand grasped my hair, pulling on it unlike when I was in the shower, when he'd let me set the rhythm.

"That feels good, Jerrica, but I want you on your hands and knees. Time to fill that pussy again."

My groan sounded almost painful, his words making it feel as if my orgasm had never happened. I moved like he was pulling my strings, hands and knees on the grass, my vest still pushed up above my breasts.

Jesse cupped them as he positioned himself behind me, his cock resting on my ass, his fingers pulling at my nipples sharply as he bit my neck, hard enough to leave a mark.

"Going to fuck you hard, baby." He moved back, one of his hands moving between my legs, cupping my sex, his finger pressing against my clit and then pushing into my centre, one finger, then two, roughly thrusting into me.

"So fucking wet for me. Let's see how much wetter you get." His hand left me, his cock replacing his fingers seconds later, his hands gripping my hips as he pushed all the way inside me in one smooth thrust.

His pace was wicked, within moments I was boneless, only his name decipherable from the words that poured from my lips, words he ignored, simply carrying on moving my hips, using me to fuck him, pulling a second and then a third orgasm out of me, telling me how good I was, how he loved being inside me. He came with my hair wrapped around his fist, the pull morphing into sharp pleasure as I felt him come, his warm wetness filling me up like he'd promised.

I expected him to pull out straight away, to do up his shorts and pass me my underwear.

He didn't.

Still inside me, still hard, he pulled me with him so we spooned on the ground, his arms wrapped around me, one cupping my breast, his mouth at my neck pressing kisses that were soft and sweet against the delicate skin there.

I turned my head, just about able to find his lips with mine and stole a messy kiss, his hand on my breast busying itself with tender touches.

He was still hard. His hips starting to move again.

"Jesse?"

I heard him exhale. "I can pull out – if you're sore or want to stop. It won't be like what we just did."

A thrill went through me, not at the fact that that I had found an actual unicorn – I could deal with that later – but that he'd moved from what I knew what his controlled comfort zone to a place that wasn't all about staying within that carefully set paradigm.

"I'm good." I was more than good.

Jesse moved slowly, careful movements that weren't as deep as before, the position on our sides didn't allow for that. His hand slipped lower to my clit, toying with it with the same rhythm as his hips, somehow working me towards another climax.

"I don't think I can come again. I'm sorry." I moved my hand back to palm his tight ass.

"Don't ever apologise. Just enjoy it. It isn't always about coming."

I did though. His release, the feel of him throbbing

inside me again triggered mine, not as powerful as before, but enough to bring tears to my eyes, my body wrapped in his, all the words either of us had, gone.

In the weeks that followed, I'd often think about that afternoon under the Mediterranean sun; how the breeze made the trees whisper stories about lovers who snuck away and how the birds sang songs about hearts that somehow found another to belong with.

And I'd wonder how it could be snatched away because of someone else's bad dream.

CHAPTER 13
Jesse

MY THERAPIST DIDN'T MAKE any observation about how I looked any different, but either that was her job, or I was simply the fucking same as I had been a couple of weeks before.

She was older than I first remembered. A stupid statement, as I'd been seeing her for years, and people aged, but today, after living a life I didn't recognise with a woman I knew I wasn't good enough for, my therapist looked like she'd aged too much.

"Will you ever retire?"

Probably not the most subtle thing to ask a woman, but Jane wouldn't tell me to fuck off.

"One day. But let's start with how you're feeling insecure about things that you have no control over." She looked up at me from eyes that already knew too much and not enough.

"What do you mean?"

Jane was good, but I didn't think she was telepathic, and I'd all but proved her guess about insecure feelings with that reaction.

I groaned.

"Jesse, you have no control over when I retire, which isn't going to be soon enough. Panicking that I might not be here is not helpful, which you know."

I stared at the coffee table between us, the usual jug of water and two glasses on it, like always. Like always, I wouldn't touch the water until about halfway through. Like always, I'd down whatever was left in it before I left her room.

I was perfectly aware of my routines. I was perfectly aware of why I had them and the function they provided.

When I started therapy I'd done so out of curiosity. I'd been wary. By the sixth session, I was starting to not look forward to seeing Jane but needing it. The space she provided for me to talk was safe. I was listened to by someone who had no agenda, someone whose job was to be only what I needed at that time.

"What happens when you retire?"

She shook her head. "If you're still having therapy by that point, I'll have someone to recommend you to. We will have a planned ending, however long that takes, and you will be fine. You know yourself better than you ever thought you could and there are days when we meet and I feel like I'm stealing your money. Then there are days like today, where I feel like you should probably pay me double, which is a very non-therapeutic thing to say, but I'm trying to provide you with an opening from which you can talk."

I inhaled. She understood that sometimes I needed another person's recognition of where I was at, otherwise I'd try to bury it and move on.

"I slept with Jerrica."

Jane already knew all about Jerrica. She knew how I lost my licence.

"Did the world end? Has her brother hired a hitman yet?"

I shook my head. "Sarcasm shouldn't become a therapist."

She smiled. "Without giving me details, talk me through how it's left you feeling."

I sat back and folded my arms. When I started these sessions I'd deviate from the point in these sorts of conversations, find something easier to talk about. Jane would let me for her given amount of time and then pull me back round to what it was I was meant to be focusing on. I stopped trying to deviate now and just considered my words instead.

"I don't know. We had sex my way, and then she, I guess she took the lead." My words faded out. Finding the right ones was hard. I'd tried not to replay parts of the last few days because I couldn't process how it had been, how I'd felt when I took away my dirty words and demands, when Jerrica had ridden me or I'd spooned her from behind.

Or I'd fallen asleep with her head on my chest and my hands wrapped around her as if she was the only thing stopping me from floating away.

"Did you like it?"

I gave a single nod. "I came, so yeah."

Jane didn't flinch. There had been a week when I'd seen her for four sessions, around the time when I'd gotten heavily into bondage and realised it was becoming something that controlled me rather than the other way round. I'd freaked the fuck out, arguing myself into a corner, but instead of repeating the mistakes of my mother, I took refuge in Jane's room, learning to talk myself down from a ledge.

"Which is irrelevant. Afterwards. Did you want to leave? Did you want to create distance?"

Because being emotionally close to someone was foreign to me. Boy Jesse hadn't had anyone to hug him, so my brain was never wired that way. Sex, when I discovered it, was great, but I couldn't cope with the aftermath, the aftercare, unless it was aftercare in the scripted sense of making sure my partner came out of subspace safely.

"No. But it's scared me that I didn't."

"Tell me more about Jerrica. How was spending so much time with her?"

"Easy. She can talk about anything, but she likes to be silent too. She didn't just talk for the sake of it and she told me what she wanted. It was like she knew I needed directions sometimes."

"Instead of it being you giving them?"

"She told me what she needed me to do."

"So she gave you a choice. Did you give her a choice?"

"Many times. She was really clear about what she wanted. She's a writer. She's good with words."

Jane nodded and left the air silent.

I knew this was one of her methods, making me think it out for myself rather than rely on her putting words in my mouth or me disagreeing for the sake of it.

"I didn't think I'd feel like that. I didn't think I would ever want to hold someone like I held her afterwards and not want it to end as soon as possible." I poured the water, maybe sooner than usual. "I didn't think I'd take whatever scraps she'd give me."

"Is that all she gave you? Scraps?"

"No. They weren't scraps at all."

"So what do you mean by scraps?"

"Any bit of her attention. We had to share a room, because the people who own the chateau had fucked up. I was cross, or at least I pretended to be, because I didn't want her to think I wanted to share with her, you know. It was only really going to lead to one thing."

"Or did you pretend to be cross so you got the first jab in? So she couldn't be the one to protest and push you away?"

That was the knowledge I didn't know how to handle.

"Not every person will treat me like an afterthought." I took a mouthful of water. I was fucking sure Jane put truth serum in it. "They're not my mother."

Jane nodded briefly. "They're not."

"Jerrica didn't treat me like an afterthought. She hasn't done since I've known her. But she's like that with everyone. She's kind to everyone." Even Jude. She was even nice to Jude.

"What's your question, Jesse?"

"She's probably no kinder to me than anyone else."

"Do you really think that? Or is that little boy Jesse who's talking, you know, that child who was never special?"

"She agreed to be my driver."

"You paid her well. Which tells you what?"

I groaned. "I didn't want her to turn it down."

"So you wanted to spend time with her. But on your terms, maybe? She wanted to spend time with you before that, didn't she? Or am I getting confused?"

She knew damn well she wasn't getting confused. "She wanted us to be something I didn't think we could."

"And you lost your licence driving away. Go back to that night. What did you feel? Were you in control?"

"No. That was why I left."

"What changed while you were in France? Tell me about what was different."

I finished the water in my glass and topped it up. "We were in France. We agreed that it was just for while we were there."

"You set a clear boundary."

"Yes." Another sip of water. "I didn't want to hurt her by suddenly ending it when we got back home."

"Do you think you've hurt her?"

I shook my head. "No. I've seen her a few times, at her brother's, but I haven't asked her to drive me anywhere yet. She's the same with me as she was before we left for France."

"Does that bother you? Did you want her to ask to carry it on, despite you setting a boundary?"

The glass felt warm in my hand now, I'd been holding it for so long. "No. No – I don't think so."

"We all have an ego, Jesse. You once told me you knew that the women you made your arrangements with would take more from you in a heartbeat if you offered it."

Which was true. The women I'd fucked had all hinted at wanting to offer me something more, but it hadn't ever flattered my ego. I didn't want them to ask for more, because I didn't want anything else from them, except that release expelled within tight boundaries.

That wasn't the point Jane was making.

"Did you want more from Jerrica?"

More water. I'd nearly finished what was in the jug.

"I – don't know." I did know. I'd found four excuses to be at Nate's house this week and then five excuses not to go. I'd composed a dozen messages to send to her and deleted every one. When I'd seen her, she'd smiled at me just like she did every time and when she walked away, I'd stared at her ass and I remembered every inch of her skin that I'd memorised, every curve a verse in a poem I could recite by heart.

Jane smiled. "You've drank a lot today."

We both knew why. It was my go to when I was edgy.

"I wanted her to want more. I thought she wanted more."

"Do you think she took you at your word then? Respected your boundaries that what you had was just for while you were away from home?" Jane picked up a fidget toy and twirled it slowly.

"Yes. Or maybe she'd had enough and she wasn't that into the sex, I mean, I think it was more than sex but we didn't label it or anything."

"You could ask her. She knows about your childhood and you seem to think she accepts how you are because of it. Would it be something to consider? Asking her how she feels?"

"But that would make me vulnerable."

"Is that such a bad thing to be?"

I put down my glass. "Apologies. I need to use the bathroom."

I left Jane's room, heading to the small bathroom next door, taking a piss I only needed because I'd drank more in our session so far than I usually did in a whole game on the pitch. And I'd done it for a reason. No one argued when you needed to piss; it was the greatest get out clause.

Jane would completely call me out for it in our next session.

I washed my hands and headed back in, aware that we only had five minutes left now. Settling back down, the jug now full again with Jane's truth serum, I avoided looking at my therapist.

"You are the person in control of what you do. You can't control how someone else feels or their actions. Even with a safe word." Her words were firm. "But you can be curious. Be curious, Jesse. Even about yourself."

"We're done for today." I stood up.

She gave me her slight nod. "We're done. I'll see you Thursday. How are you getting home?"

"Nicky's given me a lift."

She raised her brows. "Thursday. Make it work for you."

Nicky was grinning like a he'd discovered something very pleasurable for the very first time, which I figured he had. Boy had found himself a girlfriend while I was away, and she'd clearly made a man of him.

"What do you get a woman to, you know, make them feel special?" He started to reverse his car out of the worst parking space he could've picked before I'd even put my seatbelt on.

"I'm probably not the right person to ask."

A wall was narrowly avoided. "Fuck, true. You don't do relationships. I forgot."

"I'm not sure that you do driving. Have you passed your test?"

He laughed, which was Nicky's usual response to everything. He was the best natured person I'd probably ever met, and whatever baggage he should've been carrying because his childhood hadn't been filled with cake and roses either, he'd left it somewhere it couldn't do any harm.

"First time." He managed not to scratch his car or dent anyone else's, which was more of a miracle than Nate scoring a goal. "Seriously, what should I get Kitty?"

"Why are you getting her something?"

He shrugged, heading towards the training ground. We'd decided to pack in a weights session. Rowan and Ryan were meeting us there, Nate was joining us later after a check-up for Amber with her doctor-person and Matty Culver was meant to be there too, although he hadn't dropped in the group chat since last night, so there was always the chance he was waking up in some random house with an aspiring WAG.

"What's the reason to get her something?" I knew nothing about this from experience, but I had witnessed my teammates making all sorts of cock-ups with various women through the years.

Jesse swallowed. "No one ever gets her anything, she does it all for herself and I just wanted to surprise her."

That was nice of him. He was also like an over-enthusiastic puppy, which was great if Kitty liked puppies – a degree of irony was in that – and as long as that puppy didn't start to drool.

"Flowers. Have you bought her flowers yet? And by flowers, not the whole shop, just a bunch."

Jesse made a turn without indicating, incurring the wrath of whoever was behind us.

"Did you pay someone to do your test for you?"

"Fuck off, Jesse, unless you want to walk."

It might be safer.

"Do you not think flowers are a bit obvious?"

"Does she like flowers?"

Nicky shrugged, breaking far too late for lights. "I think so."

"Start with flowers. Leave the big gestures for when you've been seeing each other a bit longer. If you go all out now, she'll think you're desperate."

He laughed, shaking his head. "I kind of am, and I think she's amazing and I want to show her that."

I sat back a little deeper into the passenger seat, my jaw clenched hard enough for me to worry about crunching a tooth or two. Jerrica was amazing and I hadn't even bought her flowers. So I'd done what I'd told Nicky not to and bought her a car – under the guise of wanting to be chauffeured round in something I liked, and I was debating buying her a house with some stupid excuse to make it sound like I was getting the better deal.

Which I was.

I'd been giving her gifts, only I was pretending I wasn't. That made me more of a fool than Nicky.

"Flowers. Nice ones. Like the ones Genevieve has in her office from her secret admirer. I still think that's Guy."

"Our manager?" I frowned. Genny and Guy hated each other. She had a dartboard in her office and there was always a picture of him on it. It usually had a dart stuck out of the middle of his forehead.

Genny was also the only person who dared argue with our manager. His temper was legendary and he was known for the many ways he could hide a body. It was in your best interests to stay on his good side.

"Yeah, I'm pretty sure they're having a thing."

"Why?"

Nicky changed lanes and caused the car he'd just moved in front of suddenly to have to break.

"You're going to get us killed with the way you drive."

Nicky grinned. "Again, you can walk. So Genny and Guy – she's seeing someone, we know that."

"Do we?"

"We do. Amber is convinced and Genny's pretty much admitted that she has a friends-with-benefits arrangement with someone."

I looked at Nicky through narrowed eyes. "Do you know what one of those arrangements is?"

"I know I'm not Mr Experienced like you, but I'm not totally naïve."

"Just checking. You sounded like you were a man of the world, now you have a fully working – girlfriend." I couldn't stop my grin. I was one of the two people who knew that Nicky had been a virgin until Kitty had her wicked way with him. He'd let it slip to me and Nate one night when he'd had five too many shots.

We hadn't reminded him of what he'd said, and I didn't think he knew that we knew. Neither Nate nor I were the type of people to say anything or gossip – fuck knew we carried a lot more than Nicky's sex status – so as far as he was aware, we didn't know that Kitty was his first everything.

Boy had a lot more guts than me.

"You reckon flowers?"

"I do. Flowers and a book, if she reads. She knows you're loaded so expensive presents are easy, but ones that you have to think about will make it seem like you've put thought into it."

I wondered what gift I'd get Jerrica. Probably a book.

"Aren't we going past that bookshop? The one Ryan went to the other week?" An independent bookshop had opened up on the road between the training complex and the city centre. It had a trendy coffee shop and I'd already seen a load of hipsters hanging around there.

"You think I should get her a book?" Nicky went

through a light that had just turned red. I wasn't sure he'd noticed.

"Would you know what to get her?"

He nodded. "She likes biographies and historical stuff – like books about cities through the ages."

"Park up near it and we'll go in."

"Have we got time?"

I shrugged. "Rowan'll be late and Ryan won't notice – he has no concept of time." Unless he was on the pitch. He was my partner, feeding me passes to try and score from and vice versa. Then his timing was perfect. In real life, he was clueless, unless he was meeting his girlfriend, Otter Penhaligon, who was one of the maddest people I'd come across.

"True. I'll find somewhere to park."

We were only about five minutes from the bookstore, but it took Nicky another ten to find a space which he could actually park in without causing a grand's worth of damage.

I managed not to say anything, because Nicky genuinely didn't know how bad a driver he was, and he wasn't the one who'd lost his licence – stones and houses and all that.

The bookshop was busy, a mixture of people who looked like they were skiving from the office and students who hadn't bathed in a few days browsing the shelves. Nicky headed over to the biography section, going straight to the new releases.

I managed to find my way to the romance section.

I knew I wouldn't find either of Jerrica's books there. She self-published which meant she didn't have any mass market paperbacks in stores, as she'd explained to me, but I did remember some of the authors she liked whose books she liked to read.

I found one that was also a new release, picked it up and ignored the strange look that a woman in skinny jeans was giving me, then headed over to the sports section, specifically the biographies.

The book I was looking for was there, despite it being a few years since its release. Paul Lake had been my idol even though I'd never seen him play for real. I'd watched clips, seen that he was class, and then he'd picked up an injury that he'd never recovered from. When his autobiography came out I'd read it three times.

I didn't quite understand why I was buying it for Jerrica, apart from that my gut told me she'd enjoy it, so it went into the pile with the romance.

Nicky was waiting for me at the entrance, bag in hand.

"Successful?" I pointed at the bag.

"Yep. Good idea that, for a bloke who's never had a proper girlfriend."

I shrugged. No point arguing, although I wished I could.

"What did you get?" He eyed my bag.

"Books." It was a dickish answer.

"Who for? Because they're not for you. Jerrica?" He raised his eyebrows so high they almost disappeared into his hairline.

"What makes you think they're for her?"

"Because you've got it bad for her." He opened his car door and slid in. "You look at her like she's everything you've ever wanted, and you're not allowed even to get close enough to sniff her."

"Is it that obvious?" I muttered the words, not caring if Nicky heard or not.

"To me it is. Rowan won't have noticed, or Matty – they're too mixed up in their own dramas - but even though you're like Captain Chilled and this sound, relaxed bloke who has life all sorted with his football career, when she's around or Nate mentions her, you get this look on your face like someone told you that you weren't allowed any more chocolate." He laughed, as if he'd just realised something important that was about to change the world. "It's the same look Jude gets when he sees whatever Neva's put on his diet plan."

"Fuck that." I was nothing like Jude.

Nicky laughed again, managing to drive like a sane person for five minutes. "No one's said anything so they've not noticed, or if they have, they're too scared of you to say anything."

That did make me smile. "I do not look like Jude."

"You have the same expression, like a little kid who can't have the only thing he wants."

The words stung like the whip of stones. That little kid who didn't have anything was still there, just in a six-foot two package with tattoos and a big, expensive house.

"I don't want to mess her about."

Nicky frowned. "Not going to lie – I've got zero experience with relationships so I have no knowledge to use here, but why would you mess her about if you like her?"

"I'm not good at relationships."

He missed the turning he should've taken to get to the training complex and seemed completely unaware of it, but no one had beeped us or flashed their lights since we'd gotten back in the car, so I didn't bring that up.

"Have you ever been in a relationship? I've never

known you to, I mean, I know you've had women you've hooked up with but I've never known you to be like, into someone."

Nicky started to waffle, which was a tell he was nervous. He needn't be. He was a good kid and Kitty was lucky to have him.

Would people think that about Jerrica if she was with me? Or would they wonder why someone like her was with a man who had no idea of what it was like to be wanted?

When I first started having therapy sessions with Jane, she gave me reading material about attachment disorder, and about how children formed healthy attachments when care was given to them appropriately when they were younger, as babies.

I knew as a baby and a toddler, I'd been left for hours at a time. As a four-year-old, I'd spent two nights in the house by myself, my mother leaving me with a few sandwiches and cereal and a bottle of milk.

When she came back, she asked me if I'd missed her and I remembered saying no, because it hadn't been much different to when she was there. That was one of my earliest memories.

I didn't trust people to not leave me. I didn't understand why anyone would love me, given that my mother hadn't. At least, I didn't at the start of my therapy and at various points in the last ten years when things hadn't gone as I'd wanted.

I knew it was my mother who'd had difficulties, not me. I knew that my old coach, my friends, even my agent, all liked me. I'd been chosen as captain because I could keep the lads I played with onside and they responded well to me. I'd captained my country on a couple of occasions, and that could become a regular thing since the previous captain had now retired from international football.

I'd proven myself over and over again, but the fear of being found out was still there.

"I've never been in a relationship." I heard the words clearer than the referee's whistle at kick off.

"Why, man? You're not that ugly."

"Thanks, Nicky. Appreciate that compliment." He was grinning and had managed to find his way to the training complex without another wrong turn. "I've never been the relationship type."

"But you'd like to with Jerrica." He turned into the car park, the attendant waving him through.

"Yeah. I guess I would." Even saying the words felt scary.

"So give her the books you bought her, then let me know what she says so I know whether to give mine to Kitty or not."

I shook my head and laughed. The boy was a fucking hoot.

CHAPTER 14
Jerrica

JESSE TURNED up with my brother, looking freshly showered and a little shy. He also kept on looking at me when he thought I wasn't paying attention to him, and when I caught him, he'd look away. It was entertaining and doing wonders for my ego.

We'd spent the rest of our time in France touring the countryside and even managing a day at the beach. Our evenings – and some of our days – were spent making each other come in various ways, Jesse losing his words when I removed some of the direction he was used to giving.

He softened under my touch. Not his cock – that should've been considered a site of scientific interest and remained hard for what felt like most of the time – the rest of him. The second night I fell asleep in his arms, I woke up to find him still awake, his body utterly still. When I'd asked him if he was okay he'd barely breathed a word until I'd shifted in his arms.

"I didn't know if you'd wake if I moved. I didn't want to move in my sleep and wake you up."

I'd laughed and kissed him, telling him it didn't quite work like that, then I'd fallen back asleep with my heart feeling ten times the size it had before.

When I'd dropped him off at home after we landed, he'd become awkward, distant, as if he had no idea what to say or how to act, which I figured he didn't.

We'd agreed that it would end in France, whatever we'd been doing, it stopped when we got on that plane, and it had. I wasn't heartbroken, I'd known that we had an expiry date and I'd been prepared for that. I'd made a decision to take what he offered because if I hadn't, I'd have always wondered.

Better to have loved and to have lost than to have never loved at all.

Was I in love with him?

Yes. But I think I had been before we went to France. It hadn't taken a chateau to make me fall.

But he hadn't broken my heart, I just wished we'd had longer.

Now Jesse was in my brother's kitchen, unusually quiet and toying with a paperback, contents unknown.

Nate was going on about something – I'd tuned out minutes ago – and Amber was listening happily. She was still in the phase where she thought my brother could walk on water. I knew he was perfectly capable of falling in head first with a splash.

They were also now engaged, something that seemed to have increased the light in both of them. The girls were enthralled by it, both of them increasingly glued to Amber's side, which she seemed to love.

My spare part status was growing daily.

"Have you seen the girls' treehouse?"

I woke up to what my brother was asking Jesse.

"Not since you've put the furniture in it." Jesse's eyes flicked to me again.

"Jerrica, can you show it Jesse? I need to go through something with Nate so I can send it off." Amber smiled at me, her hand on her very large bump.

I'd given her the bare outlines of what had happened with me and Jesse. She'd asked, because Nate had mentioned my phone call with him, and gossip was her main form of sustenance at the moment. There was a lot I hadn't told her.

"Sure. Want to pretend you're Libbie's age?" I avoided the word again, because I knew six-year-old Jesse had not had a happy life.

He stood up, holding the bag. "Let's have a look."

I was positive he gave Amber a grateful look, but maybe I was reading too much into it.

It was the first time I'd properly seen him since we'd returned from France. I had hoped that when we did get home, we'd have clicked back into how we were before, however tortuous that would've been.

I wasn't surprised when it didn't happen.

I didn't feel used or led on; maybe I'd have been more concerned if he'd carried on with his tiny touches and kisses when no one was looking.

But I did want to know what was in the bag.

The summer house was on the side of the garden away from the patio, set back deep into where bushes and shrubbery and trees had been allowed to grow a little wild. A camera had been installed so Nate could keep an eye on what the girls were doing from the house, if in the future he ever let them down here alone, which maybe he would do when they were older.

It was more like another building instead of just an overlarge garden shed, even to the point of having heating installed and a lockable door.

"This is some project."

"It is. Its thunder was totally stolen though by Nate proposing the day it was built."

Jesse laughed. "His proposal went well then?"

"Not like Rowan's. Nate nailed it the first time." Dee Jones had turned Rowan down twice, which entertained everyone apart from Rowan. We all knew she'd say yes eventually, she just loved to keep Rowan on his toes.

Jesse sat down on one of the steps, the bag still in his clutches. "I got these for you." He gave me the bag.

I sat down next to him. "A gift!" I smiled at him. "I love presents." Especially unexpected ones.

I put my hand in the bag, already figuring it was book shaped. Two books. A romance by an author I loved and a football autobiography I knew of as it kind of set the bar.

"Thank you."

He nodded, looking uncertain. "I knew that you liked that author and that's one of my favourite books. The footballer, Paul Lake, didn't have his career work out for him the way he wanted, but he still managed to succeed."

I heard what he was saying. Perfect people with perfect lives didn't exist. He didn't claim to be perfect. The arrogance that some footballers carried wasn't part of his luggage.

"They're both great." I sat down next to him on the steps. "Why have you bought me them?" Everything we'd done with each other in the last few weeks, had been done with honesty. That wasn't stopping now.

Jesse laughed, like he was trying to fill the air for a second. "Nicky wanted to get Kitty a present and I suggested books. I wanted to get you something too."

"Oh. But Kitty is Nicky's girlfriend. We're friends." If I'd wanted to be cutting I could've said that I worked for him, but that wouldn't have been fair or accurate for either if us.

"Friends. Yeah." He fiddled with his hair. "About that."

I'd always been good at reading people. My gut was reliable, and I didn't see things in others just because I wanted to see what my heart was looking for.

"Do you want to be more than friends? I would like that." My heart hammered in my chest and my stomach flipped several times making me wish I hadn't finished Libbie's ice cream as well as my own. My confidence could be completely crushed here, but if it was, I'd survive.

I didn't think that was going to happen though.

"Can I take you on a date?" Jesse squeezed his hands together. "I know I said – I said a lot of things and I still don't know how to do this shit, or why the fuck you'd be interested in me, but I'd really like to go out with you."

My heart had joined my stomach in doing somersaults now. "I'd really like to go out with you. When?"

"Friday night?" He still looked nervous.

"Friday's great. What do you want to do? Restaurant? Something like bowling? What do you fancy?" My knee brushed against his leg. Considering we'd spent the best part of five days getting to know each other very intimately, this conversation made me feel like we were both fifteen-year-olds and tentatively stepping into the *I like you; do you like me?* phase of being completely clueless.

Jesse smiled. "I haven't been bowling for ages."

"I'll book a lane – the Fort Centre?"

His smile grew wider. "I'm pretty sure I'm meant to book it, seeing as I asked you out. Might need you to drive though. Or I can see if the club can book a driver."

"I'll drive. Shall we eat out?"

"Burger afterwards?"

I nodded, unsure how I was going dispose of this excitement without squeeing like the fifteen-year-old I'd reverted to.

His grin was boyish, contrasting with the tattoos that were exposed by the short sleeved T-shirt he was wearing. "Just don't tell Neva."

"Promise I won't. Do you want to see in inside the treehouse?"

He nodded, following me up the steps, the books in my hands. I typed in a code to open the door, because of course, Nate had everything secured.

"Some people would want to live in this." Jesse looked around him, slightly shocked. "Did he have Amber's sister-in-law in to do the interior design or something?"

"He and the girls chose it. We had a treehouse when we were kids – this wooden thing my dad made. Nate and I loved it, even when we were teenagers. I'd hide in there if I'd had a row with my parents, and I'm pretty sure it was where Nate lost his virginity." I grinned at the memories. "I saw him, from my bedroom window, leaving the treehouse with his then girlfriend, both of them looking dishevelled and then having a really long kiss in the garden. I did think at the time about banging on my window and making some sort of obscene gesture – I'd been about thirteen at the time – but I decided to save it to embarrass him with later."

Jesse sat down on the sofa, a pink thing that you really

could have a nap on, looking completely out of place. "I've never been in a treehouse before."

I sat down next to him and tried not to feel like shit. His childhood had been nothing like mine and I wanted to cry for the boy who never had what he should've been entitled to.

"Most aren't like this. Maybe you should build a tree cave in your garden."

He nodded, looking at the floor between his feet. "With a pink sofa."

I swallowed, really thinking before I allowed the words to come out of my mouth. "If you had a daughter. Or maybe she'd prefer a blue one. Athletic colours."

His shoulders stiffened. He stayed looking at the floor.

I didn't apologise for my words. I knew enough about trauma to understand a little about how Jesse might find the idea of being close to someone in more than a physical sense difficult. Since getting home from France, I *might* have done a little reading into that sort of trauma. I knew he went to a therapist. I knew he'd had an abusive childhood. I knew there was no cure, no easy fix for what he'd been through, no fix at all in all likelihood.

He raised his head, staring at the huge dolls' house opposite that was actually full of model cars, because that was how my nieces rolled at the moment.

"I've never thought about having kids, but maybe a treehouse would be good. I can hide in there when the team crashes mine." His smile was half-forced. "Maybe you can help me decide on what furniture it'd need." His hand slid on top of mine.

I gripped it back, a shiver running from my hand, up to my shoulder and cascading down my body.

Jesse's eyes darkened. He'd felt it too.

"I can." I moved a couple of inches closer to him, his cologne wreaking havoc with my heart rate. "We could make sure it was comfy."

The hesitation that had glimmered in him disappeared, leaving that sultry darkness I'd seen before in France.

"I want to kiss you, but it feels wrong to do it in here." He used his hand that wasn't holding mine to tip my chin, lifting my gaze to his. "Not where your nieces play."

"After our date, then."

His nod was subtle. "Date." He looked like he was almost in shock at saying the word.

"Don't overthink it. I want to ask what's made you change your mind, but I'm afraid you'll change it back." The words were laced with worry; I knew it was a stupid thing to say, by saying it I was asking the very thing I'd said I wouldn't.

"I won't change it back." His hand left mine and wrapped around my shoulders instead, pulling me closer into him.

The tension he was carrying bled into me. "It's okay if you do. I don't break." And I wouldn't.

"I don't want to break you. The idea of you hurting because I did something makes me want to - " he shook his head. "I know I'm going to fuck this up, Jerrica, because I don't know how else it works."

I tipped my head and pressed a kiss to his jaw. It was soft, barely any pressure. "Newsflash, no one really knows how it works."

"Will you hurt me?" He moved us so my back was against his chest, his chin resting on my head.

It felt so good to be held by him after a week of nothing. I hadn't let myself mope – in fact, I'd been semi-lost in the new book I was writing – but his arms wrapped around me made it feel like I could breathe deeper than I had in days.

"I can't promise that I won't hurt you, just like I know you can't promise that either. But I can promise I'll always be honest with you, and you'll hear things from me first." It was a lesson my mother had taught Nate and me when we were younger and she and our father had a blazing row that was loud enough for a neighbour to knock on and ask if we were okay.

My dad had done something really stupid, like not fixed a cupboard door after she'd asked about a dozen times, and it had eventually fallen off onto my head. My mother had hit the roof and all sorts of shit was flung between them – clearly it had been a row that had been brewing for a while.

Our parents didn't argue a lot. They would sometimes bicker and they often teased each other, but I only remembered a handful of proper arguments. After that one, my dad headed out of the house – probably to the pub – and my mother poured herself a glass of red wine and pressed an ice pack to my head, then passed on her advice.

I told Jesse about the row, knowing he would've heard and seen far worse, but then it might be easy to have the idea that normal relationships were perfect.

"You can have an argument and shout and say things that maybe you usually wouldn't, and still be okay afterwards. My dad fixed all the cupboards the next day, and my mum ended up curled next to him on the sofa, making him watch some daft Saturday night programme we knew he didn't really like." I laughed at the memory of it. "She also said most relationships don't work out and that's normal. Not everyone stays with the first person they kiss for the rest of their life."

Jesse's finger drew patterns on my forearm, the rhythmic movement almost hypnotic. "I know. I've seen healthy relationships. I know they exist."

"You have healthy relationships. With your lovers and with your friends. Your teammates." I wanted to ask if he was still seeing the women he hooked up with, if he'd been with any of them since we'd returned from France.

"But never a close relationship. Not like Nate and Amber, or Rowan and Dee. Or, fuck, even Nicky and Kitty. He's completely lovestruck."

"It's meant to be fun, you know. Dating. The excitement and the anticipation of seeing that person. Being consumed by them and agonising for them to touch you."

His finger carried on sketching on my skin.

"Let's both just enjoy a date and don't overthink it." I tipped my head back and tried to look at him, his face at the side of mine.

Footsteps thudded outside.

"It's Nate." I didn't move away. I didn't shift from Jesse's arms.

I felt him stiffen behind me, so I leaned back all the more.

"I'm nearly thirty, Jesse. He isn't my keeper and he's your friend. Hiding it would make it worse."

He didn't say anything. I prayed that Nate would have his sensible head on, like he did most of the time.

"We were going to get take – oh, hello." Nate froze in the doorway. "Thank fuck you've got clothes on. I see enough of Jesse's arse in the showers."

I started to laugh, soundless shakes of my shoulders, Jesse's arms not holding me quite as tight as they had been. "Do you make a point of looking at Jesse's arse?"

Nate raised his brows. "He has a nice arse. We once

had a vote as to whose was the best – Jesse's, Jude's or Matty's. Jesse won, actually."

"Please tell me you've never told anyone that story."

Finally, he spoke.

"Only Amber. And probably Neva. Dee might've been there too, and a couple of the other women from the team." Nate shrugged. "Take out. Do you want to eat with us? It isn't Neva approved. Amber's getting hungry so I need a quick decision."

"I'm still thinking about the arse competition." I gripped Jesse's thigh. "Did you all line up while everyone judged."

"Can we not talk about it. It was after we beat United and there were shots involved." Jesse's hand lay on my stomach.

It was a possessive gesture, although I doubted he realised that. It was also a gesture that was doing things to my insides, which I also doubted he realised.

Nate chuckled. "Final answers. I think we're having Chinese."

"I'm in." I could always eat Chinese.

"I'll join you, if it's okay." Jesse's words were quiet. They weren't about the Chinese.

My brother nodded. "It's okay. Just don't spill anything. Amber gets cranky if someone makes a mess."

"I'll try not to."

The kiss to my hair surprised me.

My brother just blinked. "Good. We both know we weren't actually talking about spilling food then, don't we?"

Jesse laughed. "We did. Make sure you order crispy chilli beef."

"Sorted. See you very soon. That pink sofa doesn't

need to see any X-rated action." He whipped around and left.

Jesse exhaled, finally relaxing. "I thought he'd hit me."

"No. He's too scared of me to do that."

"Scared of you?"

I prised myself away from Jesse, standing up and offering him my hand, not that I could pull him up. "I know all the ways to hurt Nate. I'm well-practiced."

"I thought you were all about healthy relationships." Jesse stood up and eyed me with suspicion.

"I am. My relationship with my brother is completely healthy. As long as he behaves."

We ate, the girls trying the dozen or so different dishes that Nate had ordered from the nearby Chinese restaurant. Jesse sat opposite me, Libbie to his left, keeping him occupied with her questions about the food and then about Jude, who she had the biggest crush a six-year-old could have on someone. Rowan and Dee had turned up, walking over because their house was only ten minutes or so away from Nate's.

It was an unexpected evening, my brother offering Jesse a lift home after the girls had gone to bed.

I went to the door with him, giving Nate a lethal glare and hoping he got the hint that I wanted a few more minutes alone with the man I was going on a date with.

Nate didn't get the hint, but Amber did, her smile letting me know that I was going to be telling her everything afterwards.

"So Friday. I'll pick you up at seven?"

Jesse nodded. "Seven is good. I'll book everything." He

leaned against the door frame. "Can I text you before or do I wait until then?"

"Text me all you want. There are no rules." I stepped closer to him. "So I can do this too."

I put my arms around his neck, pulling myself up to him, my lips colliding with his, starting a kiss that tasted so different than before.

Jesse's hands went to my ass, cupping me to him, his hold the possessive one I remembered. Whatever hesitation I'd seen in the treehouse had gone.

The kiss was everything that was delicious. He took charge of it, deepening it, setting the steady rhythm, keeping me where he wanted me to be, where I wanted to be.

It ended when we heard a cough from Nate.

Jesse pulled me in closer, looking at Nate over my head. I had no idea what my brother's expression would be, and part of me didn't want to know. Nate wouldn't tell me what to do, but he would at some point give me his considered opinion.

"Thanks for giving me a lift."

Jesse's hand was on the small of my back now.

"Not a problem. Are you ready to go?"

"Sure. See you Friday, Jerrica." He bent his head for another quick kiss, this one PG rated.

I watched them leave, the lack of laughter making me wonder exactly what Nate would say while he was driving Jesse home. I knew he wouldn't interfere, but I also knew that Jesse was bothered about what Nate thought and I hoped that whatever was said put both of them at ease.

I turned around to see Amber watching me with interest.

"That wasn't planned."

She nodded. "I figured that. When Nate came back from the treehouse he looked like he'd just seen a ghost."

"What did he say?"

Her smile was devilish. "I'll only tell you if you tell me exactly what happened with Jesse."

I folded my arms, closing the front door and following Amber back into the kitchen. She might not be able to drink the wine, but I could. I poured myself a generous glass and made the most of looking at her while I sipped it.

"Stop teasing and tell me about Jesse. I thought it was just a holiday hook-up." She eased herself down into the chair she'd taken to sitting in, mainly because it was easier for her to press herself out of.

"It was. But it seems he's changed his mind. He bought those books for me as a gift and asked me out on a date on Friday."

"How do you feel about him changing his mind? I get that you like him, but do you not think he might mess you about?"

I knew where Amber was coming from. Her ex, from a few years ago, had been an arsehole to her, and before Nate she'd been adamant she'd never be involved with another football player.

"He might. He's not done relationships before. In fact, I don't think he's ever been on a proper date."

She was quiet for a moment, rubbing her belly which seemed to be her new thing to do when she was deep in thought. "There's no point in telling you to be careful because he might break your heart, is there?"

"No. Because you could say that about anyone. I haven't liked anyone this much for, well, ever, really. I know this might not have a happy ending, but I don't have anything left to lose. You can recover from heartbreak, and it might not happen, anyway." I couldn't go into this thinking it was doomed, and something told me it wasn't. It might not be a smooth path, but that didn't mean it wouldn't be worth it.

"I think he really likes you. I'd go as far to say it's more than that."

My stomach trampolined with excitement. "What makes you think that?"

"The way he looks at you. How much he hung around here. Don't forget, I've known Jesse since he joined the club. I knew he was into some – I don't know how to describe it, kinky? – stuff, and I never knew of him being involved with anyone. He had a lot of interest, but never took anyone up on it." Amber stretched out her legs. "I remember a model hanging around for him, you'd know of her."

She gave me her name and I gave myself thirty seconds to wonder what Jesse saw in me that he hadn't seen in her.

"Maybe I'm the right person at the right time." I could leave it at that. My stomach wasn't as flat as it could be, and my ass definitely had a shade of wobble to it, but I liked who I was, and I also liked cake. "What did Nate say?"

Amber shrugged. "I don't think he's surprised. You had that phone call with him while you were away, and he was quiet about it when I asked him. He likes Jesse – everyone does. I know Jesse has his tastes in bed, but that's nothing to do with Nate. He also knows that Jesse's never had a girlfriend before – I think he's just worried you'll end up hurting each other and he'll be in the middle."

I took another mouthful of wine. This was a bottle I'd brought back from the chateau and I was seriously considering getting some more shipped over. "That could happen. But could doesn't mean it's a reason not to try."

"You're right. And I'm guessing you think it's got a chance of working out?"

I nodded, certain about this. "No one's ever made me feel like he does. I like him, Amber. I really like him a lot."

She pushed herself out of the chair with a groan. "I need to pee. Baby's on my bladder again. I think he thinks it's a football. When I get back I want to hear all about the size of Jesse's dick."

I laughed, drinking more wine. I was surprised it had taken her so long to ask.

CHAPTER 15
Jesse

SPORTING ability clearly ran in families.

I'd asked Nate if his sister was any decent at bowling, and he'd confessed that he didn't have a clue, it had been that long since he'd been bowling with her.

I now wondered if he'd said that to lull me into a false sense of security, because Jerrica kicked my arse, and I'd thought I was fairly decent at rolling a bowl towards twelve pins.

She'd picked me up looking like something that I thought my future might be, smiling and giddy because like she said, this was just about having fun.

Which we did. Three games, and she won two, me just about scraping a win in the second game. I claimed I was distracted by her ass in those tight jeans, but she counter claimed that she was finding it hard to not stare at my biceps.

We sat next to each other afterwards, Jerrica devouring a burger, while I was almost good, sticking with a steak and salad. She drove us back to mine afterwards, the conversation bouncing between what else she was good at and me trying to impress her in ways reminiscent of a fourteen-year-old boy.

"What happens now?" I asked as she pulled up on my driveway, the electric gates closing behind her. "What does date etiquette require?"

"You can ask me in for a coffee, or a glass of wine." She turned off the engine.

"If you have wine, you won't drive." She was strict on that. No driving if any alcohol had been drunk. "Do you want to stay? Can that happen on a first date?" I knew damn well it could, but I wanted to know where her head was at.

"I'd like to stay. This wasn't really our first date. I think we had a few dates in France, we just didn't call them that."

She was right. Meals together, touring the vineyards, lying by the pool with my fingers brushing against hers because I couldn't not touch her. "You're staying then?"

"You have to ask me first. Or invite me in and then suggest I stay. Say something that makes you sound like you couldn't possibly go on living if I didn't stay the night, so you could have your wicked way with me and then hold me while I fall asleep in your arms." She was laughing, her face creased with amusement.

"Is that what the heroes in your books say?" I knew damn well they didn't. I'd read both of them by now, which gave me a little more insight into what possibly made her tick.

"I don't want a hero in one of my books." She opened her door.

"What do you want then?" My heart pounded faster than it had done when I took a penalty in the last England game.

"To see if the man with the dark eyes and the tattoos I want to trace with my tongue was just a flash in the holiday pan or if there's something more to this."

I didn't think I could ever tear my eyes away from hers. "Do you want to come in for a glass of wine?"

Jerrica nodded. "I'd love to."

She followed me inside and through to the kitchen, discarding her shoes somewhere in the hall.

This was the first time we'd been alone since we'd come back from France, other than those stolen moments in the treehouse. Part of me wanted to order her upstairs to my bedroom, demand she bared herself for me and tell her exactly how I wanted her, how I'd bring her more pleasure than she could stand and then prove it to her over and over again.

But that was easy.

I knew we melded together perfectly already. Being back in England wasn't going to change that. The sex between us had been nothing less than mind-blowing, but I wanted to see if there was another way of getting us there, one I hadn't tried before.

"White or red?"

She sat down on the sofa in the open plan kitchen, the large living area too big for just one person.

"Red, please."

Her eyes followed me as I moved around the kitchen to find glasses and open a bottle that Carina had sent over for me.

I poured two glasses and took them over to the sofa, passing one to Jerrica and putting mine down on the coffee table.

"You never said you were fucking good at bowling. Does your brother know?

She laughed, the sound making my house feel like it finally had a soul. "I used to kick his arse on the regular when we went bowling as kids, so he knew. Did he tell you otherwise?"

"He said he didn't know."

Her smile was victorious. "He did."

"Maybe he was just trying to show me who was really in charge." My hand found hers, our fingers becoming tangled together.

I'd told Jane about my date with Jerrica when I'd seen her yesterday. I'd told her how I didn't think she would check out on me, that she was someone who saw me for what I was and she liked me, maybe because of it, because of how I'd got to this point.

That was how she made me feel.

Jane had smiled at me, then asked me her usual question. "How do you feel about this?"

Rather than drinking all the water that Jane had left on the table, I'd managed to find the words. I felt okay; that this wasn't something to run away from. I knew I could get hurt, but the fear of that wasn't as great as wanting to be with her. I told Jane all the things about Jerrica that I liked, and I found I couldn't shut up, sounding just like Nicky talking about Kitty.

I left her room feeling like I was about to jump off a building, only I had grown wings and I knew how to fly.

Jerrica leaned into me, my arm wrapping around her shoulders. I pressed my lips against the patch of skin between her shoulder and neck, feeling her shiver at the touch. "It feels like forever since I've been inside you."

"Maybe we need to remind ourselves what it feels like." She put her glass down and wriggled round so she was straddling me. "Just don't mention my brother. It kind of kills the mood."

"I think I can promise that."

She was liquid fire in my hands, her blonde hair curling over her shoulder, mouth curved in a smile and her hands were on my chest, running over the T-shirt I'd chosen because I knew it clung to my biceps and Jerrica liked my biceps.

"Tell me a story." She pulled the T-shirt up, her hands sneaking underneath so they were against my skin. "What happens when a woman sits like this on your knee?"

What was happening now was that my cock was reading this book and getting hard, all the ways I'd fucked her before rampaging through my mind like a movie on fast forward.

My front door was locked. There was no one else in the house. I wasn't expecting any visitors and my security system had been set as soon as I came in.

My first instruction for her was on the tip of my tongue, but I wanted to kiss her first, putting a hand to the back of her head, my fingers weaving through her hair, directing her mouth to mine and then claiming it as my territory.

She let me set the pace, her hands softly pressing on my skin, as if she was reading what I felt on my body. Tender lips, the taste of wine, the heat from her – I was becoming intoxicated and I was letting myself drown in it.

If this was love, then I wasn't going to fight it anymore.

I moved my hands to her waist, untucking the top from her jeans, and then pulling it up over her head. We broke the kiss, the material exposing her, just a bra barely covering her tits, her nipples visible through the lace.

I looked my fill. I brushed my fingers over her nipples, feeling them harden further.

"Take this off for me." I sat back, watching her.

Her hands went behind her back, undoing the clasp, the material slackening. She removed it slowly, letting it drop on the floor and then arching her back, her tits on display.

"You have perfect tits." I cupped them, feeling their weight, pinching her nipples. "Tomorrow morning, I want you to wear one of my T-shirts and nothing else, so I can fuck you easily when we have coffee."

She nodded, her hands by her sides, letting me touch. I'd never brought a woman back here. I'd always had it so the arrangements were that I'd go to her place, that way I could leave when I wanted. Jerrica could leave when she wanted now, which was fine because I wasn't sure that I could ever ask her to leave.

I wasn't sure I was going to ever want to.

How could it be that this one person had the ability to flip my life entirely upside down?

"Stand up and take the rest of your clothes off." I gave her nipples another pinch before she left my knee.

Her pretty mouth curved into a smile as she slid off me, her hands slipping off her jeans, pushing them down, leaving her in just a lace thong that had matched her bra.

She didn't wait for me to tell her to take it off, pushing it down over her thighs, kicking it off with her foot and then standing up, her legs slightly parted.

"Use your fingers to find out if your wet?"

She didn't say anything, just watching me as she touched her pussy, sliding her fingers through her folds. The wetness from her centre glistened on her fingers as she raised them up.

"I'm wet."

"Bring me you fingers." I patted my knee.

I undid my belt, loosened my jeans and pushed down my underwear while I was watching her, giving my cock a couple of slow fists.

Her eyes fell on it now.

She stepped back to me, her knees going either side of my thighs, one of her hands on my shoulders to steady herself, the other, the one with her fingers covered in her juices presented to my mouth.

I parted my lips, letting her touch her fingers to my lips before I sucked on them, tasting her tart nectar.

One of my hands cupped her pussy, pushing my palm against her clit, applying just enough pressure to make her start to rock her hips, seeking more.

She'd get more.

When I was ready.

I pulled her fingers away with my other hand. "Can you take my cock now? Or do you need more?"

"I can take it now."

"Good girl. Put it inside you."

She angled her hips, her small hand wrapping around the base of my dick, lining it up with her centre.

She gasped as she sank down on me, her hand that was on it, letting go and coming to my shoulder.

"How do you feel?" I pinched her nipple before setting a hand on her hip. "Don't move."

"Full. So fucking full. It's amazing." Her words were fading into moans.

"Keep your hands on my shoulders. "

She nodded, her head tipping back, back arching slightly, giving me a better view of her tits that were so full and tempting. I could spend a whole night just playing with them.

If she'd let me.

I started to move my hips, thrusting up into her, holding onto her hips to move her in time with me. She was tight and wet and a little piece of heaven on earth, her tits bouncing with the movements and my name on her lips.

My chest felt as if it was about to explode, my heart swelling as it managed to keep beating while the rest of my body was destroyed by her.

The angle worked, her clit getting enough attention to bring her to orgasm just before I couldn't hold back anymore. She pulsed around my cock, the sensation enough to yank a cry from my mouth and then I poured into her, my hands leaving her hips and circling round her back, pulling her against my chest.

My orgasm subsided. The aftershocks calming as I held Jerrica to me, our mouths managing to meet in a kiss that was messy and slow and contained all of the words I didn't know how to say yet.

"Will you stay the night?" I breathed the question against her hair when our kiss ended.

"Yes. And I'll wear your T-shirt in the morning."

I woke in the morning to an empty bed, the sheets next to me still warm and smelling of Jerrica. Summer sun tipped in through the blinds that hadn't been closed properly the night before and the sheets were mussed from night time movements that they hadn't seen before.

I usually slept like a corpse. Not moving, barely even turning during the night. I didn't sprawl out because I'd gotten used to sleeping on too many sofas or remaining as quiet and unmoving as possible so no one would notice I was there. When I moved into this house I bought a super king bed for every room, and in the first couple of weeks of living there, I slept in every one.

When I woke each morning, it was like the sheets had been barely touched. There were no creases to the sheets, no pulled out fitted sheets. The duvet hardly needed straightening.

Last night and the early hours of this morning had made sure this morning was the polar opposite. Jerrica moved in the night, which I'd already discovered, and we moved in the night, too.

I'd fucked her again when we'd gone upstairs to bed, loosely tying her wrists to the bed posts, telling her how all she had to do was pull a certain way and she'd be free.

She hadn't even tried, opening up her body for me to plunder, giving her pleasure in the best ways I knew how and finally taking mine after untying her hands so I could feel them on me when I exploded inside her.

We'd woken again just as the dawn was breaking, my body spooning hers, my hand on her breast, like I'd woken when we were in France. I'd been hard, and she'd been wet, whatever touches our sleeping selves had been indulging in leaving a need and a desperation that movements and not words had cured.

She'd moved a hand between us, guiding my hard cock between her legs, angling us so I could get inside her and somehow we moved together, still half asleep, until she found her release and I followed with mine.

At some point this morning I'd need to change the sheets. That was a practicality.

But first, I needed to find where Jerrica was, and see if she was wearing my T-shirt and nothing else.

I got out of bed, tempted to take a photo of how messed up the sheets were, and pulled a pair of sweats that were folded over the chair in the corner of the room. Part of me wondered whether she'd left already and headed back home, leaving me to a morning alone, but the intelligent part, the part where my brain functioned rationally, thought I'd find her in the kitchen, making coffee.

Wearing my T-shirt.

I brushed my teeth and splashed my face with water, aware that my hair was sticking in all directions and I definitely smelled of sex. The latter wasn't something I was worried about right now. If things went according to plan, I'd be topping up that scent.

My cock hardened as my imagination went wild, thinking about Jerrica being in my kitchen, in just a T-shirt like I'd said. My heart was going wild too, its beats per minute definitely something that the club's trainers would be monitoring if they ever became aware of it.

The radio was on in the kitchen, some pop station. I smelled coffee and heard Jerrica singing along with the track that was being played, her voice managing to carry the notes.

I paused at the doorway, watching her dancing round the breakfast bar, my T-shirt hitting her mid-thigh. She froze after about a minute, suddenly aware of my eyes on her, and a smile grew.

"Morning, sleepy head." She held up a large mug, something indecent written on it, a secret Santa gift from Jude a couple of Christmases ago. He hadn't been able to keep his mouth shut about who he'd drawn.

"You found one of my T-shirts?" There was no way she hadn't noticed the bulge in my sweats.

"I did. Coffee? I'm making more."

"Do you remember how I take it?" I strode towards the long kitchen island, the black granite worktop clear and full of possibilities.

Her eyes dipped to my cock. "I remember how you give it."

"I should spank you for being cheeky." I folded my arms, trying not to preen at how she was staring at my erection.

"How about I make you a coffee instead?" Jerrica put a hand on her hip, pushing the T-shirt up to do it, making it clear to me that she wasn't wearing underwear.

"I'll watch from here; make sure you do it properly."

Her cheeks flushed and I knew her well enough by now to know that if I was to get closer and touch her between her legs, I'd find her warm and wet.

She busied herself, bending down to pull out a coffee pot, giving me a full view of her ass and a glimpse of what else she had there.

I took another couple of steps closer. Jerrica reached across the worktop to grab hold of another mug, the T-shirt riding up again.

She turned her head to look at me. "Maybe I should've protected my modesty and wore underwear."

"Or you could just tie the T-shirt at your waist and I can see better." There was a wet spot on my sweats now, a bead of pre-cum had leaked and the sweats were light grey and thin.

"Is that what you want?"

I nodded, watching intently to see if she hesitated. There was no way anyone would be able to watch her, apart from me. As much as I liked to watch, I didn't like to share. That was why I'd never been keen on the clubs I'd been introduced to. If a woman was with me, she was *with me*.

Her hands went to her waist, pulling up the T-shirt and tying it at the side, leaving her backside completely exposed. She kept facing the kitchen unit as she turned around. "Is that better?"

"Perfect. The cafetière is on the bottom shelf."

I couldn't have arranged my kitchen shit better. She bent down again, legs slightly spread, deliberately teasing.

"Coffee in the fridge?"

"I'll get it for you." I moved behind her, my hand brushing her ass as I walked past. I found the coffee, already ground, and moved behind her, placing the bag on the worktop with the cafetière and a spoon. I caged her in, my hips pushed up against her. "Let me show you how I like it."

"Please do. I don't want to get it wrong." She turned her head to look at me, her eyes blazing. Whatever meek words had just slipped from her lips, they were all a ruse. I picked up the spoon with one hand and used the other to cup her breast through her T-shirt.

"One spoonful per person." I managed not to spill the coffee as I dug into the bag, tipping it into the pot. Jerrica pressed her ass against my erection. "Try not to waste any." I put the spoon down, pushing her closer to the worktop, my hips pressed tight against her now.

I slipped a hand down, pushing it between her legs and pressing a finger to her opening. She was soaked, the side of the top of her thighs sticky. I moved the hand that was holding her tit under her T-shirt, the knot loosening, and palmed her breast roughly. "Is this what you wanted me to do when you came down here, leaving me in bed by myself, just wearing my T-shirt?" I kissed her neck, brushing stubble over the delicate skin, then pushed two fingers into her tight channel. I wasn't gentle, knowing by now exactly how she liked this and exactly how primed she would be.

"Yes. I wanted you to do this." Her words were breathy, need having usurped any tease from them.

"And what do you want me to do exactly?"

"Fuck me like you want to."

I chuckled, removing my fingers, giving her clit a quick play with. "How do you think I want to fuck you?"

"Over this worktop. Hard."

"Is that how you want to be fucked or are you just trying to make me happy?" I pinched her nipple, using my other hand now to push down my sweats, my dick hard and angry. I ran it along her seam, resting it at her entrance.

"It's what I want. Please, Jesse - "

I could've snapped and pushed into her, but this was the point I relished most of all, where I was the one in control, where I could look after her, causing only pleasure.

"Stretch your arms out, hold onto to the edge." I dropped both hands to her hips, pushing her up so she stretched over the island, her ass now at the perfect height, her hands unable to move their grip. I bit her shoulder. "I want you to come as soon as you can. Don't hold it off."

"Please get in me." She placed her cheek on the worktop, angling to look at me.

I pushed inside her, seating myself in one go, hearing her cry out, her body tightening around me. She was every last thing right now, the very epicentre of my world and the only thing that I craved. Everything around me was at peace, the only thing that mattered was what we were doing to each other now, the rest of the world was being reassembled around us.

My hands stayed grasped hold of her hips as I moved inside her, every time feeling her tighten around me, her pussy gripping my cock and bringing me closer to the edge too quickly. I wanted longer like this, wanted to stay like this forever because if this wasn't heaven, then I didn't want to go there.

Her body bucked against me as she came, her cry loud and untamed.

"You're so fucking amazing. So fucking tight round my cock." The words spilled out of me as I reached my own release. "Want to do this to you every fucking morning. Have you come like this all over my house." I moved hard and rapid as I came, my own groans echoing around the kitchen, my arms collecting her against my chest as my release came to an end.

All I wanted to do, just like last night, was hold her. No going through the tick list of aftercare before I could leave, I wanted to keep feeling her heat, feeling her skin next to mine. Feeling her heartbeat.

Her laugh grounded me. "This is going to be messy when we move."

"It'll clean." I reached out, briefly taking my hand off her, and grabbed a piece of kitchen roll.

When she was steady on her feet and I'd pulled out, I dropped to my knees, turning her round, and carefully cleaning her up, the evidence of what I'd just done making me want to batter my fists against my chest and shout from the rooftops.

Without question, I knew I was in love with her.

I pressed a kiss to her hip and moved back up her body, my T-shirt looking worse for wear.

"Are you okay? That wasn't gentle." I wrapped my arms around her.

"That was amazing. I don't think it's about how we do it, Jesse. I think it's just you. I fucking love what you do to me."

I wanted to change her words and have her tell me that she loved me. But I could wait. I've never needed those words before, not until now.

Not until I finally felt that they could be said and meant for me.

"I fucking love what you do to me, too." Our mouths met in a kiss that was sweet, compared to the rush and roughness we'd just had.

"Go get in bed. I'll bring you coffee up." I tried to smooth the T-shirt.

"Meet me in the shower as soon as you come up." She kissed me back, her hands gripping my waist.

This felt very much like something I'd never had before; something I'd never known I wanted.

Nate, Rowan and Ryan turned up at my house just after lunch, all of them carrying kit bags and disgruntled expressions.

Pre-season was taking part in earnest, which meant we had pretty strict fitness regimes going on, including the dreaded cardio. Today we had a straightforward seven mile run scheduled, no weights. There was a suggested run rate, which was fairly steady, and nothing was put in it about how much incline was needed.

The weather forecast had been fine and not too warm,

so we'd decided yesterday to pick up a run route from my house, which meandered through the Cheshire countryside and would be relatively quiet.

Stupidly, I'd forgotten about it. Probably because I was in a sex filled haze and my one pre-occupation was wondering whether I should Google if it was possible for your balls to dry up, so when I saw on my camera two large four by fours at my gates, all I could do was groan.

"What's up?" Jerrica was lying on my bed, the sheets pulled around her because we'd just managed a third round of the morning.

"Your brother's here. I completely forgot we planned a run today."

She sat up. "Probably not a bad thing because I think my vagina would break if I let you in there again."

"Are you good with people knowing that we're – we're –"

She smiled, clearly trying to stop a laugh. "Seeing each other?"

"That." I laughed at my own discomfort. "Is that what we call it?"

She reached out and pulled me to her, something I'd discovered I liked.

"I'm not intending on going on a date or sleeping with anyone else, are you?"

I kissed her before replying. "No. You're the only girl I've ever taken on a date and I haven't slept with anyone else for months."

"In that case, I'm probably your girlfriend, but if that word makes you want to hide in a bunker, we can just say we're seeing each other." She cupped the back of my neck, bringing me in for another kiss. "It doesn't mean you have to marry me or anything, so don't break out in hives."

"I'm not worried about either. What about if the press gets hold of it?"

She shrugged. "My brother's a professional footballer for your team. I know what's involved here."

"Okay." I breathed, deep, long inhales. Panic hovered just around the corner, but I wanted this with her more than I wanted to run away and hide from being invested in another person. Or have them invested in me.

"Go let your teammates in. I'll shower quick and come down after. Just tell Nate I'm still tied to your bed or something." She laughed, a tad evilly.

"Not telling him that. He'd chop my balls off."

I heard her laughing even more evilly as I left the room to see my unwelcome guests.

CHAPTER 16
Jerrica

"WE NEED MORE DETAILS THAN THAT."

I stretched my legs out on the sun lounger in Jesse's garden. He'd only been gone about fifteen minutes and I was already fending off the inquisition about his tastes in bed.

Jude, Nicky, Nate, Rowan, Matty and Ryan had all turned up. With them had been Amber – who my brother was not happy to leave on her own, Genevieve, Neva, Dee, Otter and Kitty, who had the same sex drunk expression on her face that I was pretty sure was on mine.

I knew exactly what this was – an ambush. Last night, with Jesse and I going on a date, had clearly set the various group chats in flames with gossip, and now those mongerers wanted some more fuel for their fires.

"We went bowling. I kicked his arse. I had a burger, he had a steak and we came back here. I stayed over. That's the summary of the night." I reached down and picked up a muffin. As pre-payment, Otter had brought food, the sort of food you'd only buy when sharing with someone else, because you could never justify it to yourself.

"I want more details about the night." Genny sat back and closed her eyes. The day had turned out warmer than forecast. "So many rumours about Jesse. I once read somewhere that he never, ever kisses who he's with."

"He kisses me." I could give them that nugget.

"What about his cock? How big are we talking? I caught a glance once in the changing rooms, and it looked like your vagina would need first aid after a good seeing to from that." Neva was definitely not following her own diet plan. Her second lemon muffin was being devoured.

"He's pretty big. You do get used to it though."

"I did." Amber glanced at me. "I'm more than happy with Nate's penis."

"That's my brother. Please don't give me any more details." I glared at her. I did not need to know anything further about my brother and I was rather scared she'd try to share.

"I'll give you a detail every time you try to be vague with an answer you give us." Amber was the epitome of evil right now.

I stared at her. "I'll tell my brother everything you tell us and make it sound like you were saying he had a tiny penis and couldn't satisfy you."

She just laughed. "Feel free. He won't believe you. So what do you want to tell us about Jesse? Are you serious? Is this just research for your next book? Is he really into kinky stuff?"

"It isn't research. Does anyone want a mimosa?" I stood up. "I'll talk more with alcohol in me." One of the things I did miss about living in Manchester was that I'd lost the circle of girlfriends I had. I missed the gossip and the sharing. I'd gotten to know Amber quickly because of her getting pregnant and my brother falling head over heels for her, but it was as my brother's girlfriend, rather than my friend.

That was slowly shifting as we found our footing with each other, and I hoped we'd have a strong friendship – as long as she didn't give too much information about what my brother did with the appendage I still remembered him trying to whip round like a hose when he was eight.

"All of us apart from the pregnant lady." Otter stood up, getting off the blanket we'd thrown on the lawn. Jesse was lacking in garden furniture. "I'll give you a hand."

"Thank you."

I hadn't spent much time at Jesse's. Because of the girls, most of the hanging out was done at Nate's, so Jesse's kitchen was unfamiliar. He did have a few champagne glasses, and I'd already found champagne and orange juice in the fridge. I'd replace the champagne in the week, and I could only hope he wouldn't mind if I opened it now.

"Jesse's a nice guy," Otter said, pouring out the champagne after opening the bottle like a pro. She was an actress and was probably more used to champagne than I'd ever be. "Ryan thinks a lot of him."

I nodded, giving her a smile. I didn't know Otter well; she spent a lot of time on set and she'd only been with Ryan a year or just a little more, but when she'd hung out with us, she'd been great. "He's great." I looked over at her. "I really like him."

It was easier to say that to her than anyone else, maybe because I didn't know her as well.

"I can tell. You have it written all over you. How much sleep did you get last night?"

I topped the glasses up with the fresh orange juice, pouring one glass just of juice for Amber.

"I don't think it matters. I'm sure every orgasm makes up for an hour of missed sleep."

Otter laughed, picking up a tray I'd found and putting the glasses on it. "I second that. Last night was the first time I'd seen Ryan in a couple of weeks. I was so pissed off that he'd agreed to do this run today, and I think he would've skipped it if he wasn't so desperate for the gossip from Jesse. Not that he thinks he's going to get any."

We took the drinks outside, putting the trays on the floor and handing out the drinks. Amber scowled when she got hers.

"Let's start with the headlines. Is this serious with you and Jesse, or is it just a casual thing?" Neva leaned forward. She looked ridiculously gorgeous, her dark hair pulled into a neat twist, her make-up barely there but still making her look like a model.

"Jesse's serious. The boy's done casual behind very tightly locked doors for years and never, ever been seen out in public with a woman. There's no way he'd have gone out on a date with you if he wasn't serious." Genny was halfway through her mimosa already. "You know there's a photo of you both on gossip sites already?"

I shrugged. "I'd have been surprised if there wasn't. It doesn't bother me. I don't read them."

"Best way." Dee Jones, Rowan's fiancée sipped at her drink. "It's all a load of shit anyway. Steer clear from it and if you happen to read a comment that's bitchy, it's because they've tried to get in your fella's pants and failed. Jealously is alive and kicking from people's keyboards." Her smile was full of sunshine though. "Rowan hates any comments like that more than me, which I find kind of a turn on."

Amber nodded. "I like it when Nate gets his alpha on." She gave me the side eye. "And he gets a little bossy in bed."

I groaned. "Stop it. Just ask."

Her face lit up. "How dominant is Jesse in bed then?"

Six pairs of eyes landed on me.

I took a deep breath. There was no way they were letting me live unless I gave them some details.

I lived, long enough to go on another date with Jesse. Then another, and another after that. I'd spend the night at his, dropping him off at the training ground after, before tucking myself away, often at Kitty's café, to get all the words done. My brother mentioned that it would be okay for Jesse to stay at my house, or rather Nate's house, and while I appreciated the offer, I just didn't feel comfortable to get my rocks off with my brother's best friend while he was only a few doors down.

There wasn't just the words I had to do. I had adverts to check, a newsletter to write, the number of subscribers growing as I'd written a free novella to try and entice readers to follow my books, and there was social media. Since photos of me and Jesse had leaked out, and I'd been identified, my social media following had grown, as had my sales. I wrote a soccer romance series – soccer for my American readers – and I was now dating a soccer player. A hot one. The wannabe WAGs were loving it, although they were occasionally hating on me, and some of the reviews posted on book sites were a little too full of nastiness, accusing me of dating Jesse for the free publicity it was bringing, because my books weren't really that good.

Maybe the mistake I made was hiding this from Jesse.

The season was starting, and the team were seriously focused on winning the lead this year. They'd had a really good season last time, and this season would be a key one. There hadn't been many new signings over the summer, and only one player had left, the chairman and Guy both stating that they believed the quality of the current squad was good enough, particularly as they'd had last season to gel. The players – from what I'd seen – believed this, and their commitment that I'd seen in pre-season suggested they appreciated the faith management was showing in them. I'd been a footballer's sister for long enough to know when something special was happening too, and that was how it felt when I was around the training complex or sitting in Kitty's with whichever player turned up needing feeding and someone to talk to, or moan to, usually about Neva's diet plans.

I didn't want to bother Jesse with what people were suggesting. That I was only with him for research purposes. It wasn't true. There was no reason for me to need anyone other than my brother to tell me what actually happened at a football club or with the players and I knew enough about the game to write stories about it, even if I needed to explain the offside rule in detail.

I'd started to write a fourth book that was the beginning of a new series, one that had nothing to do with sport but was still romance, needing to prove to myself that I wasn't the sum of my acquaintances. It was going well, although I'd made sure that the hero was nothing like Jesse, not wanting anyone to be able to say that I was using him.

The first game of the season was at home. It was warm, sunny and the day before and the morning of the match had a festive like feel. The team was strong, there were no worrying niggles that had been picked up in pre-season training or the friendlies to ensure match fitness was there. The press around the club had been positive, and unlike last year, the summer hadn't been hit with scandal. Rowan Reeves had only been papped with his arm around Dee as they did their supermarket shopping together, instead of getting friendly with a wannabe WAG on holiday in Mexico; Nicky and Kitty had been focused on in celebrity gossip mags, mainly because he couldn't stop posting pictures of them together on his social media, which really was the cutest thing, and Jude had adopted a dog – a chihuahua called Mavis. To say Guy was pleased at the lack of scandal was an understatement. Genny was beaming, because her workload, usually centred around cleaning up the messes too rich, sometimes rather idiotic and egotistical footballers often made.

Which meant she had time to nosy into my name on social media and what was being said.

"Have you mentioned this to Jesse?" she said, looking at her computer screen in her office. A new photo of Guy was attached to her dart board, a dart sticking straight out of his head.

"No. He's too busy and I don't want to break his focus." I was also more than slightly worried about his reaction, given his history.

Genny took a really long exhale and studied me, inhaling steadily, which suggested she was working out which words to use to tell me I was making a mistake.

"Your boyfriend is a control freak."

"I know. Or he would be one if he didn't control it so well." It was meant to be a joke but there was too much truth in it. Jesse knew he liked control, but his awareness of that meant he moderated himself.

Genny nodded. "He's one of the good ones, but what he won't like is you cutting him out of this."

"What? The fact that a group of jealous women are accusing me of only hooking up with Jesse for 'research'?" I rolled my eyes, knowing damn well that wasn't what she was referring to.

Genny stared at me, a bit like a teacher eyeballs a naughty kid in class.

"No, Jez, the fact that you've had three threats sent, ones that contain far more detail than I'm comfortable with. This needs to go to the police."

I chewed the inside of my mouth. In the last ten days, I'd received three death threats. I'd had a few threats made already via messages on social media, all of which I'd passed over to Genny for advice. Then I'd had a few more which were more of the same, so I'd just blocked and moved on with it. None were specific, none contained any detail that made me think they could become reality, none made me think anything other than that they should get a life.

But these three – one via my personal email, another delivered to Nate's house and a third left behind my car windscreen wiper – were different.

"I don't want Jesse to know."

Genny shook her head. "You might never speak to me again, but you don't get to make that call. My conscience does. Put it this way, what if this moron decides to try to get to you while you're at Nate's, babysitting the girls?"

I blanched. My stomach turned. I'd tried not to think about the what ifs, preferring to deal in actual facts – different from what I usually did as a romance writer – which was far healthier than getting carried away with worries and suppositions.

"Nate's got a really good alarm system."

"Jerrica, I read threats on a daily basis. There are a lot of fucking psychos out there. Sometimes, someone thrust into the public domain like you've been, catches their eye. You remind them of someone they hate, and all that hate is transferred onto you. Occasionally, they have some serious mojo going on and the meds just aren't cutting it, or their relationship has ended and they just have they extra sharpened side of bite which means they'll go through with something. Most of the time, it's just words. This doesn't read like that to me."

"Are you sure you've not been reading too much true crime?" I eyeballed Genny, although I was starting to feel slightly sick.

She stared back at me. "Why won't you tell Jesse?"

I looked beyond her, fixing on the dart in photo-Guy's head. Tears were promising.

"You know what happened to his mum?"

Genny nodded. "I do."

"I don't think he'll be able to get his head around the possibility of something happening to me."

"You think he'll end it with you to keep you safe?" Her eyes narrowed, her expression telling me she already thought that was a very stupid idea.

I shrugged. I didn't know, but it was a possibility. I knew Jesse still veered on the scared side of being in a relationship, he still asked me what he should do in certain situations, making a joke of it, and I knew he'd been reading other romance books than mine to try to learn what I might like. It was sweet, just giving me all the more reasons to fall in love with him.

"Jerrica, you have to tell him."

Unfortunately, I wasn't going to get the chance.

. . .

The first game of the season started at eight in the morning, when Jesse woke, sat up bolt upright and froze. It woke me from a very nice dream where I'd been on a beach and at first, I'd been afraid someone – possibly my stalker person – had broken into Jesse's house.

"What is it?"

He turned and looked at me, his expression softening, brushing his hand through his shock of dark hair that was sticking out every which way.

"Game day. I've never woken up with someone in my bed on game day."

I settled back down, my hand going to his side, feeling the skin there. "What do you usually do on game day, apart from hang around at my brother's?"

"Breakfast. Shower. Go to Nate's if it's a home game, head to the stadium to get on the coach if it's away or wake up in a hotel if we've stayed over." He lay back down, facing me.

"Nate's at ten it is. What do you want to do before breakfast?" I toyed with his arm, my wrist being very quickly caught in his hand.

"Try a new routine."

And that was how we broke the sink in his bathroom.

We headed to my brother's house, my parents there too for a few days so they could see the start of the season like they usually did. They hadn't blinked an eye at me seeing Jesse. My mum had said before she'd been surprised that I hadn't been 'romanced' by one of Nate's teammates.

It was an easy morning; protein shakes, carbs, my

nieces running around as they picked up on the underlying excitement of the day, and Amber seeing football from a different side, as there was no way she could manage helping out in the physio department ; she looked like she had an extra-large melon attached to her front.

The first day of the season meant new kit. Nate gave each of the girls a home shirt with Morris on the back, and passed one to Amber too, her face lighting up when she saw it.

His eyes twinkled when he didn't give me one, the feeling of being left out making me angsty.

"Didn't think there was much point me getting you one." My brother grinned at me and then glanced at Jesse. "Thought you might prefer a different name this season."

I looked at Jesse, who was sitting at the breakfast bar with a huge smoothie, recipe by Neva. He was grinning, a touch of shyness about his expression.

"Nate, just pass her the damn shirt." He shook his head at my brother.

Nate stood up and gave me a bag from the club shop. I opened it with my heart dancing a jig and found a shirt in my size, Sullivan across the back. I held it up, hearing Amber laugh.

"Going to feel a bit weird seeing you with my teammates name on your shirt," Nate grumbled, glancing between me and Jesse. "I'll always have a Morris one for her, if you fuck up, Sullivan."

"I'm not going to fuck up." Jesse's eyes stayed on me as I pulled the shirt on over my T-shirt, turning round to show him the back.

I just hoped I could make the same promise.

. . .

I didn't think about the threats I'd received, lulled into what was a false sense of security because my parents were there and the weather was perfect. Athletic was playing a team that had finished mid-table last year, and would probably do the same this season too, meaning that they wouldn't be worried about a relegation battle or trying to get momentum to push for a spot at the top of the table.

We travelled to the ground separately, Nate and Jesse, along with Jude and Nicky who turned up at some point during the morning, went together; my parents drove Amber and the girls in my dad's car, leaving me to drive myself. I took the car Jesse had bought, missing him not being in it, but knowing that I'd be giving him a lift home later.

We'd planned to have dinner together at his, a takeout from the Chinese we always used, the meal already ordered for a certain time. I was staying over, the second night running, which we'd both said this morning after breaking his sink, was a sign that this was getting a little more than just having fun.

There was a lounge for the family of players, a side room that was usually full of booze and WAGs, and a bigger room that was more family orientated. The club employed a couple of children's entertainers and the woman who at some point had looked after most of the players' kids was there every home game to help look after any children who were bored.

I usually sat in family room with my nieces. It was where I had been for most of last season, taking the place of their mum and trying to help make a routine. It had been hard for the girls, especially when Nate had away games and he wouldn't be home for a couple of days. For the next six or seven years they would have the ebb and flow of the season, so this was how they were going to spend a good part of their childhood.

For some reason, during the drive to the ground, my thoughts were on the threats that had come through. They'd been crude, telling me what the author would like to do to me, and it wasn't pretty. They also described exactly where these would take place too, in enough detail to know that they were local, they knew the area and they knew the grounds.

I parked up in the secure area, recognising Keegan, one of the parking attendants. He'd started with the club last season, just before Christmas, and he'd always made a point of helping with the girls when I had them with me, which had been useful during my battles with car seats, especially when I'd needed to swap them from my car to Nate's, or my parents'.

"How's it going, Jez?" He smiled at me as I got out of the car.

I nodded, smiling back. He was about nineteen and obsessed with everything Manchester Athletic. "Good. How are you? Have you had a good summer?"

"I got a job with the grounds team here. An apprenticeship so I learn about the pitch and the maintenance." He was clearly ecstatic about this. "So I'm properly working for the club now. This is my last match doing this as I'll need to be on the pitch at half time."

"Congrats. That's amazing news." I was genuinely pleased for him, just a little surprised as he walked with me to the doors of the stadium. "I'm sad you won't be here on match days though."

"I will be. I'll just be doing a different job." His expression changed. "I'm not being weird walking you to the door, Genevieve asked me to make sure you got here okay. Following orders." He gave me a salute.

"Oh, thank you." My heart rate had started racing already, the change in his usual routine making me paranoid. Was the person who'd been sending me threats Keegan? He knew enough about the stadium and the alley next to Kitty's Café. He knew what cars I drove.

Maybe Genny was right and I needed to report it to the police, and tell Jesse and Nate. The police probably wouldn't be able to do much, but we could look at a private investigator. And security. Nate would want security.

So would Jesse.

"Enjoy the game, Jez! Everything crossed for a win." Keegan beamed at me and then headed back to where he was usually stationed.

I exhaled, feeling stupid for suspecting him, and went inside the stadium, seeing the match day staff for the first time since the season ended in May.

It was different, watching Jesse warm up on the pitch as well as Nate. Amber was happier to wait inside today, as were my parents, since the seats were comfier and they were showing the game on TVs in the family room, which meant I didn't have to feel guilty about leaving Libbie and Zara with Megs and the entertainers.

The warm up routine hadn't changed, a few of the players having exactly the same one each game as they were superstitious and wouldn't change what they did until there was an unlucky loss.

Last season, I'd watched Jesse a lot, spending far more time with my eyes on him than my brother. Jesse was our target man, the player the rest of the team tried to get the ball to, knowing that when he had it at his feet, he could create magic.

I knew only too well how much magic he could create off the pitch.

I saw women in the crowd wearing shirts with Jesse's name on the back, and a gaggle of girls in their early twenties who were talking about him, just in front of the seats we'd had reserved for us, if we wanted to sit away from the rooms. I wanted to say it didn't bother me, but it did.

"You okay?" Otter came and sat beside me, passing me a bottle of water. "You should get someone else to drive next time then we can have a few wines."

"Help pass away time?" I wasn't sure if Otter liked football or not.

She shook her head. "Helps with my nerves. I can't tell you how nervous I am. I was driving Ryan mad this morning with my pacing."

I laughed, entirely captivated by this woman who had played one of my favourite characters on TV. "You get used to it."

She nodded. "I'm sure I will next season. I can't see this easing up before May next year. And we have the World Cup too. That's going to be hard."

"The hardest thing will be them being away for nearly five weeks – if they get to the final." That I wasn't looking forward to. Not them getting to the final as I knew for both Jesse and Nate it was the last time they'd probably play in a World Cup tournament, certainly for Jesse, but the amount of time they'd be away and the time difference would make it hard to speak to them regularly, especially for Nate to FaceTime the girls and by that point, his son.

"That's the part I didn't factor in. Ryan and I can't see

each other for a couple of weeks sometimes, depending on my schedule and his games, but five weeks is too long. He doesn't want me going out either, although I'm thinking of trying to get there for two or three nights if the manager allows it." Otter looked pensive and almost heartbroken.

"Are you in Manchester at that time?"

She shook her head. "Filming in Norfolk and various places. But I'll have three or four days here and there depending on the schedule."

"Then why don't you come and stay with me and Amber? We can watch the matches together and be football widows."

Her face lit up. "That would be amazing, thank you. I think I might need the emotional support."

"I think we all will."

"Jesse's looking for you. You should stand up and wave." She stood up and started waving herself, somehow managing to get Jesse to look in the right spot.

I stood up too, waving, expecting him to give me a quick gesture back and then go back to his warm-up routine with Ryan.

He didn't. His hands came together making the shape of a heart, holding it up towards me.

The girls who'd been lusting after him turned round, giving me an appraising look followed by judging eyes. There was also a glance at Otter as well, when they quickly turned round, whispering something.

They didn't matter. Jesse's gesture filled my chest so I felt like I was about to explode. I lifted my own hands and made the same heart shape back.

Ryan slapped Jesse on the back, pulling him in for a side hug and then they started to warm up again, Jesse throwing me another glance and a smile.

I looked at Otter, who was smiling too.

"I think we should have champagne. Can't you leave the car here?"

I nodded. "Or my dad can drive it back and my mum can drive the girls. Let me check."

My parents had seen Jesse's heart gesture, my mum fanning herself and smiling as if I had just told her he'd proposed, so passing them Jesse's car keys was no problem, I just hoped he wouldn't mind. I headed back to the seats with Prosecco and two glasses, hoping we had a win to celebrate at the end of it.

CHAPTER 17
Jesse

A THREE-ONE VICTORY, two goals for me and a worldly of a strike for Ryan, meant that we were loud and on a high back in the dressing rooms once the ninety minutes was up. Nate was pissed off at the goal he'd conceded, mainly because it had definitely been offside and the ref hadn't called for VAR – the computer aided tech that checked close-to-call decisions.

But it hadn't mattered because we had the three points and a win. Everything in the world was good and I was spending the night with my girl, and I knew exactly how we were going to spend it once I'd recouped some of the calories I'd expended on the pitch, fully planning to expend just as much when I got Jerrica in bed and naked.

Or over my kitchen counter and naked. Or on the sofa. There were a variety of options.

"Fucking two goals, man!" Jude slapped my back, his fully naked self bounding around the dressing room like a possessed version of Tigger from Winnie-the-Pooh.

"I don't need to see your dick like that." I tried not to

look at the junk that he had on display, but it was difficult to miss with the strange hip-thrusting he was displaying.

"Sorry, Cap, I'm just fucking well stoked!"

His vocab was a mix of Mancunian and Australian, which made me wonder what he'd been watching.

"Captain says put some kecks on." I pointed him away, noticing Nate calling me over.

I was already showered and dressed, the motivation of getting home to Jerrica's warm, welcoming body a better celebration that the alternative, which was a night out in Alderley. Our supporters would be celebrating too, doing most of it for us, because at the end of it, this was a job and bad decisions after a win could make sure I didn't experience that win again.

"What's up?" I picked up my bag and headed to him.

He didn't look happy.

"Follow me out. Let's not piss on any parades here."

The night I walked into the place I was staying with my mother when she overdosed was something I tried not to think about. When I pressed down the handle to the room we were living in, I'd felt as if I was watching a film version of my own life, that I wasn't in my body, and instead I was seeing me walk into that room.

All the blood had rushed to my head when I saw her out cold on the sofa, her arm still with the tie-off on it. Heroin had become her new lover and I think I knew when I first saw her use it that it was the beginning of the end.

That feeling, that rush of blood, was what I had now. Adrenaline, pure and simple, mixed with fear.

"Jerrica?" Her name fell from my lips as soon as we were outside in the corridor.

"She's fine, everyone's fine. Breathe." Nate put his

hand on my shoulder. "Did you know she's been getting threats?"

"What?"

"Someone's been sending detailed threats to her, calling her a whore because of what she writes and saying shit about you. I've just seen Genny, who's given me vague details – stop."

Both hands were on my shoulders now.

"Fucking get yourself together, Jesse, or I'll punch you out cold."

I closed my mouth, unaware of what words had come out of it. Then I breathed.

"She's okay?"

Nate nodded. "There was another note left on your car windscreen and a photograph of you and her – they've caught the person on CCTV. I didn't know if you knew she'd been getting these threats."

I shook my head, starting to feel more together. "She didn't tell me. Why didn't she tell me?"

"Probably for the same reason she didn't tell me. I don't know any more details, but she's in Genny's office with the police. They're going to want to speak to both of us. Are you good to come?"

I nodded, just about holding myself together.

"We're going to get a drink first. I can't have you near my sister looking like you do right now."

I nodded, bile making its way up my throat. Jerrica was fine, everyone was okay, there was no need for me to feel this irrational, this on edge, but that sensation I'd had when I saw Nate's face and heard those words had been enough to pull me back there.

I wasn't cognisant of where he directed me, the swirl of feelings of panic, relief, fear and gratitude that Nate was so cool even though it was his sister we were also talking about.

I knew that past trauma could fuck up how you'd react when something happened to take you back to that moment. I knew that tomorrow I'd be messaging Jane and booking in a session for that day. I also knew that I could handle this.

By the time Nate had pushed me into Guy's office, my heart rate was almost back to normal, and I was with it enough to watch him take out two whisky glasses and a bottle of very nice Scotch from one of Guy's cupboards.

"Drink." He handed me a glass as soon as he'd poured the first one.

"Thank you. Is Guy going to chew us off about this?"

Nate shook his head. "He was with Genny when she told me and he was trying to chew her off because she hadn't told him. My sister is in the shit with a lot of people."

"At least she's alive and can be in the shit."

He nodded slowly. "You told me how you found your mother."

"I did. I should've been home earlier from work. If I had, I'd have been able to stop the overdose."

"Don't hit me for what I'm about to say." He knocked back the whisky in one. "That might've been the case, but there'd have been a time after that when you wouldn't have been on time, or early, or there."

I stared at the floor between my feet.

"I know."

"Here's the plan. I'm going to tear my sister a new one for keeping secrets about this. You're going to look after her." His expression told me I didn't know everything.

"What else happened, Nate?"

"Whoever it was had a crack at Keegan, the lad who works the match-day parking, the one with red hair."

My stomach turned. "What did they do?"

"Knocked him out. I'm not sure how. Genny has the details. He's okay – he's been taken to hospital to get checked out, but our doc thinks he's okay. He's a good lad." Nate poured us both another measure.

I stared at it before taking a mouthful. "Security?"

"Yep. My house and yours, and something at Kitty's too. Genny has a list of PI's." He swallowed, watching me like a hawk. "Is this going to make you ditch my sister?"

Something in my chest popped. "No." I put my glass down. "Fuck no."

He stared at me some more.

"I know I haven't dealt with getting close to someone for the fear that something will happen to them, but that's not a reason to end things." I looked at him, feeling wetness in my eyes that I didn't want to drop. "You and Chan. It didn't end you. You're still living."

When Nate's wife had died, I'd stayed away. I'd been Chan's friend too, spending time with her at their house, just like I did now. Seeing her ill and not getting better had made me run for the hills and there'd been a period of time when I just couldn't be around.

I'd got my shit together eventually, and turned back up, not knowing what to expect from a couple who were about to experience the worst of what life had to offer, but Nate had just slapped my back and told me he was glad I was there.

He nodded three or four times, finishing his whisky and putting the glass down on Guy's desk with a slam. "I am. So's my sister. So are you. She's as stubborn as hell, and she'll try and do everything by herself. There aren't many men who I know can be what she needs, even when she doesn't think she needs anything."

The door swung open before I could respond, an ashen Genevieve coming through.

"Is that Guy's whisky?"

We both managed to look twitchy.

"Poor me a double. It's his good stuff too. Make it a triple." She sat down in the leather chair facing his desk.

Nate sorted out her drink. I braced myself for words I needed to handle hearing.

Genny took a few sips before relaxing her shoulders. "It always tastes better when Guy's paid for it." She put her feet up on his desk. "You ready for the details? I've just sat in with Jez while the police have gone through everything."

"Who's with her now?" Nate asked before I could.

"Your dad. You mum's taken the girls and Amber home – they don't know anything. I've sent security over there and they still won't know anything. Jez is okay. She's shaken, but she's okay."

"What happened?" I managed to get my shit together.

Genny took a deep breath. "Keegan saw someone messing with Jez's car. He went over to them and took a blow to the head, probably from a bat. Whoever it was left a note – this is the fourth correspondence from the same person. There are various nasty threats about what they want to do to Jez, and I'm not going into more details because you don't need them."

"Is it one of the standard crazies?" Nate folded his arms.

Genny shook her head. "No. There's a difference. We had it with that girl who stalked Jude a couple of years ago – remember? Places were referenced and there was too much knowledge. It was fear-inducing and these were meant to be too."

"Okay. Why's she not said anything? Why are we - " Nate looked at me "- finding this out now?"

"Because she didn't want to worry anyone and she was worried it'd make Jesse flap." She looked over at me. "Sorry. Don't flap."

"I'm not flapping." I really wasn't. The easiest thing to do would've been to get someone to drive me home and distance myself, but that would've only been easy for twenty minutes. After that I'd have been getting a cab to find Jerrica, because I'd pretty much sussed by now that I couldn't leave her alone. I didn't want to.

She wasn't my mother. She was nothing like her.

"What's on CCTV?" Nate stood up. "Can the person be identified?"

Genny carried on drinking, sinking further into the chair. "They're small. Slight. Probably a woman, judging by how they move – I've only watched it once. Want my guess? It's the same woman who stalked Jude."

"I thought she'd moved out of the area?" I finished my drink.

She was nudging Guy's stationery around his desk with her foot. "So did I. We'll find out more in the next day or so. Jesse, you've got the same security as Nate at your house - "

"I'll feel better if Jerrica stays with me tonight. Jesse, you're welcome to stay." He turned to me. "I've got the girls and my parents with me, and Amber who's going to drop in the next few weeks. Leon's about, too, but I'd feel better – "

"We'll stay with you." I stood up, my legs no longer shaking.

Nate almost smiled. "Thanks, man."

It was okay. It was going to be okay.

Jude didn't need alcohol full stop, so we got him to drive me, Jerrica and Nate back to his, which worked, as Jude had left his car there before the game. He'd heard what had happened, and suggested himself that it was Rosie West, the woman who'd made his life a misery for a good few months a couple of years ago, offering up the information that she had moved back to Manchester because he'd hired an investigator to keep tabs on her.

Jerrica was quiet in the car on the way back to her brother's. Her hand was in mine as we sat together in the back seat, but she didn't say much and she didn't move herself closer to me.

When we got back to Nate's, our planned Chinese order now a lot larger and being delivered to Nate's address, she busied herself in the kitchen, making a fuss over Libbie and Zara, although Libbie just wanted to follow Jude around everywhere, her crush still going strong.

It was Jerrica's dad who managed to get us back to some sort of normality, talking about the win, picking up on bits of play he was curious about. Jude wasn't fazed by the possible return of Rosie, or Libbie's infatuation, and indulged Jerrica's dad in the game talk, as well as pouring over the rest of the results in the Premier League and yesterday's championship.

Tomorrow, or Tuesday, I'd find some way to thank him because right now, he was the one keeping our heads up and stopping fear and anger from kicking up a stink.

Jerrica didn't sit next to me at dinner. She didn't sit

next to me on the sofas afterwards, taking her nieces upstairs to bed with Nate instead. I waited for her to come back down, but she didn't appear, Nate coming into the room on his own.

"Is she okay?" I asked him in front over everyone, stopping already with the keeping things on the quiet.

"She's feeling guilty and blaming herself, which like I said, there's an element to that which is true. If she'd told us, it might not have happened." He sat down next to Amber, his arm going around her shoulders, his other hand resting on her belly. "Go and see her."

I stood up, looking at her parents. "Thank you for everything this evening."

Her father nodded, her mother gave me a beam and raised her hands, making the same heart shape I'd made at Jerrica.

I couldn't stop the smile or the slight heat of embarrassment, especially when I turned to see Nate and Jude doing exactly the same thing.

"Fuckers, the lot of you. Except Jerrica's mum."

I left the room to the sound of laughter, which at least made me feel a little better.

I knew there was the chance that someone had targeted Jerrica because she was seeing me, in which case, I'd inadvertently put her at risk. I also knew that even with that knowledge, I wouldn't have done anything differently, just maybe hired a team of bodyguards or something slightly less dramatic.

I didn't knock on her door, but I did open it slowly.

Jerrica sat on her bed, her face wet with tears, her eyes staring out of the window, watching the sunset.

"Hey." I kept my voice low trying to sound soothing, not sure if it was working.

She didn't turn to look at me. "Hey."

I wanted to hold her. I wanted to bring her close to me so she knew she wasn't alone. I wanted to tell her that everything would be okay and there was no way anyone would ever hurt her or anyone she loved, but that was something that couldn't be promised.

It didn't stop me wanting to try to make that happen.

I sat down on the bed next to her and put my hands on her shoulders, pulling her back gently so she could rest against my chest.

For a moment, she was solid rock, unmoving, then something in her relented and she shifted back into me.

"I'm sorry."

"For not telling me?" My arms went round her, just as I'd wanted. This was me being able to take care of someone in a way I'd never imagined. Those broken synapses in my head that formed attachments started to fix, or feel like they were fixing.

"If I had, Keegan wouldn't have been hurt."

"I'm not sure that's true." Genevieve had known; she'd sent Keegan to meet Jerrica so she didn't walk across the car park on her own. I'd have asked for the same, or for Jerrica to have gone in the car with her dad, or a fucking security guard, but that wouldn't have stopped what happened to Keegan. It wouldn't have stopped someone putting another note on the windscreen, one that detailed exactly how they'd like to tear her apart. "I don't think you can blame yourself for him. I don't think anything would've happened differently today. But I wish you'd told me and Nate what was going on."

She shrugged, another veil of tears falling. "I just thought it was normal. I write books, people message me, sometimes to tell me how much they've enjoyed it, sometimes to tell me that I need a better editor, sometimes it's because they've got some of their own weird stuff going on, and I know the crap Dee got and even Chan, when they started seeing footballers. People think because you're in the public eye, you're fair game." She shook her head. "I'm telling someone how to suck eggs here."

"Why didn't you tell me about the messages you were getting? That's the bit I don't get. We've been together three or four nights a week – was I not doing something I should've been?" She should've been able to tell me; that was the bit I didn't understand.

Jerrica turned around, her eyes too fucking sad.

"Some of the messages said that I was only with you because it boosted the publicity my books were getting." She hiccupped, trying to stop her tears. "I worried you'd think I was using you."

I raised my brows and moved my head back, staring at her. "Really?"

She nodded. "I've had a decent bump in sales since you put that picture of us on Instagram and tagged me. Do you never read your comments?"

"No. I stopped doing that a long time ago because that's where the madness lies. Jerrica, I didn't think you'd use me. I don't think you're that good an actress." She'd made it clear in the beginning that she was interested, but she hadn't gone out on a limb to let me know that; she'd read the vibes off me.

"I was also worried you'd start to blame yourself for me being threatened and maybe worry that you wouldn't be able to protect me or something." Her back stiffened again.

We'd found the crux of the problem here, and she was

right. I didn't know what my reaction would've been, I only knew what it was now.

"You're not my mother. I don't need to save you. You can save yourself, but I can help you when you need it. I want to be your person. I want to be the man who you can call home; the man you can rely on. The man who gives you seriously good orgasms." I wasn't sure that last part was the right thing to say, but I was calm enough now, now I had her safe in my arms, to at least try to ground her.

Life wasn't about just surviving the dark times. It was about dancing in the light.

"Does that mean I can't scare you away?"

She looked at me, tears tracing down her cheeks. I wiped them away and shook my head. "I don't think so."

There was a nod and her chin tipped up, just like it did when she was feeling stubborn. "So I if I told you I loved you, you wouldn't run a mile?"

I'd never heard those words before. No one had ever said them to me in thirty years of being on this planet. My mother had never uttered them to me and no woman had ever been close enough to fall in love with me.

Until Jerrica.

"Say it." I was suddenly desperate to hear them out loud.

Her face lit up with a smile that was brighter than any dawn. "I love you, Jesse Sullivan."

When I told Jane about this moment, which I would, she would ask me to find a word to describe it. I didn't know how I could use just one, but if I had to it would be joy. Simple, unadulterated joy. I hadn't known it before. I hadn't known I could feel it before, not if it wasn't from winning a game or scoring a goal. Not because of another person.

"I love you back." They were words I'd never said. This was the first time, not the last though.

"I'm so glad you said that." She wrapped her arms around me, still crying, but I had a feeling that these weren't sad tears anymore. "I'm sorry."

"What the fuck for?"

"Not telling you. Making this mess of things."

I shook my head slowly. "You remember how I told you I'd fuck things up and you said it was okay. Well, same goes, and you haven't fucked things up, Jerrica." I kissed her forehead, then the tip of her nose, then her lips. "This isn't fucking something up, it's just being human."

She pressed her head against my chest, her arms around me now, and we just held each other, the feeling warm and comforting, and although my dick was getting some ideas, it seemed to know that this wasn't the time to make a grand entrance.

"How about going downstairs? I think Nate and your parents want to make sure you're okay."

She nodded, moving her head back to look at me. "My parents like you. And I don't think my brother wants to maim you either."

My grin was anything but fake. "I'm aiming to keep it that way. You want a few minutes to freshen up?"

"Do I look a mess?"

"You look like you've been crying, but you're still beautiful." I brushed her cheek with my thumb, her skin soft.

"You're biased." She gave a half-laugh. "You'd think I was beautiful even if you saw me three chapters before I was about to write the end and I hadn't showered for four days straight."

"And your point?"

"There isn't one." She touched my jaw with her fingers. "I thought you'd end things after finding out today."

"I think it's going to take more than that."

Jerrica washed her face and came downstairs, looking slightly apprehensive as she sat down with her family, this time taking a seat next to me. I slid my arm round her back and she leaned into me. This was the first time we'd touched like this in front of her brother in this way, and definitely in front of her parents. I glanced round at their faces, trying to read their thoughts, wondering if they'd think I was good enough for her.

"Genny's called me with an update from the police." Nate had his feet up on the coffee table, Amber's legs over his. She looked half asleep and very, very pregnant. Nate also looked very relaxed.

"What've they said?" Jerrica had her head resting on my chest. She didn't tense up like I thought she would, instead staying relaxed, soft.

"They went to Rosie West's address – Jude was right, she had moved back to Manchester. They've brought her in for questioning." Nate slid his hand up and down Amber's leg. "Nothing is certain right now, but Genny seemed to think the police reckoned it was her."

I felt tension pour out of Jerrica, my arms tightening round her so she knew I was there.

"I hope she gets support." Jude was sat in a reclining chair, looking half asleep already.

I was surprised he hadn't headed out with some of the others, heading to a few bars and then a club to celebrate.

Nate shook his head. "I just hope that if it's her, she doesn't get the chance to do this again." He looked at his sister. "And you tell us if anything like this comes up."

Her nod was barely there, but it was there. "I will. Don't blame Genny. She wanted me to go to the police and I wasn't up for it. But I'll just hand anything over to the club like this going forward and take their advice."

Nate nodded, sitting upright. "Sounds like Libbie's out of bed." He glared at Jude. "She'll want to see you."

"Girl's got good taste." Jude grinned. "Tell her to bring a book down and she can read to me."

Which was what ended up happening, Jude sitting next to Libbie, helping her sound out words then reading her a story about a princess who saved everyone, no princes needed, before adding an extra ending where the princess went to bed without any arguments.

I watched Jude as he sat back down on the recliner, looking smug, like he should be christened the child whisperer or something.

"I always knew you liked princess stories." I waited for his backlash.

All I got was a smile.

Jerrica and I made our way up to bed shortly after Libbie disappeared back up the stairs. I tried to stand tall, feeling incredibly self-conscious in front of her parents that I was sleeping in the same bed as their daughter.

No one in the room knew anything much about what we did in private. Nate may have had his suspicions, but I doubted he even gave them much of a detailed thought. I figured Amber would know something; Jerrica had already said she'd been hounded by some of the other women for details, but had managed to not say too much. Even so, I felt awkward until we got into Jerrica's room and locked the door.

She sat down on the bed and looked at me with big eyes. "Can you tell me what to do?"

I froze, my hand still on the door handle.

"I want you to fuck me so I forget about today. Tell me what to do so I don't have to think."

For a moment, I lost my words. I had no idea what to say, my brain short circuiting and my body freezing. I'd experienced enough therapy in the last decade to have an understanding of where her head was at.

Sex was cathartic. It was a release. It could be a safe place to experiment with boundaries that had no bearing on a day-to-day life. For me, it had given me a space to take control, to look after, to bring pleasure and find mine afterwards.

Later, when the timing was better, we'd have a conversation about this, about what was driving her right now, because when you understood why you wanted something it was easier to ask for it.

Right now though, I didn't want to be the lover I was used to. My drives, my needs, were different. I wanted to hold her closer and touch her like she was made of delicate glass.

I swallowed. I found those words. "How do you want me to fuck you?"

"Hard." Her voice was husky, filled with too much of something.

I moved to the bed, pulling off my T-shirt, seeing her eyes flicker over my chest. I crawled over her, Jerrica leaning back onto her mattress, her hands coming to my shoulders. I took her lips in a rough kiss, bracing myself over her.

Her hands trailed from my shoulders down my chest, her fingers playing near the waistband of the sweats I was wearing. I was hard, there was no way I couldn't be. Instinct was kicking in, the adrenaline from the win, from what happened after, from hearing those words. I let it take over, knowing that this would remind me that we were both still breathing, that we were both still present.

I knelt up, staring down at her, her face still pale and her eyes red from the tears that she'd shed, but the light was back there.

"Take your top off."

She sat up, pulling off her top, leaving her in just her bra, a white lacy thing that looked designed to drive me mad.

"And bra. I want to see your tits."

Her hands went to between her breasts, the fastening there. She took her sweet time to undo it, pulling it away with more tease than shyness.

I looked my fill, the swell of her breasts tipped with those hard nipples that had become one of my favourite things to daydream about.

"Pinch them for me." I was lost to what was happening now, the fact we were in her brother's house now completely irrelevant.

She brought her hands up to her tits, cupping them before doing as I asked. My cock throbbed, my hands itched to touch her myself, but I kept my control and watched.

"Take off your leggings."

She pulled them off, leaving her in just her underwear, a thong that matched the bra now on the floor.

"Good girl. I love how you do as you're told."

Her smile was my reward.

Hers was coming - literally.

"How do you want to come? On my face or on my hand?"

Her cheeks flushed. "Your hand. On your knee. Please."

Like the first time. I turned round so I was sitting on the edge of the bed, sweats tented, the lamplight illuminating her profile when I turned to her.

"Sit here." I pointed to my knee.

Jerrica slid over to me, getting close enough so I could pull her over, place her where I wanted her.

I started with another kiss, one of my hands going to her waist, the other cupping a breast. I teased and toyed controlling her mouth, exploring her skin, my hands reading the twine of muscle and sinew and smoothness, the soft roundness of her stomach, the slope between her thighs to where heat and wetness accrued.

I whispered praise into her ear, pressing kisses, not giving her the roughness she'd asked for, not yet. I needed this first, this gentle prelude playing before we hit a crescendo where neither of us would know where one ended and the other began.

My fingers pushed inside her panties, sliding from her centre to her clit, coaxing her to an orgasm that had her holding onto me, whimpering as she came.

I stopped thinking, running on instinct, not waiting for her aftershocks to come to a stutter.

"I want you on your hands and knees. Face your mirror."

She looked at me, half stunned that I wasn't giving her time to come down, but we didn't have that yet, I didn't want that.

Jerrica looked at me as she moved, my hands steering her into position so she was looking into the floor length mirror, her ass up in the air, me behind her, kneeling up. I pushed my sweats down, releasing my cock and giving it a couple of hard fists, watching her eyes in the mirror.

This position could be completely anonymous, unless you had a mirror in front to make that eye contact, to see the other person's expression. To have that same moment and find electricity in that connection.

It might be rough. It might be hard and fast and raw, but this wasn't just about fulfilling a basic need.

I toyed with my cock at her entrance, moving it down through her folds and back again, her wetness slick over the sensitive tip.

My hands gripped her hips, steadying her as I pushed inside with one wicked movement, her groan echoing through the room, her eyelids dropping. I started to move steadily, using my grip on her hips to get deeper, harder, filling her up and filling the room with words telling her how good she felt, how tight she was around my cock, how much I fucking loved her.

The reversal of those words was what I'd said before.

Now they were in the right order.

She came with my fingers on her clit and her eyes on mine through the mirror. I followed her with a groan, my arms holding her back against my chest, a hand on her breast, the sensation of us being so fucking close I didn't know if it was going to be possible to separate. I didn't know if I wanted to.

Words came out of my mouth that I'd never heard

before, praise, love, wants, needs. How she was mine, and possessive utterings that I thought were reserved for my teammates whose balls were kept in cases owned by their girlfriends.

I knew there would be times when I felt that panic, when I doubted myself, when I had no idea what I was meant to do because my early life lessons in love had never been taught. But I could learn now.

We collapsed onto our sides, my cock still buried deep inside her, her head turned so I could press messy kisses to her lips, invading her mouth with my tongue, wondering how the hell I could get closer to her.

Eventually we slowed. Heart rates coming down and breath settling back to normal. Her body curled into mine and my arms wrapped around her, holding, touching.

This wasn't like the first time we had sex. It wasn't the same as in that hotel room in France, when we started to learn each other. This was something I'd never had; never known I needed.

"I love you." The words came easily now. "I don't think a day's going to go by where I don't say those words to you."

"I love hearing them from you. I love you. Every bit. Even the ones you want to hide from me. Especially those."

I think, there, in her bed in her brother's house, I found peace for the first time.

It wouldn't be the last.

Epilogue
JERRICA

BABY OLIVER MORRIS was big and chunky and incredibly good natured. He also weighed a ton, which was why I was holding him on my knee, listening to him gurgle, while Jesse attempted to warm up a bottle.

This was our third time on babysitting duty, just for an hour or so, while Amber and Nate took the girls to see the puppy that would join their family in a few weeks' time.

Personally, I thought a puppy would add even more to the madness, but my unflappable brother had simply shrugged and taken the idea in his stride.

Oliver's birth had been traumatic and there had been a moment when Nate had thought he might lose both Amber and their son. It had been Jesse who'd talked him out of that dark spot, made him find the light that the doctors had told us was there. The birth had not been straightforward, sudden labour that Amber's body hadn't been prepared for, and Oliver had been big. There had been blood loss and a drop in heart rates, and emergency caesarean being called.

Nate had driven him and Jesse from the training

ground, although I was pretty sure Jesse had done the actual driving as my brother would not have been in any fit state. I was also sure that I'd never find that out for certain.

I'd been with Amber, at the hospital, calling Nate, my voice hysterical when I tried to relay what was happening. Afterwards, I'd realised just how Jesse had held everyone together – me, Nate, Jude, Nicky – we all knew and loved Amber. Jesse had been calm, reassuring, practical.

It was only when we were at Nate's house afterwards, Libbie and Zara in bed, that he told me how he'd felt inside, how he'd had that same sensation when he'd found his mother's body.

We made love that night in a different way, for different reasons, and then we'd fallen asleep knowing that somehow, all was well and would be.

It would be if Jesse sussed out how to work a bottle warmer.

"You okay there?" I so wanted to laugh.

He glared at me. "Fine. I think this is working."

Oliver gurgled again. He was such a placid boy, a replica of his dad in so many ways, apart from having Amber's eyes.

"To be fair, I think he can skip a meal." My nephew was weighty.

"Want me to take him and you can sort this bottle?"

There was Jesse taking the get out.

"Absolutely. Go be carried by Uncle Jesse." I eyeballed him as I said the title, standing up with the baby in my arms. Jesse came over and took him straight away, carrying him with ease, and for a moment I indulged myself with watching him.

I'd already told him he looked good with a baby, to

which he'd gone all mumbly and shy, but then we'd had really good sex later, so I didn't think he'd disliked the compliment.

He focused on the baby while I sorted out the bottle, most of it done already.

"Hey, Olly." Jesse grinned. "What did you think of that goal against Spurs? Pretty decent wasn't it? Shame your daddy didn't manage to keep a clean sheet."

I smothered a giggle. The game had ended in a draw because Nate had conceded a goal, which had infuriated him. Jesse hadn't stopped winding him up about it yet.

They'd come back from the World Cup, a long few weeks apart, full of the joys of life and confidence. Athletic were having a good season and the players who'd had international call ups had managed to stay relatively injury free. The club had a real buzz about it and had gone into the New Year as league leaders.

"Genny had an update about Rosie West today." I'd been waiting for a moment like this to tell him, when he was distracted and getting high on that clean baby smell.

"Is it one I'm going to like?" He was too fixed on Oliver to look at me.

I fully suspected that Jesse's biological clock would start ticking before mine did. "She's been admitted for treatment in a hospital in Suffolk. She should get the treatment she needs and the care."

Jesse muttered something that I knew would be to do with exactly what care, because he had very little sympathy for Rosie West. She had been behind the vile threats I'd received, and the attack on Keegan. After that first match of the season, the police had spoken to her, but not had enough evidence to charge her. Two days later she'd managed to break into the training complex changing rooms and hid in one of the lockers, jumping out at Jesse with a hammer in her hand.

Luckily Nate had been there with Nicky, and the changing rooms had CCTV installed, which was another story altogether. She'd been arrested and detained under the Mental Health Act, which had made Jesse and Nate finally relax some.

Jude had sent Jesse a hammer as a birthday present last month, which had gone down exactly as expected, but that was Jude.

"Still not lapsing the extra security." He rubbed his nose against Oliver's, which was cute to the extent an ovary melted. "So don't bother asking."

"Wasn't going to." I walked over to him with the bottle. "Dinner time. Then burps and bed."

Jesse's eyes darkened. "For Oliver or me?"

I laughed. "Both, if you're lucky."

He sat down, positioning Oliver so he could administer the bottle easily, something Uncle Jesse had become rather smooth at.

I sat next to him, not needing to help, enjoying the whispers of the man I'd fallen head over heels for as he talked my nephew through his dinner.

Tomorrow I had another book release, my readership growing well enough to make the call that it was my career. In the summer, I'd probably move into Jesse's. He'd asked at least once a week, and I'd found that various belongings had somehow found their merry way to his place without my help. I now had a bookcase in one of his downstairs rooms, full of romance paperbacks and cloth bound classics that I would find in paper bags next to where I sat on his couch, because I now had my own spot.

I repaid the favour by sending him photos of things he

liked: my boobs, screenshots of paragraphs I'd written, my hands making a heart.

Life was good. It was an adventure. And it was better for having Manchester Athletic's target man by my side.

Oliver let go of a massive burp a minute or so after Jesse finished with the bottle, his eyes starting to close as a milk coma started.

"I'm sure he's copying Jude when he does that." Jesse frowned, looking up at me. "Maybe Nate should reduce the amount of time Jude spends here."

I laughed because that wasn't going to happen. Jude was our boomerang, bless him. "Libbie would have words to say if she heard you suggest that."

Jesse grinned. "She would. And so would someone else."

I raised my brows. I'd learned that Jesse was excellent at finding out gossip.

"But if you want me to tell you, you'll have to persuade me." He stood up with Oliver, putting him down in his cot that was kept in the kitchen area.

"I'm pretty sure I can find ways to do that."

So I did, ways we both enjoyed.

The End

Want more Jesse and Jerrica? Get a bonus epilogue when you sign up to my newsletter via my website www.writeranniedyer.com. You also get a couple of free novellas!

Not sure what to read next? Want more Manchester Athletic? Carry on for a taste of Penalty Kiss, a feisty enemies-to-lovers, found family, sports romance!

Love small town? Visited Severton in Sleighed!

Want to start a binge read? Begin the Callaghan Green series in Engagement Rate!

Penalty Kiss

CHAPTER ONE - DEE

Nothing could turn a warm, summery Mancunian morning into a shit-tastic fuckery of a mess like a nine o'clock meeting.

With my manager. And agent. Plus, no hint of what this meeting was about, although I could guess. It wouldn't take a genius to work out exactly which parts of the last two weeks they were pissed about, and it wasn't the photos of me doing extra training on the beach where two of the lads and I had been on holiday.

Oh no. There would be no pats on the back for that, or the fact I'd had more goal assists than anyone else last season, or sold more shirts with my name on than anyone else at Manchester Athletic, including Nate Fleming, who was the team's golden boy.

I was about to be torn a new asshole, and then have it rammed without lube.

Nothing good came of Monday morning meetings when you were still meant to be on holiday, enjoying a leisurely morning dreaming up how to spend the rest of the day without being bored. A trip to the gym maybe, or a dip in the indoor pool to stretch a few muscles. Perhaps lunch somewhere given that my usual rigid diet plan was slightly less rigid with just another few days to go before pre-season training started. Didn't mean I could go completely rogue with carbs and sugar, just that I was less likely to get a rollocking off from our chief meal spoiler, also known as the club's nutritionist.

We never asked her out for team meals, or to parties, but I don't think she cared. I wasn't entirely sure what she cared about.

The stadium was the shining diamond in the campus Manchester Athletic's new owners had built when they took over half a decade ago, investing money into an area that needed to be developed. It was now the place I spent most of my time, enough to wonder why I didn't just live in one of the suites at the hotel there.

I nodded at Mandy, the woman who ran the reception at the entrance to part of the building dedicated to offices and the business side. She didn't like footballers, despite her job existing because of the football team, but then I didn't think she liked most people. Still, I was never rude to her when I saw her on the few occasions I came in this part. In fact, I made a point of being especially friendly to her, because I figured that pissed her off even more.

The team's manager, Guy Babin, had an office on the second floor, with a meeting room next to it. I'd been here exactly four times before: the day I came for talks about joining the team, the day I signed, two days after I scored my first hat trick for the club, and after I ended up in the media for being thrown out of a bar for fighting. That last time was admittedly the most uncomfortable – the fight was with a bloke who just happened to support our main rivals, and it looked bad.

In reality, that fight had nothing to do with what team I played for and everything to do with how he was speaking to his girlfriend. Unfortunately, that wasn't the take the press had, especially after he sold his story to a Sunday tabloid.

The door to the meeting room was open revealing Guy and my agent, sitting opposite each other, a huge, polished rosewood desk in between them. They were both laughing.

Until they saw me come in.

"Rowan. Good of you to be on time."

Only Guy Babin could make being on time sound like you were late.

I looked at Rhys, the man I paid to have my back. He folded his arms and sat back in his chair, expression grim. He had a suit on too, which made me take a deep inhalation. A cleansing breath, something our yoga instructor would be proud of.

Shit was about to hit the fan, and that fan was about to spread it all over me.

I sat down next to Rhys, bracing myself, not sure what to say. There was no point going on the defensive – that would just make me sound guilty. Or more guilty than I actually was.

"We have a problem." Guy didn't sit back. He didn't look relaxed, but he did look tanned.

I fucking hoped he hadn't come back off his holiday to wherever it was just to deal with this.

The door opened again, and Genevieve Casson, our Head of Player Support waltzed in, looking like she'd just stepped out of a modelling shoot. "So sorry I'm late. I had to deal with a call from the press." She sent a look my way. Something that was obviously my fault.

"Not an issue."

Clearly Guy didn't have the same standards about tardiness with her.

I glanced at Rhys again, who just shook his head, opened his mouth a few times and then closed it, as if he didn't have the words to express how utterly I'd disappointed him.

If we'd been elsewhere, I'd have laughed – Rhys was only a couple of years older than me. We'd played on the same football team back when we were kids in Newcastle, only he'd ended up shattering his knee coming off a skateboard, so he'd found another way to be involved in the game.

Guy's gaze was back on me, his eyes piercing. "Rowan, the last two days have been something of a shit-show. Since Saturday morning, I've had phone calls and emails asking me for comments about the story in the press, and the photos of you in the pool with the young lady have added an additional layer of difficulty. We have to look at how this situation is managed."

He wasn't wrong, apart from the young lady part. There had been nothing lady-like about the girl in the pool, whose name I'd only found out when I'd seen the picture on social media, but she had been all woman.

I didn't smile at the memory. I wished it hadn't happened.

"I had no idea Jade was going to go to the press." Which was the truth. We'd split at the end of the season when I'd gotten tired of her being so fame hungry. There were more photos of me on her Instagram than there were on mine, and the pressure from her to spend all of my free time doing stuff that involved being seen.

"I did warn you." Rhys always liked to say *I told you so*, usually with a big shit-eating grin on his ugly face, which he was managing to hide right now under the pretence of being professional.

There was no point responding. Jade had made up a story to sell, painting herself in the light she wanted to be seen in, casting me as the villain. I'd read it at stupid o'clock this morning, when I'd been woken by Rhys' assistant telling me I had to get to the stadium ground for this meeting. When I'd asked why, she'd told me to Google myself.

I'd ignored the media while we were on holiday. I hired someone to manage my social media accounts, adding the odd post when it was something more personal, and even though my season had been a hundred-percenter, after ten years as a professional footballer, I'd learned not to read pundits' opinions in the press.

Which meant this morning had been a bit of a surprise.

"Rowan's solicitor is involved already. We're researching if we can sue Ms Young. The timing of the other photos are unfortunate." Rhys reached under the table and pinched what he could of the skin on my thigh hard – a sign to shut the fuck up.

I had no idea my solicitor was involved, clearly something else Rhys was taking care of.

Rhys continued without missing a beat, "But this is all solvable, and we can use it to our advantage."

He was trying to gloss over it.

Guy stared at me in a way that made me feel he was

analysing my soul. "You should pursue it with Ms Young and the paper. You do need to defend your image on this one, Rowan. Goals and assists aren't going to be enough to clear up the image you now have." His accent sounded even more French than usual. "Genevieve, where are you up to with the media?"

Pretty green eyes looked up from the tablet in front of her. "The party line is that Rowan was single – Jade doing a tell-all has actually helped in that case – and entitled to enjoy himself, and that he's also entitled to his privacy." Her eyes narrowed. "Having sex with a woman on a sun lounger in full view probably wasn't your wisest move though."

I rubbed my forehead. "It was a private party. I didn't know her friend was going to take photos and post them."

"That's the problem, Rowan, you can never know when someone's going to do that. You were our record signing, you're on our record wages. We've taught you to always think the worst of people who you don't know well, or can't be vouched for, until you know them better. You're not stupid, but the holiday photos are damaging to your image, as is Jade's interview. We have damage control to do." Guy's jaw stiffened and his eyes had that dark gleam to them that usually made me want to stay well away.

I shrugged. "I understand what you've said – I have shit taste in women and I didn't make a good choice at the party." No point in trying to bullshit my way through that.

Genevieve shook her head. "How can you have sex in front of other people? Never mind, you're a footballer. Therefore, you have a whole different set of rules."

She was right. Money, fame and adoration were a toxic combination. When you heard fans chanting your name in the stadium, saw your name on banners and shirts, encountered women making themselves available for you when you wanted, you couldn't be untouched by it. For a kid who grew up playing footy on the fields of Newcastle, whose mam couldn't afford to buy him new boots, it was a lot.

"I apologise on behalf of all footballers. What damage has been done?" I had the sense not to argue with her. You didn't argue with Genevieve.

"There's questions in the press whether you can handle the pressure of your price tag – but that's been on and off since you joined us." She checked her tablet. "A lot of backlash from fans about your behaviour on holiday – 'you're paid to be an example', which you are." She looked up at me, still glaring. "And a lot of negativity from women's groups following on from Jade's interview and the photographs. That's not what you need. Or what the club needs."

I took another deep breath. She was right. Manchester Athletic portrayed itself as being family friendly and a community-based club. Rory Baines, the owner, had invested not only in the campus, but the surrounding area, regenerating what had been a run-down, historically industrial area of the city, only the industry wasn't there anymore. Families were encouraged, the club had a ton of junior football schools for kids too.

"We have a few weeks until the season starts…"

That wasn't a sentence I was going to let Genevieve finish. "We have one week until pre-season training starts. You know how intensive that gets. Whatever you're about to say, keep that in mind."

Rhys' hand patted my back. "I'm sure Genevieve has

taken all that into consideration. We all have an interest in how you're perceived – just like your sponsors."

I wanted to tell Rhys that I didn't give a shit about my sponsors, but that wasn't true. My mam had brought me up on her own – me, my little brother, and our younger sister. My wages and the income from sponsorships made sure the life we'd lived back then was just a bad dream, and the future, especially my sister's, was comfortable. She had severe learning difficulties and required round the clock support. While our mam was heavily involved, she couldn't manage on her own, so the first thing my income did was provide for them. I had no intention of their quality of life changing, unless it was for the better.

I swallowed again. "What's your plan?"

Genevieve glanced at Guy. She'd probably not had chance to run this past him yet. "There are two options. You lie low and keep out of the media, hoping it blows over, go legal with Jade. But that will take longer and after the issue with the fight last season, where we used that tactic, it's going to leave you open to a lot more speculation and scrutiny. We've already had journos digging for comments on your sister, and your ex before Jade." Genny had always managed to stop the media from digging into my family's background. I had no idea how. Maybe she baked them cakes or sent choirs round to serenade them; I didn't know how. I was just grateful.

"What's the second option?" Rhys leaned forward.

She glanced again at Guy. "We work proactively. Get Rowan in front of the cameras but in situations that promote the image we all want him to have. I do know how intensive pre-season training can be and we won't be looking at cutting into any of that."

Guy nodded. "And if you're busy with this, you won't have a chance to get in any more trouble."

"What do you want me to do?"

The look Genevieve gave Rhys did not fill me with joy.

"The answer's no."

Rhys laughed. "You don't have an answer to give. You're doing it. End of. And I think it's a great idea."

"Because you'll have something to take the piss out of me about for the next five years."

"I've already got plenty of things to take the piss out of, Ro. This is just extra."

He helped himself to coffee from the machine in my kitchen that I'd never learned to work. Rhys was an expert at using it. Adding the beans, knowing which setting to use for the perfect coffee, and just the right amount, so he could squeeze his milk in. Precision. Very Rhys.

"I'm not doing it. Anything – I can do the kids football school by myself, and the hospital stuff. Jones doesn't need to be involved." I swore this was a punishment.

Rhys sat down at the table that came with the house. Since I'd transferred to Athletic, I'd been living in one of the properties the club owned, renting it off them while I found my own place. My contract was five years, with various options to extend, so buying somewhere was at the top of my to do list and probably something I should be doing this week before pre-season started.

I was about to get a new housemate too. Ryan O'Connell had signed for us last week from Arsenal, and I'd been told he was moving in here since security and all that shit was at its best.

I'd played against him plenty of times but didn't know him. We'd both been capped by England, but never in the same squad. With the World Cup next summer, we'd both be looking to be involved, so playing together at club level would hopefully boost us both.

Rhys had been my agent since I was twenty-one, and my previous one had tried shafting me with a contract that even a nursery kid would've known was corrupt. Rhys had been twenty-three and an apprentice agent. I'd been his first big name. But unlike the first guy, he had more than money as his motivation – he'd spent more time growing up at my house than his own.

Right now, Rhys was far too fucking amused for his own good.

"It's one week coaching kids, which you're good at. You never know, you might actually get along this time." He sniggered, reminding me of the fourteen-year-old version of him who caught me kissing a girl round the back of the garages.

"Dee Jones hates me." I took a mouthful of the protein smoothie I'd made myself, thinking about the not-so-lovely Dee. "She thinks she's Miss Perfect, so she's going to fucking love me being in trouble."

Dee was captain of Manchester Athletic's Women's Team. We played the same position – attacking midfield – and we both wore the number ten shirt.

No love was lost between us.

Rhys grinned. I could almost see the thought bubbles bursting from his head. He'd been there a few months back when Miss Dee and I had exchanged a few words about her parking in my space.

"I'll remember to wear ear plugs. And bring a first aid kit for after she's finished chewing you up." Rhys finished his coffee, which must've been hot enough to take off a layer of his mouth. "What did you do to piss her off? Have you figured it out yet?"

I had no idea what I'd done to earn the wrath of Dee Jones. I hadn't slept with her, I'd never said anything negative about women's football – I actually thought it was more skilful than men's football most of the time – and I hadn't done anything to any of her teammates that I was aware of.

It wasn't the parking incident. She'd been unimpressed with me before that, a little like a raincloud that liked to piss on my parade whenever I had something to celebrate, to mix my metaphors.

I scored a brace, she'd get a hat-trick. I won man of the match, she ended up in team of the week. I bought a new car; she did an interview where she discussed how cars were killing furry animals.

"I was born."

Rhys banged down his coffee cup and headed back to the machine, choking on a laugh. "She's a nice person. We've got her as a client now."

"Really?"

He shook his head at me, turning on the coffee machine again and then heading to the fridge for more milk. "We do take on female clients, you know."

"I didn't mean that. Just – *her*. She probably bathes in hand sanitiser to keep herself so squeaky clean." I finished the rest of my shake. "And you know I'd rather focus on pre-season than have to do all these appearances."

I saw his sigh, his chest rising, nose flaring slightly. "Rowan, you've fucked up. I know Jade was a bitch to go to the press, and I know half of what she said wasn't true – you didn't cheat, and you weren't partying all the time, but you did pretty much ignore her rather than just break up with her…"

"Until I did break it off."

"Yeah, well. She was desperate to be a WAG. Next time, listen to what I say and don't go there with women who're just after one thing. Men are so much more straight forward." He found a jug I didn't know I owned, filled it with milk and stuck it in the microwave. Clearly we were feeling classy today.

Rhys had come out when he was eighteen, not that he'd needed to. He'd never had a girlfriend, despite being scouted by a modelling agency, and had politely turned down every girl that had asked him out.

My mum inquired one day if he was going to ever go on a date with a girl called Katy, who lived across the road from us, and was always hanging around in the hope that Rhys would ask her out.

His response? *I'm actually interested in her brother.*

And that was that. Nothing more was said. And Rhys did end up dating her brother for about eighteen months.

"And Mexico – what the fuck were you thinking, Ro? I get you were on holiday, but you've been too much in the media. You've had your face everywhere. Fucking a girl on a sun lounger isn't classy, mate."

The microwave pinged.

I pushed the glass away. He had a point. The media loved a story about WAGs, footballers wives and girlfriends. Some magazines would devote whole pages to them.

"Please tell me only alcohol was involved."

"Only alcohol was involved. I still don't touch anything else. You know that." Rhys' dad had been a user. Coke had been his drug of choice.

He nodded. "Good. I just needed to hear it." He sat back down, coffee to his liking. "You need to manage your mouth with Dee. There's been a ton of shit about how you treat women after what Jade said, and those photos."

"I know. I will."

Somehow.

Maybe with superglue.

Carry on reading Penalty Kiss

Sleighed

Zack Maynard rubbed at the thick stubble that had accumulated since that morning and debated which incompetence he should yell about first. He was spoilt for choice given that one of his staff had failed to lock a door that should be kept locked and bolted at all times, and a resident had gone exploring. His cousin, Jake, had delivered a truck full of alpacas to the field next to Severton Sunlight Care and Nursing Home and had neglected to tell his farmhand to ensure the gate was shut. And the world's slowest builders had seemingly been employed to take as much time as possible to erect the extension to the dementia care unit and entertainment hall, and the words coming out of the site manager's mouth were not the ones he wanted to hear.

"We're looking at mid-January."

Zack stuffed his hands in his coat pockets. "I'm sorry. Can you repeat that?"

"It's unlikely to be finished before mid-Jan. I realise that's a bit of a pain…"

His accent was broad, thickly Northern and Zack knew he needed to be careful not to mimic it.

"You realise there's a clause in the contract if the building wasn't fit for purpose on December twentieth so we can use it for Christmas dinner?" He managed to ignore an alpaca that was lingering nearby. He was going to kill his fucking cousin.

Jez Hammond, site manager non-extraordinaire, nodded and made a noise that could be interpreted as an agreement. "I realise that, as does the company. However, there was some issues with laying the foundations that's slowed us down and we've encountered a problem with labour."

Zack looked at the site, the half-finished shell of a building and the surrounding rubble. "What's the issue with labour?" He could see maybe four men at work and even though he wasn't an expert on construction, even he knew that this wasn't enough.

"The usual shortage. Contractors, you know?"

The alpaca made an odd snorting noise and edged closer, its mouth slightly hung open, displaying large teeth.

Jake was going to die.

And then possibly be used as alpaca food.

"I don't know. I manage a care home for the elderly. Working with builders, electricians, plasterers, plumbers —*that* isn't my speciality. It's what I'm paying *you* for. And right now, I can count the number of people working on this project on *one* hand."

The alpaca came closer. It nudged Jez's arm and made a strange sound again. A rather excited sound. One Zack was wary of. He was going to fucking kill Jake, even if it would upset his aunt.

"I'm doing what I can, son. We were running behind, but we should've been done in time for Christmas so you could use the hall for your do, but the lass at the hotel on the hill has paid over the odds for labourers so we're down. If these bloody schools would stop encouraging kids to go to university to study bleeding Harry Potter and get them in proper work instead, we wouldn't be so far behind." Jez patted his shapely beer belly.

Zack's words froze in his mouth. Not because the temperature was skating lower than normal for this time of year, but because the alpaca's expression had turned to one of sheer delight as it started to sink its teeth into the thick fleece of the site manager's coat. It was an action Zack could only attribute to fate.

"Holy fuck!" Jez yelled, yanking his arm away. But the alpaca's teeth were firmly sunk into the material. "Get this bastard animal off my bleeding arm? I thought this was a care home, not a freaking petting zoo with sadistic fucking beasts." He carried on pulling his arm away from the set jaws of the alpaca.

"I'm going to feed Jake limb by limb to his new fucking pets," Zack muttered under his breath, trying to entice the alpaca away.

He saw Lee Barnes, Jake's farmhand trying to round up the rest of the escaped animals and shouted him over. Lee strode over, taking his own sweet time. He was dressed in just a T-shirt and ripped jeans, oblivious to the cold.

"We have a situation." Zack pointed at the animal. "Please let my cousin know he's going to be in a situation later. Where the hell have these creatures come from? And why?"

Lee shrugged. He was a man of few words at the best of times, preferring to communicate through the set of drums he hit most weekends. He leaned over to the creature and blew at its nose. The alpaca gave a gentle snort and released its death chomp.

"Sorry about that." Lee didn't look that sorry. "I'll get rounding them up."

"Make sure you do." Zack turned back towards Jez. "Why can't you stop your contractors from working on the hotel and get them back down here?"

Jez rubbed at his arm. "We don't have the budget to pay them what the lass up there has agreed to. And they'll only be a couple of weeks, then they'll come back down here and finish off. I'm sorry, Zack, but there ain't much more I can do."

"I'll see about upping the budget." Zack rubbed his face. He hadn't slept well the night before, which wasn't unusual, but he could do with climbing into bed in one of the unoccupied rooms—or hell, even May Pearson's room because she didn't move from her sofa in front of the TV—and collapsing for an hour or six. "Find out how much more she's paying them and let me know."

Jez shook his head. "But then you'll be stuck paying that rate until the job's done. It's not just extra cash over two weeks, you'll end up going right over. If I were you, I'd hang on till the lass has had her work done. It's only an extension and from what I hear it's pretty straightforward." He looked to where Lee was herding the alpacas, apparently turning into the animal whisperer. "How do you think those animals taste?"

"Not as good as revenge will when I get hold of Jake."

Zack felt the heat smother him as he entered the care home. It was always warmer than he liked but he wasn't important here: the sixty-three residents were, and if you were elderly or not in the best of health then heat was important.

Unless you were Mr McNeild. In which case you had every window open, plus the door to your patio propped wide and a fan on. It was a room where Zack would find refuge on a warm summer's day, and maybe at the end of a shift partake in something to take the edge off. Mr McNeild still had every one of his marbles, and possibly a few of someone else's. The only thing he didn't have was mobility, although Zack had seen him race across the bowling green to chase off the odd cat more than once before now. And he was pretty speedy then.

"I heard there's a delay on the ballroom."

He stopped in his tracks, not sure if the dulcet tones of Veronica Moore were welcome right now or not. He also wasn't sure how she knew, given that he'd only just found out himself.

"Afternoon, Gran," he said, spinning round to see the small but sturdy old lady he'd known pretty much all his life. He'd been in the same primary school class as her granddaughter, Vanessa, and had felt the power of Gran's right hand on the back of his head when he'd tried sneaking out a dirty magazine from the post office that she'd always run.

"I notice you didn't put the 'good' on the front of afternoon there, Zack Maynard," Gran said. "I also notice you look like you developed a new way to murder someone and dispose of the body without being caught."

He found himself smiling. "Jake. And his fu… flipping alpaca monsters. And that stupid site manager. Plus, the idiot woman who bought the old building and is trying to set up a boutique hotel in Severton." His smile faded, knowing that the list could continue. His mood darkened to the same colour as the river during a night-time storm.

Gran eyed him. "So where do you start? I'm not sure your dad would thank you if he lost Jake any time soon. Best let him live a little longer and maybe stuff his exhaust with manure like you did last time."

"He's still checking his exhaust every time he takes the Range Rover out. It didn't help that Scott stuffed it full of mashed potatoes two weeks after the manure," Zack said.

He truly loved his family. His two brothers, Scott and Alex and his cousins, Jake and Rayah, were the reason he'd come back to Severton after working in Manchester for three years once he'd graduated. They'd all drifted back to their hometown, even after swearing as teenagers that they were going to leave and never return, but the small town pulled them back home like a magnet.

Gran nodded sagely. "He never was as stupid as he made out. Have you met Sorrell?"

"Sorrell?" Zack squinted. "What's sorrel? I thought it was a herb?"

"It is. But it's also an unusual name. It's the woman who's turning the old care home into a boutique hotel. I'm having to start stocking up on more knick-knacks in the post office to cater for all the overnighters it's going to bring in."

Zack rolled his eyes and walked with Gran down to the main lounge. It was a brand-new purpose-built building with one wing dedicated to residents who had dementia. He was proud of it: three years of researching, planning and persuading the local council for permits had resulted in an environment he knew was the best it could be. And he was passionate about his job. As a social worker, he'd specialised in care for the elderly; now he got to be hands-on, making sure that the care they received was as good as it could be; as good as they deserved.

"I thought it was a man who bought it." He hadn't paid too much attention to the sale of the old building where the care home had previously been housed. His uncle, Jake's dad, was the conglomerate, and he oversaw the larger financial operations.

"Hmmm." Gran raised an eyebrow. "I think it was a man involved initially. Not sure of the finer details—Davey would have those."

Gran, of course, knew his uncle, and his father. Hell, she knew everyone and probably had more information on them than they had on themselves. Rumour had it that she was the great-great granddaughter of a witch and she'd inherited those powers, but this was a rumour from when he'd been ten and contemplating pinching sweets from the post office and his mother had caught him.

"All I know is that they got it for a steal." Zack did a quick check of what was going on around them and whether there were any more alpacas hovering. "And because of that, my budget got lowered. Whoever did the negotiating isn't getting a drink bought from me."

Gran shook her head. "You've done a good job, Zacky-boy. It's a fine place to visit and I can see from how Glenda's doing that it's a fine place to live. I've had a really good chat with her today—she even asked about Vanessa. Mind you, next time she might be shouting at me for the time when I took Frankie Morrow round the back of the sheds when she liked him."

Zack decided that by not asking, he wouldn't have to bleach his brain later. Glenda Roberts was a childhood—and adulthood—friend of Gran's who had started with dementia when she was in in her late fifties. For a few years, she managed to remain in her home, thanks to her friends and family and the people of Severton, but after she'd gone missing from home overnight, causing a mass search party to hunt for her, the decision had been made to move her somewhere she could get the support she was starting to need.

And that had led to the birth of the Sunlight Wing, a specialist part of the care home for people with dementia and it had grown to the extent that Severton Sunlight Care Home needed to grow physically as its reputation spread —hence the move to a purpose built campus where the dementia wing had specific rooms set up from various eras where people could find the familiar items from their living memories.

"That's what keeps it entertaining here," Zack said. "You never know what your day is going to bring: crockery being thrown at you, impromptu parties and your cousin walking down the corridor with an alpaca... What the fuck, Jake?" The volume of Zack's voice increased so that old Peter Musgraves who used hearing aids and always had his TV sound on full put his hands over his ears.

The alpaca made a noise that sounded like a disgruntled cluck and shot Jake a look that could've killed him, which would've saved Zack the trouble.

"One of your staff left the door open again that leads on to the field. Apparently there's another one roaming around the Netherwood wing." Jake patted the alpaca on the back of its neck.

"Does that mean it's shitting all over the corridors?" Zack folded his arms. "Where have these creatures come from, Jake? Why have thirty odd alpacas just landed in one of the fields? Shouldn't they be in South America somewhere?"

Jake shook his head and gave the lopsided grin that had once persuaded several girls to go behind the same sheds where Gran had taken Frankie Morrow. "They don't shit everywhere. They're really clean animals—they all use the same spot in a field to do their business, which is more than you can say for a lot of humans. And I got them from a place in Halifax. The farmer was moving to France and needed to get rid of them in a hurry. I offered to take them off his hands."

Zack groaned. "What's Dad said?"

Jake shrugged. "Not much. Think he's more concerned with Rayah."

"What's she done?"

"Spent a night in the cells. She's in work today, so she's fine."

Zack shook his head. His only female relative apart from his mother had always been a wild child, despite now being the town's nursery school teacher. She was great with little kids, mainly because she hadn't mastered adulting yet.

Gran laughed. "She wasn't arrested, so you needn't worry."

"I'm not worried about my sister." Jake looked to the heavens as if praying for sanity. "She can take care of herself. I'm more concerned with the cop she persuaded to let her into the police station overnight and his gullibility."

"Holy fuck," Zack said. "Sorry for swearing, Gran."

"What about apologising to me, young Zachariah? She's heard it all before! My ears are sensitive!" May Pearson said as she doddered past on her walking frame, cursing quietly under her breath.

"Never changed, that woman." Gran shook her head. "I'll leave you to it. I'm going to see about taking the post down with me. Hopefully catch the van before he buggers off to the depot." She strutted off, quicker than anticipated, leaving the cousins and an alpaca watching her and shaking their heads.

"Are you getting that thing out of here or are we finding it a room and a suitable health package?" Zack said, aware that the alpaca was making another snorting noise and now head-butting Jake's shoulder.

"You could use him as a therapy pet," Jake said. "But I'm not sure he could cope with continual reruns of *Love Boat* and *Baywatch*."

Zack snorted. "Like you would ever turn off *Baywatch*. I remember when your Saturday evenings were spent studying those red swimsuits and what filled them."

Jake nodded, not even attempting to deny it. "At least I moved on. I'm pretty sure Alex still spends most evenings doing that. Maybe he should save paying for the electricity and watch with Mr McNeild. Come with me while I put Emery here back in the field."

Zack watched his cousin shift the pack of alpacas towards the shed that would be their night time quarters, away from the care home. He did it with ease and without any apprehension around the animals, which Zack understood. He'd grown up on his father's farm and had worked the land and looked after the animals, but neither he nor his two brothers had been interested in carrying it on. Luckily for their father, Jake had. Stupidly bright and ridiculously charismatic, he'd only agreed to go to university because he'd been told he wouldn't be allowed to get a job running the family farm without a degree, so he'd spent three years passing modules easily and sleeping his way around Sheffield.

Zack had been there too, studying social policy and planning to be a social worker in a big city where he could help children in crisis, but he'd ended up broken-hearted and working in adult social care instead, trying to avoid his ex who was with children's social services. And then his uncle had needed a manager for Sunlight so he'd followed Jake home.

"It's a shitter about the hotel manager nicking all your builders," Jake said after he'd locked the shed and headed back to Zack. It was near to the end of October and dark already, even though it wasn't yet dinner time. "I heard in the pub she'd asked around to find out how much they were getting per day from working on Sunlight and then offered fifty percent more."

Zack felt his shoulders tense. "She offered them what?"

Jake shrugged. "I heard it was fifty percent per day more than what they were getting. It's only for three weeks though and then they're back on your job. It isn't the end of the world."

"No, it's the end of fucking Christmas." Zack started to walk away from Sunlight and the fields. He didn't need to confirm with Jake where they were going, it was the same place they went most Fridays: the Buffer Stop for a beer, before going home to shower and head to Scott's bar for food and drinks and, occasionally, a woman.

"That's a bit Scrooge-like."

Zack shook his head. "We needed the hall finished to be able to hold the Christmas dinners. There's not another room big enough. When we were in Litton Manor, there was the ballroom."

"So what'll you do?"

"I don't know. We've more residents than last year as it is. I could see about using one of the hotels towards Manchester or Sheffield, but I'm not sure some of the residents would cope with the travelling. Seriously, the only answer I've got at the moment is beer and tequila. Or having words with the hotel princess. Stupid idea anyway, setting up a boutique hotel in Severton. Who's going to stay here?" Zack pushed his fingers through his thick hair. He knew it would be stuck up in every direction by now, due to alpacas, site managers, and open doors, plus an unknown hotel manager, but he didn't care.

"I think it's a good idea. In summer, the tourist season's booming. Especially now the steam trains are running up here. Scott's considering buying the property next door and expanding the bar and there's talk of a festival being held next year. The town's growing again, and not just the over seventy sector." Jake shrugged strong shoulders. "I'm gutted we didn't think of turning the Manor into a hotel."

"Because you would've given up your sheep and cows to run it?" Zack knew full well the answer to that was no.

"Fuck off. It's your round."

Zack stopped, looking towards the road they'd just passed, the one that led to Litton Manor. "Actually, I'm going to have a word first about poaching my builders."

Jake groaned. "Really? What's it going to achieve? You'll just piss her off. Leave it and let's get to the pub. I'm dying for a beer."

"It's go now, or go when I've finished at Scott's and I'm telling you, now is the better option. Doesn't she realise that she's alienating herself by blackmailing my builders to go to her? She'll need the support of local businesses to be successful…" Zack carried on talking as he paced through the gates towards the imposing building, sheltered by old, tall oak trees and manicured shrubbery.

"This isn't the best idea you've ever had," Jake said. "You smell of disinfectant and I smell of alpacas and I'm pretty sure I have straw in my hair."

"Jake, it's some crony old woman who's probably only ever close to a man when she's trying to hex him. She's not going to be the source of your next fucking blow job," Zack said and banged heavily on the door.

There was no sign of life. If she had poached his builders, they were all packed up for the night, which given it was Friday, didn't surprise him.

"Leave it, Zack. She's probably out for the night. Or gone away for the weekend. Would you want to stay in this place on your own?" Jake said, turning back towards the road.

Zack knocked again, swearing under his breath. He was pissed and he needed someone to argue with. She—Sorrell, or whatever stupid name it was—would fill that need.

"She's not in. Let's leave it and go get that beer. Seriously, I'm parched and I want to go home and get ready. Amy Canning's mate from Sheffield is meant to be out tonight," Jake said.

Zack looked up to the heavens and prayed once more for the patience to not use his cousin for animal feed. "Stop thinking with your dick all the time."

"Just because you've taken your vows to become a monk."

Zack banged again and a light flicked on.

"Just a moment. The lock's a bit stiff…" a light, tuneful voice called back.

"Push the door to when you turn," he shouted back. He'd battled with that door for eight years.

"Oh." There was a click and then a squeal as the door opened. "That's helped. Thank you. How did you know?"

The woman in front of him was not an old crone but she did look like she could hex men, just not with spells. She was slight, just to his shoulder in bare feet, and had long straight red hair that fell down her back. Her face was dusted with white, probably from scraping plaster and there was a piece of wallpaper stuck to the side of her head that she was completely unaware of.

Zack was sure Jake had let out a low whistle behind him, probably because she was wearing a thin grey vest and the cold air was doing nothing to help the fact that she was braless.

"You've poached my builders." He stepped forward over the threshold. "You've ruined Christmas for a hundred senior citizens and their families."

She folded her arms, which did nothing to distract his eyes from her chest. He glanced down once and then caught her smiling viciously. "I have a hotel to get ready for a wedding in five weeks' time, otherwise I'm screwed. I need builders."

"Then find some. But not mine. I have an entire building that's only half done. They've left their jobs because Miss-Flashy-Pants has flashed money at them."

"It's a bonus if they get the job down in three weeks. Then you can have them back! Nice to meet you by the way."

"The pleasure's all yours, sweetheart. You want to run a business in this town, you need to have some respect for your fellow residents. Poaching workers like you've done is not the way to do things. When your hotel's out of food for your guests' breakfasts and you want to serve local, don't bother coming to my family's farm to fill their plates." Zack wanted to kick something. Forget the pub, after this he needed to go to the gym or something and lift heavy.

Sorrell's arms dropped from her chest and her hands landed on her hips. "If I'd known how rude the people were who lived around here, I'd have found somewhere else for my hotel. Maybe I need signs up telling people to beware of the local residents, not to watch out for cows on the road!"

"Or alpacas," Jake said quietly.

Sorrell frowned, looking confused.

"Shut up, Jake." Zack glared. "Maybe you should think about stopping your pet project here and finding somewhere else for your fancy hotel." He gave a look that would've murdered anything slightly timid. "And you have Mrs Gibbons' wallpaper in your hair."

She lifted a hand, small fingers searching for the offending item.

"Come on, Jake, let's go." Zack heard Jake mutter something and start to step away. "By the way, the key for the cellar door looks the same as the one for the small outhouse. I forgot to write it down in the pack."

He turned around and walked off, refusing to think about long red hair and plump lips.

Carry on reading Sleighed*!*

Engagement Rate

Engagement Rate is the first in the Callaghan Green series. Here's a taste!

Read the rest free in Kindle Unlimited or download from the Amazon store.

CHAPTER ONE - JACKSON

I'd never considered that watching a woman do pull ups was a way to get rid of jet lag. This woman was wearing a sports bra that did nothing to hide the shape of perfect breasts and exposed a toned, smooth stomach; her yoga pants outlining long, long legs that would look fucking amazing around me as I thrust into her.

But sleep deprived, jet lagged and being travel-fresh wasn't the best way to be caught staring at the dark-haired mystery currently working out in the gym. I was a professional: a lawyer and a businessman. Or at least I tried to give that impression at first. Staring at her tits was not the best start.

I kept a change of gym gear at work: trainers and

shorts, but today I hadn't bothered with a vest as I didn't think anyone else was likely to be around for an hour or so, unless Seph, my youngest brother turned up to train. Deadlifts, bicep curls, tricep extensions and a chest press too heavy to be doing without a spotter took my focus away from obsessing exactly how her long dark hair would look wrapped around my fist.

I had missed this space in the past three weeks; it was my retreat, my sanctuary. The place where I could be me and not just the man who ran his family's law firm. I focused on the music that was blaring out of the speakers, and tried to stop staring at the woman who I should probably know. She was on the other side of the room, my main view of her via a mirror, the perfect place to creep at her, which I gave up trying not to do.

"Fuck me," she said, as she half collapsed to the ground from the pull up bar, shaking her arms.

I managed to bite my tongue, stopping myself from offering to do just that. I watched her as she began another set of pull ups, waiting for her to realise I was there. She was tall, around 5'9, with dark hair pulled into one of those messy bun things; all lean muscle and the best pair of tits I'd seen for years. She was pretty: large blue eyes and high cheekbones.

I turned my back to head for the showers, needing to escape. I had no idea who she was – Maxwell tore through secretaries like he did girlfriends only with less pleasure – so she could've been a temp or equally the marketing woman we'd recently hired. Either way, she didn't need to know about the tent she'd caused in my shorts.

"Sorry," I heard her say and I turned back, my neck twisting like an owl's and my brain trying to conjure up images of Granny Callaghan without her teeth in. "I was oblivious to anyone else being in here. Sorry if you heard me swear like an Irish navvy." She massaged her hands and I wasn't sure whether it was a nervous reaction or they were hurting from the grip she had to use to do the pull ups.

I shrugged, the images of Granny doing their job. "Not like I never use those words. I'm Jackson Callaghan. I don't think we've met before."

She stepped forward, beads of sweat glistening on her skin. I was conjuring up several different ways to get her equally as sweaty. "Vanessa Moore. I'm from Cole Henderson. Claire said it was okay to use the gym down here…" She looked a little nervous, although I was pretty sure she knew who I was, even though I looked a lot different half naked than the photos on the website. Shirts and suits went a long way to covering up most of my tattoos and I generally looked more presentable when my hair was not tied up in a shitty man bun and my scruff was tamed instead of looking as if garden birds were nesting there. She was the marketing consultant. I congratulated myself on remembering.

"It's absolutely fine while you're working with us. How've you found the first few days?" Vanessa seemed to have managed my grump of a mood even better than the weights. She was close enough now for me to see that she wasn't wearing a scrap of make-up, her cheeks red from the exercise and blue eyes bright.

God forbid she was a morning person.

"Good. There's a lot to do to rebrand and get everything ready for your father's retirement ball but the firm's got a clear direction and ethos so it's volume of tasks rather than having to come up with the creative." She tightened the pony tail and I sensed again that she was nervous of me. I didn't mind that – at thirty-four I was young to have this sort of role, managing and directing an extremely profitable and noteworthy law firm, so I didn't need anyone to think I was a soft-touch.

"How about staff? I hope Kirsty's been accommodating."

Vanessa's eyes dropped to my chest and I couldn't resist the urge to very slightly flex my muscles. Her cheeks grew redder and I smirked. Also at thirty-four I was too much of a child to always be professional, especially when a pretty lady was standing in front of me. "It's different for her. She's not used to someone else directing. But she's got a decent skill set and it's a case of trying to develop her a little more so once we've finished you've got a good employee."

This confirmed some of my concerns. "Look, Vanessa." I didn't even bother with the formality of calling her Ms Moore, partly because she could be married, partly because I had enough stuffy clients to be uber-polite to. "Here probably isn't the best place for this conversation and I probably smell of planes as well as sweat. How about we get showers and I'll spot us breakfast? We can discuss your ideas and how they align with the brief so far. And probably introduce ourselves."

"I can do that," she gave me a slight nod. "I'll leave a note for Kirsty to let her know I might be running a few minutes late to meet her." There was a smile that turned into a grin, with, God forbid, a dimple. "I have a huge appetite, by the way, and I don't do prissy food."

"Noted." I shot back a smile back. "I don't do prissy anything. See you in reception in – 30 minutes?" I wondered how much time she needed to shower and dress. I'd had two longish relationships in the past, both ran their natural course and we grew apart - no fault of either party - and both women took forever to get ready.

"Sure," she nodded, her eyes drifting down to my chest again and I struggled not to preen. She headed to the female changing rooms and I tried to casually walk away, my mind totally conjuring up images of her naked in the shower with water pouring over those tits and all the ways I could help get her clean.

And then dirty again.

I showered quickly, turning the temperature onto Baltic cold to get rid of any lingering hardness in my cock. I needed to focus on work and getting involved with a contractor was not good business practice. Yes, she was beautiful and probably intelligent given she ran her own business but I'd need to find my relief elsewhere. Vanessa Moore was off-limits. So why the fuck was I taking her to breakfast?

Continue reading Engagement Rate here!

Also by Annie Dyer

The Callaghan Green Series

In Suggested Reading order (can be read as stand-alones)

Engagement Rate

What happens when a hook up leaves you hooked? Jackson Callaghan is the broody workaholic who isn't looking for love until he meets his new marketing executive? Meet the Callaghans in this first-in-series, steamy office romance.

White Knight

If you're in the mood for a second chance romance with an older brother's best friend twist, then look no further. Claire Callaghan guards her heart as well as her secrets, but Killian O'Hara may just be the man to take her heart for himself.

Compromising Agreements

Grumpy, bossy Maxwell Callaghan meets his match in this steamy enemies-lovers story. Mistaking Victoria Davies as being a quiet secretary is only Max's first mistake, but can she be the one to make this brooding Callaghan brother smile?

Between Cases

Could there be anything better than a book boyfriend who owns a bookstore? Payton Callaghan isn't sure; although giving up relationships when she might've just met The One is a dilemma she's facing in BETWEEN CASES, a meet-cute that'll have you swooning over Owen Anders.

Changing Spaces

Love a best friend's younger sister romance? Meet Eli, partner in the Callaghan Green law firm and Ava's Callaghan's steamy one-night stand that she just can't seem to keep as just one night. Independent, strong-willed and intelligent, can Eli be the man Ava wants?

Heat

Feeling hungry? Get a taste of this single dad, hot chef romance in HEAT. Simone Wood is a restaurant owner who loves to dance, she's just never found the right partner until her head chef Jack starts to teach her his rhythm. Problem is, someone's not happy with Simone, and their dance could be over before they've learned the steps.

Mythical Creatures

The enigmatic Callum Callaghan heads to Africa with the only woman who came close to taming his heart, in this steamy second-chance romance. Contains a beautifully broken alpha and some divinely gorgeous scenery in this tale that will make you both cry and laugh. HEA guaranteed.

Melted Hearts

Hot rock star? Enemies to lovers? Fake engagement? All of these ingredients are in this Callaghan Green novel. Sophie Slater is a businesswoman through and through but makes a pact with the devil – also known as Liam Rossi, newly retired Rockstar – to get the property she wants - one that just happens to be in Iceland. Northern lights, a Callaghan bachelor party, and a quickly picked engagement ring are key notes in this hot springs heated romance.

Evergreen

Christmas wouldn't be Christmas without any presents, and that's what's going to happen if Seph Callaghan doesn't get his act together. The Callaghan clan are together for Christmas, along with a positive pregnancy test from someone and several more surprises!

The Partnership

Seph Callaghan finally gets his HEA in this office romance. Babies, exes and a whole lot of smoulder!

The Green Family Series

The Wedding Agreement

Imogen Green doesn't do anything without thinking it through, and that includes offering to marry her old - very attractive - school friend, Noah Soames, who needs a wedding. The only problem is, their fauxmance might not be so fake, after all…

The Atelier Assignment

Dealing with musty paintings is Catrin Green's job. Dealing with a hot Lord who happens to be grumpy AF isn't. But that's what she's stuck with for three months. Zeke's daughter is the only light in her days, until she finds a way to make Zeke smile. Only this wasn't part of the assignment.

The Romance Rehearsal

Maven Green has managed to avoid her childhood sweetheart for more than a decade, but now he's cast as her leading man in the play she's directing. Anthony was the boy who had all her firsts; will he be her last as well?

The Imperfect Proposal

Shay Green doesn't expect his new colleague to walk in on him when he's mid-kiss in a stockroom. He also doesn't expect his new colleague to be his wife. The wife he married over a decade ago in Vegas and hasn't seen since

Puffin Bay

Puffin Bay

Amelie started a new life on a small Welsh island, finding peace and new beginnings. What wasn't in the plan was the man buying the building over the road. She was used to dealing with arrogant tourists, but this city boy was enough to have her want to put her hands around his neck, on his chest, and maybe somewhere else too...

Manchester Athletic FC

Penalty Kiss

Manchester Athletic's bad boy needs taming, else his football career could be on the line. Pitched with women's football's role model pin up, he has pre-season to sort out his game - on and off the field.

Hollywood Ball

One night. It didn't matter who she was, or who he was, because tomorrow they'd both go back to their lives. Only hers wasn't that ordinary.

What she didn't know, was neither was his.

Heart Keeper

Single dad. Recent widow. Star goal keeper.

Manchester Athletic's physio should keep her hands to herself outside of her treatment room, but that's proving tough. What else is tough is finding two lines on that pregnancy test...

Target Man

Jesse Sullivan is Manchester Athletic's Captain Marvel. He keeps his private life handcuffed to his bed, locked behind a non-disclosure agreement. Jesse doesn't do relationships – not until he meets his teammate's – and best friend's – sister.

Red Heart Card

It's tough being talented and from a footballing legacy, every move you make is under scrutiny. Jude has always been the spoilt baby of the team, which is why he needs to keep what he's up to in private, under wraps.

Severton Search and Rescue

Sleighed

Have a change of scenery and take a trip to a small town. Visit Severton, in Sleighed; this friends-to-lovers romantic suspense will capture your heart as much as Sorrell Slater steals Zack Maynard's.

Stirred

If enemies-to-lovers is your manna, then you'll want to stay in Severton for Stirred. Keren Leigh and Scott Maynard have been at daggers drawn for years, until their one-night ceasefire changes the course of their lives forever.

Smoldered

Want to be saved by a hot firefighter? Rayah Maynard's lusted over Jonny Graham ever since she came back to town. Jonny's prioritised his three children over his own love life since his wife died, but now Rayah's teaching more than just his daughter – she's teaching him just how hot their flames can burn.

·Shaken

Abby Walker doesn't exist. Hiding from a gang she suspects is involved in the disappearance of her sister, Severton is where she's taken refuge. Along with her secrets, she's hiding her huge crush on local cop, Alex Maynard. But she isn't the only one with secrets. Alex can keep her safe, but can he also take care of her heart?

Sweetened

Enemies? Friends? Could be lovers? All Jake Maynard knows is that Lainey Green is driving him mad, and he really doesn't like that she managed to buy the farm he coveted from under his nose. All's fair in love and war, until events in Severton take a sinister turn.

Standalone Romance

Love Rises

Two broken souls, one hot summer. Anya returns to her childhood island home after experiencing a painful loss. Gabe escapes to the same place, needing to leave his life behind, drowning in guilt. Neither are planning on meeting the other, but when they do, from their grief, love rises. Only can it be more than a summer long?

Bartender

The White Island, home of hedonism, heat and holidays. Jameson returns to her family's holiday home on Ibiza, but doesn't expect to charmed by a a bartender, a man with an agenda other than just seduction.

Tarnished Crowns Trilogy

Lovers. Liars. Traitors. Thieves. We were all of these. Political intrigue, suspense and seduction mingle together in this intricate and steamy royal romance trilogy.

Chandelier

Grenade

Emeralds

Crime Fiction

We Were Never Alone

How Far Away the Stars (Novella)

About the Author

Annie Dyer enjoys her alarm to be off, her books to be steamy, and her gin to be dry. Her stories are set in the UK and filled with more heat than an English summer. She writes about strong women and the men who are men enough to make them happy! Her books are made to binge read, and guarantee a happily ever after. Annie lives in Manchester, England with her husband and pets, in a Victorian house with leopard print carpet!

Made in the USA
Columbia, SC
12 November 2022